2 1⁰⁰

D0290114

ALL HALLOWS' EVE

by the same author

★

WAR IN HEAVEN
MANY DIMENSIONS
THE PLACE OF THE LION
THE GREATER TRUMPS
DESCENT INTO HELL
SHADOWS OF ECSTASY

★

THE DESCENT OF THE DOVE
TALIESSIN THROUGH LOGRES: REGION OF
THE SUMMER STARS; THE ARTHURIAN TORSO
(With C. S. Lewis)

Charles Williams

ALL
HALLOWS' EVE

Introduction by T. S. Eliot

Grand Rapids

WILLIAM B. EERDMANS PUBLISHING COMPANY

Copyright © 1948 by Pellegrini & Cudahy
First Eerdmans edition 1981

Reprinted, June 1989

All rights reserved

Library of Congress Cataloging in Publication Data
Williams, Charles, 1886-1945.
All Hallow's Eve.

Reprint of the 1963 ed. published by Noonday Press,
New York.
I.   Title.
PR6045.I5A8   1981   823'.912   80-29072
ISBN 0-8028-1250-3

CONTENTS

INTRODUCTION

It was in the late 'twenties, I think, that I first met Charles Williams; and it was through the friend who first called my attention to his work that the introduction was effected. A woman with a notable flair for literary talent, who liked to bring together the authors whose work interested her, and who was in a position to do so, made me read Williams's two first novels, *War in Heaven* and *The Place of the Lion,* and at the same time, or a little later, invited me to tea to meet him. I remember a man in spectacles, who appeared to combine a frail physique with exceptional vitality; whose features could be described as "homely"—meaning by that word a face which is immediately attractive and subsequently remembered, without one's being able to explain either the attraction or the persistence of the impression. He appeared completely at ease in surroundings with which he was not yet familiar, and which had intimidated many; and at the same time was modest and unassuming to the point of humility: that unconscious humility, one discovered later, was in him a natural quality, one he possessed to a degree which made one, in time, feel very humble oneself in his presence. He talked easily and volubly, yet never imposed his talk; for he appeared always to be at the same time preoccupied with the subject of conversation, and interested in and aware of, the personalities of those to whom he was talking. One retained the impression that he was pleased and grateful for the opportunity of meeting the company, and yet that it was he who had conferred a favour—more than a favour, a kind of benediction, by coming.

From that time, I read all of Charles Williams's novels as they were published; and I saw him, from that time, at the same house and elsewhere. It was not, however, until the middle 'thirties that I much improved the acquaintance. My play *Murder in the Cathedral* was produced at the Canterbury Festival in 1935; Williams's *Cranmer* was the play for the following year, and I went down with a party of mutual friends to see the first performance. Thereafter I saw Williams more and more frequently until the outbreak of war. He was a member of the staff of the London office of the Oxford University Press, which, when the war came, was removed to Oxford. He was rarely free to come to London. I saw him only on my own occasional visits to Oxford, where he cheerfully carried on his official duties in a converted bath-room in which the tub had been provided with a cover to make an improvised table. In May of 1945 I went over to Paris to give a lecture. I returned late in the afternoon to my office in London, to find a message that Sir Humphrey Milford wanted me to telephone him at once in Oxford. It was too late to get through to the University Press; so it was not until the next morning that I learned that Charles Williams had died in hospital in Oxford the day before, after an operation which had not been expected to be critical. He died only a few days after the capitulation of Germany.

Such is the outline of an acquaintance of some twenty years, which I am proud to think became a friendship—though I was only one of an increasing circle of friends, and though, in his last years, there were others who saw much more of him. There are some writers who are best known through their books, and who, in their personal relations, have little to give beyond what more commonplace, uncreative minds can give; there are others whose writings are only the shadow of what the men have given in direct intercourse. Some men are less than their works, some are more. Charles Williams cannot be placed in either class. To have known the man would have been enough; to know his books is enough; but no one who has known both the man and his works would have willingly foregone either experience. I can think of no writer who was more wholly the same man in his life and in his writings. What he had to say was beyond his resources, and probably beyond the resources of language, to say once for all through any one medium of expression. Hence, probably, the variety of forms in which he wrote: the play, the poem, the literary or philosophical essay, and the novel. Conversation was for him one more channel of communication. And just as his books attract and hold the reader's interest from the start, but have a great deal in them which only reveals itself on re-reading, so the man himself had an immediate charm and likeability, a radiation of benevolence and amiability which, while it concealed nothing, yet left the best of him to disclose itself gradually on better acquaintance.

As I have already suggested, Williams never appeared to wish to impress, still less to dominate; he talked with a kind of modest and retiring loquacity. His conversation was so easy and informal, taking its start from the ordinary trifles and humorous small-talk of the occasion; it passed so quickly and naturally to and fro between the commonplace and the original, between the superficial and the profound; it was so delightfully volatile, that one was not aware, until after several meetings, of any exceptional quality about it; and appreciation of its value came all the more slowly because of his quickness to defer and to listen. There was also a deceptive gaiety in his treatment of the most serious subjects: I remember a bewildering and almost hilarious discussion in which we considered the notion, propounded by some early Christian heretics, that the world had been created at the Nativity. (It was characteristic of his adventurous imagination, that he should like to put himself at the point of view from which a doctrine was held, before rejecting it.) Amongst a small group of friends, on a leisurely evening over beer or port, his talk would flash from one level to another, never apparently leading the thought of his companions, but seeming rather to respond instantly to the mood or tone of the last speaker. When it was pertinent to the matter in hand, he could declaim long quotations from one or another of his favourite poets, for his memory for poetry was prodigious and accurate. He was, furthermore, a very successful lecturer. His means were always straitened; for many years he supplemented his income by conducting evening classes; and in his pupils he aroused, not only a warm devotion to himself, but an excited interest in the literature to which he introduced them. After his removal to Oxford, he lectured to undergraduates with, I believe, the same success. As a platform speaker, he was certainly unusual, and had, to an exaggerated degree, some of those mannerisms which uninspired speakers should most sedulously avoid. He was never still: he writhed and swayed; he jingled coins in his pocket; he sat on the edge of the table swinging his leg; in a torrent of speech he appeared to be saying whatever came into his head from one moment to the next. But what would have been the ruin of another lecturer contributed to Williams's success; he held his audience in rapt attention, and left with them the contagion of his own enthusiastic curiosity.

How, with his exacting daily work in a publisher's office, with his evening lectures and with his economic anxieties, he managed to write so much and so well as he did, remains incomprehensible to me. Some of his books—such as his *Life of Henry VII*—were frankly pot-boilers; but he always boiled an honest pot. And besides what could be considered (if it had been less well done) merely hack-work, and besides the financial lash on his back in writing even what he wanted to write, much of his work, especially for the theatre, was done without expectation of adequate remuneration and often without expectation of payment at all. He would respond to almost any appeal, and produce a masque or play for a particular occasion for some obscure group of amateurs. Yet he left behind him a considerable number of books which should endure, because there is nothing else that is like them or could take their place.

I have already tried to indicate the unity between the man and the work; and it follows that there is a unity between his works of very different kinds. Much of his work may appear to realize its form only imperfectly; but it is also true in a measure to say that Williams invented his own forms—or to say that no form, if he had obeyed all its conventional laws, could have been satisfactory for what he wanted to say. What it is, essentially, that he had to say, comes near to defying definition. It was not simply a philosophy, a theology, or a set of ideas: it was primarily something imaginative. Perhaps I can give some hint of it by returning for a moment to the man. I have said that Williams seemed equally at ease among every sort and condition of men, naturally and unconsciously, without envy or contempt, without subservience or condescension. I have always believed that he would have been equally at ease in every kind of supernatural company; that he would never have been surprised or disconcerted by the intrusion of any visitor from another world, whether kindly or malevolent; and that he would have shown exactly the same natural ease and courtesy, with an exact awareness of how one should behave, to an angel, a demon, a human ghost, or an elemental. For him there was no frontier between the material and the spiritual world. Had I ever had to spend a night in a haunted house, I should have felt secure with Williams in my company: he was somehow protected from evil, and was himself a protection. He could have joked with the devil and turned the joke against him. To him the supernatural was perfectly natural, and the natural was also supernatural. And this peculiarity gave him that profound insight into Good and Evil, into the heights of Heaven and the depths of Hell, which provides both the immediate thrill, and the permanent message of his novels.

While this theme runs through all of Williams's best work, it is made most apprehensible in this series of novels, from *War in Heaven* to *All Hallows' Eve*. Not having known him in his earlier years, I do not know what literary influences were strongest upon him at the beginning. I suspect some influence from Chesterton, and especially, in connection with the novels, an influence of *The Man Who Was Thursday*. If this influence is present, it is most present in the first novel, *War in Heaven*, and becomes fainter in the later work. (Chesterton may also have influenced the early verse; Williams's poetry became more and more modern and original in form.) But I suggest a derivation only to point a difference. Chesterton's *The Man Who Was Thursday* is an allegory; it has a meaning which is meant to be discovered at the end; while we can enjoy it in reading, simply because of the swiftly moving plot and the periodic surprises, it is intended to convey a definite moral and religious point expressible in intellectual terms. It gives you *ideas*, rather than *feelings*, of another world. Williams has no such "palpable design" upon his reader. His aim is to make you partake of a kind of experience that he has had, rather than to make you accept some dogmatic belief. This gives him an affinity with writers of an entirely different type of supernatural thriller from Chesterton's: with writers as different as Poe, Walter de la Mare, Montague James, Le Fanu and Arthur Machen. But the danger of this second type of story is that its thrills are apt to turn into pure sensationalism. If Poe, at his best, as in *The Fall of the House of Usher* or *Ligeia,* escapes this accusation, it is because the symbolism of nightmare has its reference in the psychological ailment of Poe, which is itself a serious matter. If De la Mare escapes it, at his best, it is because he gives you a perception of something which you can interpret as you please. But with inferior stories of supernatural horror of this type, you feel that the supernatural world is not really believed in, but is merely being exploited for an immediate but very transient effect upon the reader. The nearest approximation to Williams's effects that I can think of, is given by Stevenson's *Dr. Jekyll and Mr. Hyde;* and even here, I feel that the literary craftsman is too obviously the manipulator of the scene.

The stories of Charles Williams, then, are not like those of Edgar Allan Poe, woven out of morbid psychology —I have never known a healthier-minded man than Williams. They are not like those of Chesterton, intended to teach the reader. And they are certainly not an exploitation of the supernatural for the sake of the immediate shudder. Williams is telling us about a world of experience known to him: he does not merely persuade us to believe in something, he communicates this experience that he has had. When I say that we are persuaded to believe in the supernatural world of Charles Williams, I do not mean that we necessarily give complete credence to all the apparatus of magic, white or black, that he employs. There is much which he has invented, or borrowed from the literature of the occult, merely for the sake of telling a good story. In reading *All Hallows' Eve,* we can, if we like, believe that the methods of the magician Simon for controlling mysterious forces could all be used with success by anyone with suitable natural gifts and special training. We can, on the other hand, find the machinery of the story no more credible than that of any popular tale of vampires, were-wolves, or demonic possession. But whether credulous or incredulous about the actual kinds of event in the story, we come to perceive that they are the vehicle for communicating a para-normal experience with which the author is familiar, for introducing us into a real world in which he is at home.

The conflict which is the theme of every one of Williams's novels, is not merely the conflict between good and bad men, in the usual sense. No one was less confined to conventional morality, in judging good and bad behaviour, than Williams: his morality is that of the Gospels. He sees the struggle between Good and Evil as carried on, more or less blindly, by men and women who are often only the instruments of higher or lower powers, but who always have the freedom to choose to which powers they will submit themselves. Simon, in this story, is a most austere ascetic, but he is evil; Evelyn is a woman who appears too insignificant, too petty in her faults, to be really "bad," but yet, just because she is no more than pettiness, she delivers herself willingly into the hand of evil. Her friend, who makes the other choice, is also a rather commonplace woman; but, having lived just well enough to be able to choose the good, she develops in the light of that good she follows, and learns the meaning of Love. Williams's understanding of Evil was profound. Had he himself not always seen Evil, unerringly, as the contrast to Good—had he understood Evil, so far as it can be understood, without knowing the Good—there are passages in this book, and in other books (notably in *Descent Into Hell*) which would only be outrageous and foul. He is concerned, not with the Evil of conventional morality and the ordinary manifestations by which we recognise it, but with the essence of Evil; it is therefore Evil which has no power to attract us, for we see it as the repulsive thing it is, and as the despair of the damned from which we recoil.

It would be easy, but not particularly profitable, to

classify Williams as a "mystic." He knew, and could put into words, states of consciousness of a mystical kind, and the sort of elusive experience which many people have once or twice in a life-time. (I am thinking of certain passages in *The Place of the Lion,* but there is no novel without them.) And if "mysticism" means a belief in the supernatural, and in its operation in the natural world, then Williams was a mystic: but that is only belief in what adherents of every religion in the world profess to believe. His is a mysticism, not of curiosity, or of the lust for power, but of Love; and Love, in the meaning which it had for Williams—as readers of his study of Dante, called *The Figure of Beatrice,* will know—is a deity of whom most human beings seldom see more than the shadow. But in his novels he is as much concerned with quite ordinary human beings, with their struggle among the shadows, their weaknesses and self-deceptions, their occasional moments of understanding, as with the Vision of Love towards which creation strives.

His personages have a reality, an existence in their own right, which differentiates them from the ordinary puppets of the usual adventure story. Only as much of the reality of each character is given as is relevant: the rest could be supplied. In *All Hallows' Eve,* we are given only enough of the characters of Richard Furnival and his friend Jonathan to establish their relations with Lester and Betty respectively; the character of Betty is necessarily not more vivid than it is, because of the conditions of the twilight world in which her mother has kept her; and the mother herself is inevitably simplified in terms of the control over her exercised by the magician. And Simon himself is defined by his function of representing the single-minded lust for unlawful and unlimited power. It is to the two young women whose destinies are so different, Lester and Evelyn, that Williams devotes his analysis; and a study of these two figures will reveal his understanding of the depths and intricacies of human nature. And the delineation of the relationship between Lester and her husband, as seen by Lester after she has begun her journey towards enlightenment, shows great psychological insight.

I hesitated before writing this introduction, for the very fact of an introduction might, I felt, give a false impression of the book to be introduced. It might suggest that the book is hard reading, or that it is perhaps a book for some other type of reader than that to which the prospective reader belongs. So I want to make clear that these novels of Williams, including *All Hallows' Eve,* are first of all very good reading, say on a train journey or an air flight for which one buys a novel from a bookstall, perhaps without even noticing the name of the author. They are good reading even for those who never read a novel more than once, and who demand only that it should keep them interested for two or three hours. I believe that is how Williams himself would like them to be read, the first time; for he was a gay and simple man, with a keen sense of adventure, entertainment and drollery. The deeper things are there just because they belonged to the world he lived in, and he could not have kept them out. For the reader who can appreciate them, there are terrors in the pit of darkness into which he can make us look; but in the end, we are brought nearer to what another modern explorer of the darkness has called "the laughter at the heart of things."

T. S. ELIOT

London, August 14, 1948

ALL HALLOWS' EVE

Chapter One

THE NEW LIFE

She was standing on Westminster Bridge. It was twilight, but the City was no longer dark. The street lamps along the Embankment were still dimmed, but in the buildings shutters and blinds and curtains had been removed or left undrawn, and the lights were coming out there like the first faint stars above. Those lights were the peace. It was true that formal peace was not yet in being; all that had happened was that fighting had ceased. The enemy, as enemy, no longer existed and one more crisis of agony was done. Labor, intelligence, patience—much need for these; and much certainty of boredom and suffering and misery, but no longer the sick vigils and daily despair.

Lester Furnival stood and looked at the City while the twilight deepened. The devastated areas were hidden; much was to be done but could be. In the distance she could hear an occasional plane. Its sound gave her a greater sense of relief than the silence. It was precisely not dangerous; it promised a truer safety than all the squadrons of fighters and bombers had held. Something was ended and those remote engines told her so. The moon was not yet risen; the river was dark below. She put her hand on the parapet and looked at it; it should make no more bandages if she could help it. It was not a bad hand, though it was neither so clean nor so smooth as it had been years ago, before the war. It was twenty-five now and to her that seemed a great age. She went on looking at it for a long while, in the silence and the peace, until it occurred to her that the silence was very prolonged, except for that recurrent solitary plane. No one. all the time she had been standing there, had crossed the bridge; no voice, no step, no car had sounded in the deepening night.

She took her hand off the wall and turned. The bridge was as empty as the river; no vehicles or pedestrians here, no craft there. In all that City she might have been the only living thing. She had been so impressed by the sense of security and peace while she had been looking down at the river that only now did she begin to try and remember why she was there on the bridge. There was a confused sense in her mind that she was on her way somewhere; she was either going to or coming from her own flat. It might have been to meet Richard, though she had an idea that Richard, or someone with Richard, had told her not to come. But she could not think of anyone, except Richard, who was at all likely to do so, and anyhow she knew she had been determined to come. It was all mixed up with that crash which had put everything out of her head; and as she lifted her eyes, she saw beyond the Houses and the Abbey the cause of the crash, the plane lying half in the river and half on the Embankment. She looked at it with a sense of its importance to her, but she could not tell why it should seem so important. Her only immediate concern with it seemed to be that it might have blocked the direct road home to her flat, which lay beyond Millbank and was where Richard was or would be and her own chief affairs. She thought of it with pleasure; it was reasonably new and fresh, and they had been lucky to get it when Richard and she had been married yesterday. At least—yesterday? well, not yesterday but not very much longer than yesterday, only the other day. It had been the other day. The word for a moment worried her; it had been indeed another, a separate, day. She felt as if she had almost lost her memory of it, yet she knew she had not. She had been married and to Richard.

The plane, in the thickening darkness, was now but a thicker darkness, and distinguishable only because her eyes were still fixed on it. If she moved she would lose it. If she lost it, she would be left in the midst of this— this *lull*. She knew the sudden London lulls well enough, but this lull was lasting absurdly long. All the lulls she had ever known were not as deep as this, in which there seemed no movement at all, if the gentle agitation of the now visible stars were less than movement, or the steady flow of the river beneath her; she had at least seen that flowing—or had she? was that also still? She was alone with this night in the City—a night of peace and lights and stars, and of bridges and streets she knew, but all in a silence she did not know, so that if she yielded to the silence she would not know those other things, and the whole place would be different and dreadful.

She stood up from the parapet against which she had been leaning, and shook herself impatiently. "I'm moithering," she said in a word she had picked up from a Red Cross companion, and took a step forward. If she could not get directly along Millbank, she must go round. Fortunately the City was at least partially lit now. The lights in the houses shone out and by them she could see more clearly than in the bad old days. Also she could see into them; and somewhere in her there was a small desire to see someone—a woman reading, children playing, a man listening to the wireless; something of that humanity which must be near, but of which on that lonely bridge she could feel nothing. She turned her face towards Westminster and began to walk.

She had hardly taken a dozen steps when she stopped. In the first moment, she thought it was only the echo of her own steps that she heard, but immediately she knew it was not. Someone else, at last, was there; someone else was coming, and coming quickly. Her heart leaped and subsided; the sound at once delighted and frightened her. But she grew angry with this sort of dallying, this over-consciousness of sensation. It was more like Richard than herself. Richard could be aware of sensation so and yet take it in its stride; it was apt to distract her. She had admired him for it and still did; only now she was a little envious and irritated. She blamed Richard for her own incapacity. She had paused and before she could go on she knew the steps. They were his. Six months of marriage had not dulled the recognition; she knew the true time of it at once. It was Richard himself coming. She went quickly on.

In a few moments she saw him; her eyes as well as her ears recognized him. Her relief increased her anger. Why had he let her in for this inconvenience? had they arranged to meet? if so, why had he not been there? why had she been kept waiting? and what had she been doing while she had been kept? The lingering lack of memory drove her on and increased her irritation. He was coming. His fair bare head shone dark-gold under a farther street lamp; under the nearer they came face to face.

He stopped dead as he saw her and his face went white. Then he sprang towards her. 'She threw up her

4

hand as if to keep him off. She said, with a coldness against her deeper will, but she could not help it, "Where have you been? what have you been doing? I've been waiting."

He said, "How did you get out? what do you mean —waiting?"

The question startled her. She stared at him. His own gaze was troubled and almost inimical; there was something in him which scared her more. She wondered if she were going to faint, for he seemed almost to float before her in the air and to be far away. She said, "What do *you* mean? Where are you going? Richard!"

For he was going—in another sense. Her hand still raised, in that repelling gesture, she saw him move backwards, uncertainly, out of the range of that dimmed light. She went after him; he should not evade her. She was almost up to him and she saw him throw out his hands towards her. She caught them; she knew she caught them, for she could see them in her own, but she could not feel them. They were terrifying and he was terrifying. She brought her hands against her breast and they grew fixed there, as, wide-eyed with anger and fear, she watched him disappearing before her. As if he were a ghost he faded; and with him faded all the pleasant human sounds—feet, voices, bells, engines, wheels—which now she knew that, while she had talked to him, she had again clearly heard. He had gone; all was silent. She choked on his name; it did not recall him. He had vanished and she stood once more alone.

She could not tell how long she stood there, shocked and impotent to move. Her fear was at first part of her rage, but presently it separated itself, and was cold in her, and became a single definite thought. When at last

5

she could move, could step again to the parapet and lean against it and rest her hands on it, the thought possessed her with its desolation. It dominated everything—anger and perplexity and the silence; it was in a word—"Dead," she thought, "dead." He could not otherwise have gone; never in all their quarrels had he gone or she; that certainty had allowed them a license they dared not otherwise have risked. She began to cry—unusually, helplessly, stupidly. She felt the tears on her face and peered at the parapet for her handbag and a handkerchief, since now she could not—O despair!—borrow his, as with her most blasting taunts she had sometimes done. It was not on the parapet. She took a step or two away, brushed with her hand the tears from her eyes, and looked about the pavement. It was not on the pavement. She was crying in the street and she had neither handkerchief nor powder. This was what happened when Richard was gone, was dead. He must be dead; how else could he be gone? how else could she be there, and so?

Dead, and she had done it once too often. Dead, and this had been their parting. Dead; her misery swamped her penitence. They had told each other it made no difference and now it had made this. They had reassured each other in their reconciliations, for though they had been fools and quick-tempered, high egotists and bitter of tongue, they had been much in love and they had been fighting their way. But she felt her own inner mind had always foreboded this. Dead; separate; forever separate. It did not, in that separation, much matter who was dead. If it had been she——

She. On the instant she knew it. The word still meant to her so much only this separation that the knowledge did not at first surprise her. One of them was;

6

she was. Very well; she was. But then—she was. On that apparent bridge, beneath those apparent stars, she stood up and knew it. Her tears stopped and dried; she felt the stiffness and the stains on her apparent flesh. She did not now doubt the fact and was still not surprised. She remembered what had happened—herself setting out to meet Evelyn at the Tube, and instead coming across her just over there, and their stopping. And then the sudden loud noise, the shrieks, the violent pain. The plane had crashed on them. She had then, or very soon after, become what she now was.

She was no longer crying; her misery had frozen. The separation she endured was deeper than even she had believed. She had seen Richard for the last time, for now she herself was away, away beyond him. She was entirely cut off; she was dead. It was now a more foreign word than it had ever been, and it meant this. She could perhaps, if it was he who had been dead, have gone to him; now she could not. She could never get back to him, and he would never come to her. He could not: she had thrown him away. It was all quite proper; quite inevitable. She had pushed him away, and there was an end to Richard. But there was no end to her.

Never in her life had she contemplated so final an end which was no end. All change had carried on some kind of memory which was encouragement. She had not always supposed it to be so; she had told herself, when she left school, when she was married, that she was facing a new life. But she had, on the whole, been fortunate in her passage and some pleasantness in her past had always offered her a promise in the future. This however was a quite new life. Her good fortune had preserved her from any experience of that state which is—almost adequately—called "death-in-life"; it had consequently little prepared her for this life-in-death. Her heart had not fallen—ever, ever—through an unfathomed emptiness, supported only on the fluttering wings of everyday life; and not even realizing that it was so supported. She was a quite ordinary, and rather lucky, girl and she was dead.

Only the City lay silently around her; only the river flowed below, and the stars flickered above, and in the houses lights shone. It occurred to her presently to wonder vaguely—as in hopeless affliction men do wonder—why the lights were shining. If the City were as empty as it seemed, if there were no companion anywhere, why the lights? She gazed at them, and the wonder flickered and went away, and after a while returned and presently went away again, and so on for a long time. She remained standing there, for though she had been a reasonably intelligent and forceful creature, she had never in fact had to display any initiative—much less such initiative as was needed here. She had never much thought about death; she had never prepared for it; she had never related anything to it. She had nothing whatever to do with it, or (therefore) in it. As it seemed to have nothing to offer her except this wide prospect of London, she remained helpless. She knew it was a wide prospect, for after she had remained for a great while in the dark it had grown slowly light again. A kind of pale October day had dawned and the lights in the apparent houses had gone out; and then it had once more grown dark and they had shone—and so on—twenty or thirty times. There had been no sun. During the day she saw the River and the City; during the night, the stars. Nothing else.

Why at last she began to move she could not have said. She was not hungry or thirsty or cold or tired—well, perhaps a little cold and tired, but only a little, and certainly not hungry or thirsty. But if Richard, in this new sense, were not coming, it presently seemed to her useless to wait. But besides Richard, the only thing in which she had been interested had been the apparatus of mortal life; not people—she had not cared for people particularly, except perhaps Evelyn; she was sincerely used to Evelyn, whom she had known at school and since; but apart from Evelyn, not people—only the things they used and lived in, houses, dresses, furniture, gadgets of all kinds. That was what she had liked, and (if she wanted it now) that was what she had got. She did not, of course, know this, and she could not know that it was the sincerity of her interest that procured her this relaxation in the void. If Richard had died, this would have remained vivid to her. Since she was dead, it remained also, though not (stripped of all forms of men and women) particularly vivid.

She began to walk. It did not much matter which way. Her first conscious movement—and even that was hardly a movement of volition—was to look over her shoulder in the seeming daylight to see if the plane were there. It was, though dimmer and smaller, as if it were fading. Would the whole City gradually fade and leave her to emptiness? Or would she too fade? She did not really attempt to grapple with the problem of her seeming body; death did not offer her problems of that sort. Her body in life had never been a problem; she had accepted it, inconveniences and all, as a thing that simply was. Her pride—and she had a good deal of pride, especially sexual—had kept her from commitments except

9

with Richard. It was her willingness to commit herself with Richard that made her believe she (as she called it) loved Richard, though in her bad moments she definitely wished Richard, in that sense, to love her more than she loved him. But her bad moments were not many. She really did want, need and (so far) love Richard. Her lack and longing and despair and self-blame were sincere enough, and they did not surprise her. It had been plain honest passion, and plain honest passion it remained. But now the passion more and more took the form of one thought; she had done it again, she had done it once too often, and this was the unalterable result.

She began to walk. She went up northward. That was instinct; she at least knew that part of London. Up from the bridge, up Whitehall—no one. Into Trafalgar Square—no one. In the shops, in the offices—no one. They were all full and furnished with everything but man. At moments, as she walked, a horrible fancy took her that those at which she was not, at the moment, looking were completely empty; that everything was but a façade, with nothing at all behind it; that if she had walked straight through one of those shops, she would come out into entire nothing. It was a creeping sensation of the void; she herself could not have put it into words. But there the suspicion was.

She came to the bottom of Charing Cross Road and began to go up it. In front of her she saw the curtains of brick that hid the entrances to Leicester Square Tube Station. By one of them, on the opposite side of the road, someone was standing. She was still not conscious of any shock of surprise or of fear or even of relief. Her emotions were not in action. There had been no one; there was now someone. It was not Richard; it was another young woman. She crossed the road towards the unknown; it seemed the thing to do. Unknown? not unknown. It was—and now she did feel a faint surprise—it was Evelyn. In the sudden recollection of having arranged to meet Evelyn there, she almost forgot that she was dead. But then she remembered that their actual meeting had been accidental. They had both happened to be on their way to their appointed place. As she remembered, she felt a sudden renewal of the pain and of the oblivion. It did not remain. There was nothing to do but go on. She went on.

The figure of Evelyn moved and came towards her. The sound of her heels was at first hideously loud on the pavement as she came, but after a step or two it dwindled to almost nothing. Lester hardly noticed the noise at the time or its diminution; her sense was in her eyes. She absorbed the approaching form as it neared her with a growing intensity which caused her almost to forget Richard. The second best was now the only best. As they drew together, she could not find anything to say beyond what she had said a hundred times—dull and careless, "O hallo, Evelyn!" The sound of the words scared her, but much more the immediate intolerable anxiety about the reply: would it come? It did come. The shape of her friend said in a shaking voice, "O hallo, Lester!"

They stopped and looked at each other. Lester could not find it possible to speak of their present state. Evelyn stood before her, a little shorter than she, with her rather pinched face and quick glancing black eyes. Her black hair was covered by a small green hat. She wore a green coat; and her hands were fidgeting with each other. Lester saw at once that she also was without a handbag. This lack of what, for both of them, was almost, if not quite, part of their very dress, something without which they were never seen in public; this loss of handkerchief, compact, keys, money, letters, left them peculiarly desolate. They had nothing but themselves and what they wore—no property, no convenience. Lester felt nervous of the loss of her dress itself; she clutched it defensively. Without her handbag she was doubly forlorn in this empty City. But Evelyn was there and Evelyn was something. They could, each of them, whatever was to happen, meet it with something human close by. Poor deserted vagrants as they were, they could at least be companions in their wanderings.

She said, "So you're here!" and felt a little cheered. Perhaps soon she would be able to utter the word *death*. Lester had no lack of courage. She had always been willing, as it is called, "to face facts"; indeed, her chief danger had been that, in a life with no particular crisis and no particular meaning, she would invent for herself facts to face. She had the common, vague idea of her age that if your sexual life was all right you were all right, and she had the common vague idea of all ages that if you (and your sexual life) were not all right, it was probably someone else's fault—perhaps undeliberate, but still their fault. Her irritation with her husband had been much more the result of power seeking material than mere fretfulness. Her courage and her power, when she saw Evelyn, stirred; she half prepared a part for them to play—frankness, exploration, daring. Oh if it could but have been with Richard!

Evelyn was speaking. Her quick and yet inaccurate voice rippled in words and slurred them. She said, "You *have* been a long time. I quite thought you wouldn't be coming. I've been waiting—you can't think how long. Let's go into the Park and sit down."

Lester was about to answer when she was appalled by the mere flat ordinariness of the words. She had been gripping to herself so long her final loss of Richard that she had gripped also the new state in which they were. This talk of sitting down in the Park came over her like a nightmare, with a nightmare's horror of unreality become actual. She saw before her the entrance to the station and she remembered they had meant to go somewhere by Tube. She began, with an equal idiocy, to say, "But weren't we——" when Evelyn gripped her arm. Lester disliked being held; she disliked Evelyn holding her; now she disliked it more than ever. Her flesh shrank. Her eyes were on the station entrance and the repulsion of her flesh spread. There was the entrance; they had meant to go—yes, but there could not now be any Tube below; or it would be as empty as the street. A medieval would have feared other things in such a moment—the way perhaps to the *città dolente*, or the people of it, smooth or hairy, tusked or clawed, malicious or lustful, creeping and clambering up from the lower depths. She did not think of that, but she did think of the spaces and what might fill them; what but the dead? Perhaps—in a flash she saw them—perhaps there the people, the dead people, of this empty City were; perhaps that was where the whole population had been lying, waiting for her too, the entrance waiting and all below the entrance. There were things her courage could not face. Evelyn's clutch on her arm was light, light out of all proportion to the fear in Evelyn's eyes, but in her own fear she yielded to it. She allowed herself to be led away.

They went into the Park; they found a seat; they sat down. Evelyn had begun to talk, and now she went on. Lester had always known Evelyn talked a good deal, but she had never listened to more than she chose. Now she could not help listening, and she had never before heard Evelyn gabble like this. The voice was small and thin as it usually was, but it was speedier and much more continuous. It was like a river; no, it was like something thrown about on a river, twisted and tossed. It had no pressure; it had no weight. But it went on. She was saying—"that we wouldn't go to see it today, after all. I mean, there aren't many people about and I do hate an empty theater, don't you? Even a cinema. It always seems different. I hate not being with people. Should we go and see Betty? I know you don't much care for Betty, or her mother. I don't like her mother myself, though of course with Betty she must have had a very difficult time. I wish I could have done more for her, but I did try. I'm really very fond of Betty and I've always said that there was some simple explanation for that odd business with the little German refugee a year or two ago. Naturally I never said anything to her about it, because she's almost morbidly shy, isn't she? I did hear that that painter had been there several times lately; what's his name? Drayton; he's a friend of your husband, isn't he? but I shouldn't think he——"

Lester said—if she said; she was not certain, but she seemed to say, "Be quiet, Evelyn."

The voice stopped. Lester knew that she had stopped it. She could not herself say more. The stillness of the City was immediately present again and for a moment she almost regretted her words. But of the two she knew she preferred the immense, the inimical stillness to that insensate babble. Death as death was preferable to death mimicking a foolish life. She sat, almost defiantly, silent; they both sat silent. Presently Lester heard by her side a small and curious noise. She looked round. Evelyn was sitting there crying as Lester had cried, the tears running down her face, and the small noise came from her mouth. She was shaking all over and her teeth were knocking together. That was the noise.

Lester looked at her. Once she would have been impatient or sympathetic. She felt that, even now, she might be either, but in fact she was neither. There was Evelyn, crying and chattering; well, there was Evelyn crying and chattering. It was not a matter that seemed relevant. She looked away again. They went on sitting.

The first shadow of another night was in the sky. There was never any sun, so it could not sink. There was a moon, but a moon of some difference, for it gave no light. It was large and bright and cold, and it hung in the sky, but there was no moonlight on the ground. The lights in the houses would come on and then go out. It was certainly growing darker. By her side the chattering went on; the crying became more full of despair. Lester dimly remembered that she would once have been as irritated by it as all but the truly compassionate always are by misery. Now she was not. She said nothing; she did nothing. She could not help being aware of Evelyn, and a slow recollection of her past with Evelyn forced itself on her mind. She knew she had never really liked Evelyn, but Evelyn had been a habit, almost a drug, with which she filled spare hours. Evelyn usually did what Lester wanted. She would talk gossip which Lester did not quite like to talk, but did rather like to hear talked, because she could then listen to it while despising it. She kept Lester up to date in all her less decent curiosities. She came because she was invited and stayed because she was needed. They went out together because it suited them; they had been going out that afternoon because it suited them; and now they were dead and sitting in the Park because it had suited someone or something else—someone who had let a weakness into the plane or had not been able to manage the plane, or perhaps this City of façades which in a mere magnetic emptiness had drawn them to be there, just there.

Still motionlessly gazing across the darkening Park, Lester thought again of Richard. If Richard had been in distress by her side—not, of course, crying and chattering, more likely dumb and rigid—would she have done anything? She thought probably not. But she might, she certainly might, have cried to him. She would have expected him to help her. But she could not think of it; the pang took her quickly; he was not there and could not be. Well . . . the pang continued, but she was growing used to it. She knew she would have to get used to it.

The voice by her side spoke again. It said, through its sobs, the sobs catching and interrupting it, "Lester! Lester, I'm so frightened." And then again, "Lester, why won't you let me talk?"

Lester began, "Why——" and had to pause, for in the shadow her voice was dreadful to her. It did not sound like a voice; only like an echo. In the apparent daylight, it had not been so bad, but in this twilight it seemed only like something that, if it was happening at all, was happening elsewhere. It could not hold any meaning, for all meaning had been left behind; in her flat perhaps which she would never occupy again; or perhaps with the other dead in the tunnels of the Tube; or perhaps farther away yet, with whatever it was that had drawn them there and would draw them farther; this was only a little way— Oh what else remained to know?

She paused, but she would not be defeated. She forced herself to speak; she could and would dare that at least. She said, "Why. . . . Why do you want to talk *now?*"

The other voice said, "I can't help it. It's getting so dark. Let's go on talking. We can't do anything else."

Lester felt again the small weak hand on her arm and now she had time to feel it; nothing else intervened. She hated the contact. Evelyn's hand might have been the hand of some pleading lover whose touch made her flesh creep. She had, once or twice in her proud life, been caught like that; once in a taxi—the present touch brought sharply back that other clasp, in this very Park on a summer evening. She had only just not snapped into irritation and resentment then; but in some ways she had liked the unfortunate man and they had been dining pleasantly enough. She had remained kind; she had endured the fingers feeling up her wrist, her whole body loathing them, until she could with sufficient decency disengage herself. It was her first conscious recollection of an incident in her past—that act of pure courtesy, though she did not then recognize it either as recollection or as a courtesy. Only for a moment she thought she saw a taxi race through the Park away before her, and she thought it could not be and was not. But she stiffened herself now against her instinctive shrinking and let her arm lie still, while the feeble hand clutched and pawed at her.

Her apprehension quickened as she did so. To be what she was, to be in this state of death, was bad enough, but at the same time to feel the dead, to endure the clinging of the dead, being dead to know the dead—the live man in the taxi was far better than this, this that was Evelyn, the gabbing voice, the chattering teeth, the helpless sobs, the crawling fingers. But she had gone out with Evelyn much more than with the man in the taxi; her heart acknowledged a debt. She continued to sit still. She said in a voice touched by pity if not by compassion, "It's no good talking, especially like that. Don't you understand?"

Evelyn answered, resentfully choking, but still holding on. "I was only telling you about Betty, and it's all quite true. And no one can hear me except you, so it doesn't matter."

No one could hear; it was true enough—unless indeed the City heard, unless the distant façades, and the nearer façade of trees and grass, were listening, unless they had in them just that reality at least, a capacity to overhear and oversee. The thin nothingness could perhaps hear and know. Lester felt all about her a strange attention, and Evelyn herself, as if frightened by her own words, gave a hasty look round, and then burst again into a hysterical monologue: "Isn't it funny—we're all alone? We never thought we'd be alone like this, did we? But I only said what was quite true, even if I do hate Betty. I hate everyone except you; of course I don't hate you; I'm very fond of you. You won't go away, will you? It's nearly dark again and I hate it when it's dark. You don't know what the dark was like before you came. Why are we here like this? I haven't done anything. I haven't; I tell you I haven't. I haven't done *anything*."

The last word rose like a wail in the night, almost (as in the old tales) as if a protesting ghost was loosed and fled, in a cry as thin as its own tenuous wisp of existence, through the irresponsive air of a dark world, where its own justification was its only, and worst, accusation. So high and shrill was the wail that Lester felt as though Evelyn herself must have been torn away and have vanished, but it was not so. The fingers still clutched her wrist and Evelyn still sat there, crying and ejaculating, without strength to cry louder. "I haven't done anything, anything. I haven't done anything at all."

And what then could be done now? If neither Evelyn nor she herself had ever of old done anything, what could or should they do now—with nothing and no one about them? with only the shell of a City, and they themselves but shell and perhaps not even true shell? only a faint memory and a pang worse than memory? It was too much to bear. As if provoked by an ancient impetuosity of rage, Lester sprang to her feet; shell or body, she sprang up and the motion tore her from the hand that held her. She took a step away. Better go alone than sit so companioned; and then as her foot moved to the second step she paused. Evelyn had failed again, "Oh don't go! don't go!" Lester felt herself again thrusting Richard away and she paused. She looked back over her shoulder; half in anger and half in pity, in fear and scorn and tenderness, she looked back. She saw Evelyn, Evelyn instead of Richard. She stared down at the other girl and she exclaimed aloud, "Oh my God!"

It was the kind of casual exclamation she and Richard had been in the habit of throwing about all over the place. It meant nothing; when they were seriously aggressive or aggrieved, they used language borrowed from bestiality or hell. She had never thought it meant anything. But in this air every word meant something, meant itself; and this curious new exactitude of speech hung there like a strange language, as if she had sworn in Spanish or Pushtu, and the oath had echoed into an invocation. Nothing now happened; no one came; not a quiver disturbed the night, but for a moment she felt as if someone might come, or perhaps not even that—no more than a sudden sense that she was listening as if to hear if it was raining. She was becoming strange to herself; her words, even her intonations, were foreign. In a foreign land she was speaking a foreign tongue; she spoke and did not know what she said. Her mouth was uttering its own habits, but the meaning of those habits was not her own. She did not recognize what she used. "I haven't done anything. . . . Oh my God!" This was how they talked and it was a great precise prehistoric language forming itself out of the noises their mouths made. She articulated the speech of Adam or Seth or Noah and only dimly recognized the intelligibility of it. She exclaimed again, despairingly, "Richard!" and that word she did know. It was the only word common to her and the City in which she stood. As she spoke, she almost saw his face, himself saying something, and she thought she would have understood that meaning, for his face was part of the meaning, as it always had been, and she had lived with that meaning—loved, desired, denounced it. Something intelligible and great loomed and was gone. She was silent. She turned; she said, more gently than she had spoken before, "Evelyn, let's do something now."

"But I haven't done *anything*," Evelyn sobbed again. The precise words sounded round them and Lester answered their meaning.

"No," she said, "I know. Nor have I—much." She

had for six months kept house for Richard and herself and meant it. She *had* meant it; quarrels and bickerings could not alter that; even the throwing it away could not alter it. She lifted her head; it was as certain as any of the stars now above her in the sky. For the second time she felt—apart from Evelyn—her past present with her. The first had been in the sense of that shadowy taxi racing through the Park, but this was stronger and more fixed. She lived more easily for that moment. She said again, "Not very much. Let's go."

"But where can we go?" Evelyn cried. "Where are we? It's so *horrible.*"

Lester looked round her. She saw the stars; she saw the lights; she saw dim shapes of houses and trees in a landscape which was less familiar through being so familiar. She could not even yet manage to enunciate to her companion the word *death.* The landscape of death lay round them; the future of death awaited them. Let them go to it; let them do something. She thought of her own flat and of Richard—no. She did not wish to take this other Evelyn there; besides, she herself would be, if anything at all, only a dim shadow to Richard, a hallucination or a troubling apparition. She could not bear that, if it could be avoided; she could not bear to be only a terrifying dream. No; they must go elsewhere. She wondered if Evelyn felt in the same way about her own home. She knew that Evelyn had continuously snubbed and suppressed her mother, with whom she lived; once or twice she had herself meant to say something, if only out of an indifferent superiority. But the indifference had beaten the superiority. It was now for Evelyn to choose.

She said, "Shall we go to your place?"

Evelyn said shrilly, "No; no. I won't see Mother. I hate Mother."

Lester shrugged. One way and another, they did seem to be rather vagrants, unfortunate and helpless creatures, with no purpose and no use. She said, "Well . . . let's go." Evelyn looked up at her. Lester, with an effort at companionship, tried to smile at her. She did not very well succeed, but at least Evelyn, slowly and reluctantly, got to her feet. The lights in the houses had gone out, but a faint clarity was in the air—perhaps (though it had come quickly) the first suggestion of the day. Lester knew exactly what she had better do and with an effort she did it. She took Evelyn's arm. The two dead girls went together slowly out of the Park.

Chapter Two

THE BEETLES

It was a month or so since Lester Furnival had been buried. The plane crash had been explained and regretted by the authorities. Apologies and condolences had been sent to Mrs. Furnival's husband and Miss Mercer's mother. A correspondence on the possibility and propriety of compensation had taken place in the Press, and a question or two had been asked in the House. It was explained that nothing could be done, but that a whole set of new instructions had been issued to everyone connected with flying, from Air Marshals to factory hands.

The publicity of this discussion was almost a greater shock to Richard Furnival than his wife's death; or, at least, the one confused the other. He was just enough to see that, for the sake of the poor, the Crown ought always at such times to be challenged to extend as a grace what it refused as a claim. He was even conscious that Lester, if the circumstances had been reversed, might properly have had no difficulty in taking what he would have rejected; not that she was less fastidious or less passionate than he, but it would have seemed to her natural and proper to spoil those whom he was content to ignore.

The Foreign Office, in which through the war he had been serving, pressed on him prolonged leave. He had been half inclined to refuse, for he guessed that, after the first shock, it was not now that his distress would begin. The most lasting quality of loss is its unexpectedness. No doubt he would know his own loss in the expected places and times—in streets and stations, in restaurants and theaters, in their own home. He expected that. What he also expected, and yet knew he could not by its nature expect, was his seizure by his own loss in places uniquely his—in his office while he read Norwegian minutes, in the Tube while he read the morning paper, at a bar while he drank with a friend. These habits had existed before he had known Lester, but they could not escape her. She had, remotely but certainly, and without her own knowledge, overruled all. Her entrance into all was absolute, and lacking her the entrance of the pain.

He went away; he returned. He went away to spare his office companions the slight embarrassment of the sight of him. He returned because he could not bear to be away. He had not yet taken up his work; in a few days he would. Meanwhile he determined unexpectedly one afternoon to call on Jonathan Drayton.

He had known him for a number of years, long before Jonathan became a well-known painter. He was also a very good painter, though there were critics who disapproved of him; they said his color was too shrill. But he had been appointed one of the official war-artists, and two of his paintings—*Submarine Submerging* and *Night Fighters over Paris*—were among the remarkable artistic achievements of the war. He also had been for some time on leave, in preparation (it was understood) for the grand meetings after the peace, when he would be expected to produce historic records of historic occasions. He had been once or twice, a little before the accident, at the Furnivals' flat, but he had then gone to Scotland and written to Richard from there. A later postcard had announced his return.

Richard had come across the card accidentally on this particular afternoon and had suddenly made up his mind to go round. Jonathan had been living, or rather had left his things while he was away, on the top floor of a building in the City, not far from St. Paul's, one room of which was sufficiently well-lit to be used as a studio. It was to the studio that he took Richard after a warm welcome. He was shorter and stockier than his friend, and he had a general habit of leaving Richard the most comfortable chair and himself sitting on the table. He settled himself there, and went on. "I've got several things to tell you; at least, I've got one to tell you and two to show you. If I tell you first . . . the fact is I'm practically engaged."

"Splendid!" said Richard. Such things were unlikely to distress him, as Jonathan guessed; one could not altogether say what might, but not that. He was quite simply pleased. He said, "Do I know her? and what do you mean by 'practically'?"

"I don't know if you know her," Jonathan said. "She's Betty Wallingford, the daughter of the Air Marshal. She and her mother are coming here presently."

"I remember hearing her name," Richard said. "She was a friend of Lester's—or rather not a friend, but they knew each other some time ago. But I rather gathered she was ill or something and her mother didn't let her go out much."

"That's true enough," Jonathan answered. "It was the Air Marshal who asked me to dine one night after I'd painted him. He's a nice creature. though not interesting to paint. Lady Wallingford keeps Betty rather close, and why I say 'practically' is because, when things came to a head with Betty the other day, she didn't seem very keen. She didn't exactly refuse, but she didn't encourage. They're both coming here presently. Don't go, whatever you do. I've a particular reason for asking you to stay."

"Have you?" Richard said. "What is it?"

Jonathan nodded at an easel on which was a canvas covered by a cloth. "That," he said, and looked at his watch. "We've an hour before they come and I'd like you to see it first. No; it's not a painting of Betty, or of her mother. It's something quite different, but it may— I don't know, but it just may—be a little awkward with Lady Wallingford. However, there's something else for you to see first—d'you mind? If you hadn't come along, I was going to ring you up. I'm never quite happy about a thing till you've seen it."

This, as Richard knew, was a little extreme. But it had a basis of truth; when Jonathan exaggerated, he exaggerated in the grand style. He never said the same thing to two people; something similar perhaps, but always distinguished, though occasionally hardly anyone but he could distinguish the distinction. Richard answered, "I've never known you take much notice of anything I said. But show it to me all the same, whatever it is."

"Over here," Jonathan said, and took his friend round to the other side of the room. A second easel was standing back to back with the first, also holding a canvas, but this uncovered. Richard set himself to look at it.

It was a part of London after a raid—he thought, of the City proper, for a shape on the right reminded him dimly of St. Paul's. At the back were a few houses, but the rest of the painting was a wide stretch of desolation. The time was late dawn; the sky was clear; the light came, it seemed at first, from the yet unrisen sun behind the single group of houses. The light was the most outstanding thing in the painting; presently, as Richard looked, it seemed to stand out from the painting, and almost to dominate the room itself. At least it so governed the painting that all other details and elements were contained within it. They floated in that imaginary light as the earth does in the sun's. The colors were so heightened that they were almost at odds. Richard saw again what the critics meant when they said that Jonathan Drayton's paintings "were shrill" or "shrieked," but he saw also that what prevented this was a certain massiveness. The usual slight distinction between shape and hue seemed wholly to have vanished. Color was more intensely image than it can usually manage to be, even in that art. A beam of wood painted amber was more than that; it was light which had become amber in order to become wood. All that massiveness of color was led, by delicate gradations almost like the vibrations of light itself, towards the hidden sun; the eye encountered the gradations in their outward passage and moved inwards towards their source. It was then that the style of the painting came fully into its own. The spectator became convinced that the source of that light was not only in that hidden sun; as, localized, it certainly was. "Here lies the east; does not the day break here?" The day did, but the light did not. The eye, nearing that particular day, realized that it was leaving the whole fullness of the light behind. It was everywhere in the painting—concealed in houses and in their projected shadows, lying in ambush in the cathedral, opening in the rubble, vivid in the vividness of the sky. It would everywhere have burst through, had it not chosen rather to be shaped into forms, and to restrain and change its greatness in the colors of those lesser limits. It was universal, and lived.

Richard said at last, "I wish you could have shown the sun."

"Yes?" said Jonathan. "Why?"

"Because then I might have known whether the light's in the sun or the sun's in the light. For the life of me, I can't be certain. It rather looks as though, if one could see the sun, it would be a kind of container . . . no, as if it would be made of the light as well as everything else."

"And very agreeable criticism," Jonathan said. "I admit you imply a whole lot of what I only hope are correct comments on the rest of it. You approve?"

"It's far and away the best thing you've done," Richard answered. "It's almost the *only* thing you've done—now you've done it. It's like a modern Creation of the World, or at least a Creation of London. How did you come to do it?"

"Sir Joshua Reynolds," said Jonathan, "once alluded to 'common observation and a plain understanding' as the source of all art. I should like to think I agreed with Sir Joshua here."

Richard still contemplated the painting. He said slowly, "You've always been good at light. I remember how you did the moon in that other thing—*Doves on a Roof,* and there was something of it in the *Planes* and the *Submarine.* Of course one rather expects light effects in the sea and the air, and perhaps one's more startled when the earth becomes like the sea or the air. But I don't think that counts much. The odd thing is that you don't at any time lose weight. No one can say your mass isn't massive."

"I should hope they couldn't," said Jonathan. "I've no notion of losing one thing because I've put in another. Now to paint the massiveness of light———"

"What do you call this?" Richard asked.

"A compromise, I fear," Jonathan answered. "A necessary momentary compromise, I allow. Richard, you really are a blasted nuisance. I do wish you wouldn't always be telling me what I ought to do next before I've been let enjoy what I've done. This, I now see, is compromising with light by turning it into things. Remains to leave out the things and get into the light."

Richard smiled. "What about the immediate future?" he asked. "Do you propose to turn Churchill into a series of vibrations in pure light?"

Jonathan hummed a little. "At that———" he began and stopped. "No, I'm babbling. Come and see the other thing, which is different."

He led the way back round the easels. He said, "Have you ever heard of Father Simon?"

"Have I not?" said Richard. "Is he or is he not in all the papers, almost as much as the Peace? The Foreign Office has been taking a mild concern in all these new prophets, including this one. Then there's the Russian one and the Chinese. You get them at times like these. But they all seem, from our point of view, quite innocuous. I've not been very interested myself."

"Nor was I," said Jonathan, "till I met Lady Wallingford. Since then I have read of him, listened to him, met him and now painted him. Lady Wallingford came across him in America when she was there soon after the last war and I gather fell for him then. During this war he became one of their great religious leaders and when he came over she was one of—or rather she was—his reception committee. She's devoted to him; Betty—not so much, but she goes with her mother." He paused frowning, as if he were about to make a further remark about Betty and her mother, but he changed his mind and went on. "Lady Wallingford thought it would be a privilege for me to paint the Prophet."

Richard said, "Is that what they call him?"

His hand on the covering of the canvas, Jonathan hesitated. "No," he said, "I don't want to be unfair. No. What she actually calls him is the Father. I asked her if he was a priest, but she took no notice. He's got a quite enormous following in America, though here, in spite of the papers, he's kept himself rather quiet. It's been suggested that he's the only man to evangelize Germany. It's also been suggested that he and his opposite numbers in Russia and China shall make a threefold World Leadership. But so far he's not done or said anything about it. He may be just waiting. Well, I did the best I could. Here's the result."

He threw the covering back and Richard was confronted with the painting. It was, at first glance, that of a man preaching. The congregation, of which there seemed a vast number, had their backs to the spectator. They were all a little inclined forward, as if (Richard supposed) in the act of listening, so that they were a mass of slightly curved backs. They were not in a church; they were not in a room; it was difficult to see where they were, and Richard did not particularly mind. It was in an open space somewhere; what he could see of the ground was not unlike the devastation in the other picture, though more rock-like, more in the nature of a wilderness than a City. Beyond them, in a kind of rock pulpit against a great cliff, was the preacher. He seemed to be a tallish dark man of late middle age, in a habit of some sort. His face, clean-shaven, heavy, emaciated, was bent a little downward towards his audience. One hand was stretched out towards them, also a little downward, but the hand was open and turned palm upward. Behind him his shadow was thrown on the rock; above, the sky was full of heavy and rushing cloud.

Richard began to speak and checked himself. He looked more closely at the preaching figure, especially at the face. Though the canvas was large the face inevitably was small, but it was done with care, and as Richard studied it, the little painted oval began to loom out of the picture till its downward-leaning weight seemed to dominate and press on the audience below, and to make all—clouds and crowds and rock-pulpit—grayer and less determined around it. If it was a pulpit; Richard was not clear whether the figure was casting a shadow on the rock or emerging from a cleft in the rock. But the face—it was almost as if the figure had lowered his face to avoid some expression being caught by the painter, and had failed, for Jonathan had caught it too soon. But what exactly had Jonathan caught? and why had Jonathan chosen to create precisely that effect of attempted escape and capture?

Richard said at last, "It's a wonderful effect—especially the color of the face. I don't know how you got that dark deadness. But what——" He stopped.

"Richard," Jonathan said accusingly, "you were going to ask what it *meant*."

"I don't think I was," Richard answered. "I may

have been going to ask what *he* meant. I feel as if there was something in him I hadn't grasped. He's—" and again he paused.

"Go on!" Jonathan said. "The ladies won't be here just yet, and you may now have got a general idea of why I'd like you to be here when they do come. Anyhow, go on; say anything that occurs to you."

Richard obediently renewed his study and his reverie. They had done this together on a number of occasions before a new painting. Richard did not mind sounding foolish before his friend and Jonathan did not mind being denigrated by his friend; in fact, he always swore that one soliloquy of this kind was worth a great deal of judicious criticism. Painting was the only art, he maintained, about which it could be done; one couldn't hear a poem or a symphony as one could look at a painting; in time one could never get the whole at once, but one could in space—or all but; there was bound perhaps to be a very small time lag even there. Except for that, all the aural arts aspired to escape from recollection into the immediate condition of the visual.

Richard said, "The skin looks almost as if it were painted; I mean—as if you were painting a painted effect. Very dark and very dull. Yet it's a sort of massive dullness—much like your mass *and* light; only the opposite. But what I don't get is the expression. At first he seems to be just a preacher driving his point home—convicting them of sin or something. Only, though that mass makes him effective enough—even his hand seems to be pressing down on them, though it is back downwards; it might almost be pulling the sky down on them by a kind of magic—a sort of Samson and the pillars of cloud—yet the more I look at what I can see of the face,

32

the more I think that it doesn't mean anything. It seems to be as near plain bewilderment as anything I ever saw."

"Ho!" said Jonathan, getting off the table to which he had retired. "Ho! You're a genius, Richard. I thought that too. But I've looked at it so often that I can't make out now who's bewildered—him or me."

Richard looked a question.

"I began painting the damned fellow, as one does," Jonathan went on, pacing up and down the room and frowning at the floor. "Of course, he wasn't sitting for me, so I had to do the best I could from one meeting at St. Bartholomew's, a couple of orations, seven photographs in *Picture Post,* a dozen daily papers and other oddments. Lady Wallingford says he won't sit because of his reserve, which may of course be true. But at a pinch I can manage to get something out of such a general hodge-podge fairly well, tiresome as the whole business always is, and this time I took particular notice. I wasn't trying to paint his soul or anything; I just wanted to get him done well enough to please Betty's mother. And when I'd done it I stared at it and I thought, 'Either I don't know *what* he is or he doesn't know *where* he is.' But a fellow who's put it over all America and bits of England is likely to know where he is, I suppose, so I must just have got him completely wrong. It's odd, all the same. I generally manage to make something more or less definite. This man looks as if he were being frightfully definite and completely indefinite at the same moment—an absolute master and a lost loony at once."

"Perhaps he is," said Richard doubtfully.

Jonathan came to a stop by the easel and sighed

drearily. "No," he said, "no. I'm afraid not. In fact, I'm afraid it's a complete give-away for me. The main point is—do you think Lady Wallingford will notice it? And what will she say if she does?"

"I shouldn't think she would," said Richard. "After all, I only just did myself and I'm far more used to your style than she is."

"She may not be used to me, but she's extremely used to him," Jonathan said gloomily. "She's one of the real inner circle. Betty and I will have a much more difficult time if there's any trouble. Otherwise, I shouldn't mind in the least. What *do* you people know about him, Richard?"

"We know," said Richard, "that his name is Simon Leclerc—sometimes called Father Simon and sometimes Simon the Clerk. We gather he's a Jew by descent, though born in France, and brought up in America. We know that he has a great power of oratory—at least, over there; he hasn't tried it much here so far—and that it's said he's performed a number of very remarkable cures, which I don't suppose we've checked. We know that quite intelligent people are attached to him—and that's about all we do know; at least, it's all I know. But, as I told you, I've not been particularly interested. You say you've heard him preach; what does he preach?"

"Love," said Jonathan, more gloomily than ever as he looked at his watch. "They'll be here in a minute. Love, so far as I can gather, but I was more looking at him than listening to him and it's almost impossible for me really to do both at once. I could sort of feel his effect going on all round. But it was mostly Love, with a hint of some secret behind, which Love no doubt could find out. He sometimes gives private interviews, I know, but I really felt it'd be too embarrassing to go to one. So I can only generalize from the bits I caught while I was staring. Love, and something else."

There was a ring at the front door bell, Jonathan threw the cover again over the painting, and said, "Richard, if you go now, I'll never forgive you. And if you don't say the right thing, I'll never listen to a word of yours again." He went hastily out.

He was back so soon that Richard had hardly time to do more than feel at a distance within him that full and recollected life which, whenever it did show itself, threatened to overthrow all other present experiences. It was his first experience of such a nature, of "another" life. Almost, as he too turned from the easel, he saw Lester's dead face, as he had seen it, floating, dim and ill-defined, before his eyes; and the two women who came into the room, though more spectacular, were more empty and shell-like than she.

They were not unlike, with thirty years between. They were both smallish. Lady Wallingford was gray and thin, and had something almost of arrogance in her manner. Betty was fair and thinner than, at her age, one would have thought she ought to be. She looked tired and rather wan. Her eyes, as she entered, were turned on Jonathan, and Richard thought he saw her hand drop from his. Jonathan presented him. Lady Wallingford took him, so to speak, for granted—so granted as to be unnecessary. Betty gave him a quick little glance of interest, which for the moment he did not quite understand; having forgotten that she was supposed to have known Lester. He bowed twice and stepped back a pace. Jonathan said, "You'll have some tea first, Lady Wallingford? It's not too warm today."

Lady Wallingford said, "We'll look at the picture first. I'm anxious to see it."

"I'm very cold, Mother," Betty said—a little nervously, Richard thought. "Couldn't we have tea?"

Lady Wallingford entirely ignored this. She said, "Is that covered thing it? Let me see it."

Jonathan, with the faintest shrug, obeyed. He went to the easel; he said, over his shoulder, "You'll understand that this is rather an impression than a portrait," and he pulled aside the covering. There was a silence, concentrated on the painting. Richard, discreetly in the background, waited for its first quiver.

The first he observed was in Betty. She was just behind her mother and he saw her yield to a faint shudder. Jonathan saw it too; he almost made a movement towards her and checked it before Lady Wallingford's immobility. After what seemed like minutes, she said, "What is our Father coming out of, Mr. Drayton?"

Jonathan pinched his lip, glanced at Betty, and answered, "What you choose, Lady Wallingford."

Lady Wallingford said, "You must have some idea. What is he standing on? rock?"

"Oh yes, rock," said Jonathan readily; and then, as if reluctantly truthful, added, "At least, you might as well call it rock."

The private view was not going very well. Betty sat down as if her power had failed. Lady Wallingford said, "*Is* he standing on it?"

Jonathan answered, "It doesn't much matter, perhaps." He glanced rather anxiously at Richard. Richard took a step forward and said as engagingly as he could, "It's the whole impression that counts, don't you think?"

It was quite certainly the wrong remark. Lady Wallingford took no notice of it. She went on, still addressing herself to Jonathan, "And why are the people so much like insects?"

Betty made an inarticulate sound. Jonathan and Richard both stared at the painting. It had not occurred to either of them—not even apparently to Jonathan—that the whole mass of inclined backs could be seen almost as a ranked mass of beetles, their oval backs dully reflecting a distant light. Once the word had been spoken, the painting became suddenly sinister. Jonathan broke out but his voice was unconvincing, "They're not . . . they weren't meant . . . they don't look like beetles."

"They look exactly like beetles," Lady Wallingford said. "They are not human beings at all. And Father Simon's face is exactly the same shape."

Richard saw that there at least she was right. The oval shape of the face differed only in its features and its downward inclination from the innumerable backs, and in the fact that it reflected no light. It was this lack of reflection which gave it its peculiar deadness; the backs had that dim reflection but this face none. But now he saw it as so similar in shape that it seemed to him for half a second not a face at all, but another back; but this eyed and mouthed as if the living human form ended in a gruesomeness and had a huge beetle for its head, only a beetle that looked out backward through its coat and had a wide speaking mouth there also; a speaking beetle, an orating beetle, but also a dead and watching beetle. He forgot the aesthetic remark he had been about to make.

Jonathan was saying, "I think that's rather reading things into it." It was not, for him, a particularly intelligent remark; but he was distracted by the thought of

Betty and yet his voice was as cold as Lady Wallingford's own. He could manage his words but not his tone.

Lady Wallingford moved her head a little more forward. Richard saw the movement and suddenly, as she stood in front of him, she too took on the shape of an overgrown insect. Outside the painting her back repeated the shapes in the painting. Richard suddenly found himself believing in the painting. This then was what the hearers of Father Simon looked like. He glanced at the face again, but he supposed he had lost that special angle of sight; it was now more like a face, though of that dead artificiality he had remarked before. Lady Wallingford leaned towards the picture as if she were feeling for it with invisible tentacles. But she was feeling with a hideous and almost dangerous accuracy. She now said, and her voice was more than cold; it was indignant, "Why have you painted our Father as an imbecile?"

Here, however, Jonathan was driven to protest more strongly. He turned his back on the painting and he said with some passion, "No, really, Lady Wallingford, I have not. I can see what you mean by complaining of the shapes, though honestly I never thought of anything of the sort, and I'll do something. . . . I mean, I'll paint something different somehow. But I never had the slightest intention of painting Father Simon in any displeasing way. . . ."

Lady Wallingford said, "You intended. . . . Look at it!" Jonathan stopped speaking; he looked at the woman; then he looked beyond her at Betty. She looked back despairingly. Richard observed the exchange of their eyes, and the full crisis became clear to him. He felt, as they did, Betty swept away on Lady Wallingford's receding anger; he saw her throw out a hand towards Jonathan and he saw Jonathan immediately respond. He saw him move away from the painting and go across to Betty, take her hands and lift her from her chair so that she stood against him. His arm round her, he turned again towards the painting. And again Richard's eyes went with his.

It was as he had last seen it. Or was it? Was the face not quite so down-turned? was it more lifted and already contemplating the room? Had he misjudged the angle? of course, he must have misjudged the angle. But to say it was "contemplating" was too much; it was not contemplating but only staring. What he had called bewilderment was now plain lack of meaning. Jonathan's phrase—"an absolute master and a lost loony at the same time"—recurred to him. The extended hand was no longer a motion of exposition or of convincing energy, holding the congregation attentive, but rather drawing the congregation after it, a summons and a physical enchantment. It drew them towards the figure, and behind the figure itself perhaps to more; for the shadow of the figure on the cliff behind was not now a shadow, but the darkness of a cleft which ran back very deeply, almost infinitely deep, a corridor between two walls of rock. Into that corridor the figure, hovering on its shadowy platform, was about to recede; and below it all those inclined backs were on the point of similar movement. A crowd of winged beetles, their wings yet folded but at the very instant of loosing, was about to rise into the air and disappear into that crevice and away down the prolonged corridor. And the staring emaciated face that looked out at them and over them was the face of an imbecile. Richard said impatiently to himself, "This

is all that old woman talking," because, though one did
get different angles on paintings, one did not usually so
soon see on the same canvas what was practically a different painting. Blatant and blank in the gray twilight,
where only a reflection of the sun shone from the beetles'
coats, the face hung receding; blank and blatant, the
thousand insects rose towards it; and beyond them the
narrow corridor hinted some extreme distance towards
which the whole congregation and their master were on
the point of unchecked flight. And yet the face was not
a true face at all; it was not a mockery, but the hither
side of something which was hidden and looking away,
a face as much stranger than the face they saw as that—
face or back—from the other insect backs below it.

They had all been silent; suddenly they all began
to speak. Richard said recklessly, "At least the coloring's
superb." Betty said, "Oh Jon, *need* you?" Jonathan said,
"It's a trick of this light. Don't cry, Betty. I'll do something else." Lady Wallingford said, "We won't keep you,
Mr. Drayton. If that's serious, we have very little in
common. If it's not serious, I didn't expect to be in-
sulted. We'll go, Betty. My daughter will write to you,
Mr. Drayton."

"This is quite absurd," Jonathan said. "Ask Mr.
Furnival, and he'll tell you that it wasn't in the least like
that until you talked us into believing it. I'm extremely
sorry you don't like it and I'll do something different.
But you can't think that I meant to show you a painting
of a madman and a mass of beetles as a portrait of your
Father Simon. Especially when I know what you think
about him. Is it likely?"

"It appears to be a fact," said Lady Wallingford.
She had turned her back on the canvas and was looking

bitterly at Jonathan. "If we are nothing more than vermin to you—Betty!"

Betty was still holding on to Jonathan. It seemed to
give her some strength, for she lifted her head and said,
"But, Mother, Jonathan is going to alter it."

"Alter it!" said Lady Wallingford. "He will alter it
to something still more like himself. You will have
nothing more to do with him. Come."

Jonathan interrupted. "Lady Wallingford," he said,
"I've apologized for something I never thought or in-
tended. But Betty's engagement to me is another matter.
I shan't accept any attempt to interfere with that."

"No?" Lady Wallingford said. "Betty will do what
I tell her and I have other plans. This pretended engagement was always a ridiculous idea and now it is
finished."

"Mother——" Betty began. Lady Wallingford, who
had been looking at Jonathan, turned her eyes slowly
to her daughter. The slight movement of her head was
so deliberate that it concentrated a power not felt in that
room till then. Her eyes held Betty as in the painting
behind her the outstretched hand held the attentive congregation; they summoned as that summoned. Jonathan
was thwarted, enraged and abandoned. He stood, helpless and alone, at the side of an exchange of messages
which he could not follow; he felt Betty flag in his arm
and his arm was useless to her. He tightened it, but she
seemed to fall through it as a hurt dove through the air
by which it should be supported. Richard, as he saw that
slow movement, was reminded suddenly of Lester's way
of throwing up her hand; the physical action held something even greater than the purpose which caused it. It
was not only more than itself in its exhibition of the

mind behind it, but it was in itself more than the mind. So killing, though it may express hate, is an utterly different thing from hate. There was hate in the room, but that particular hate was not so much hate as killing, as pure deliberate murder. As a man weak from illness might try to wrestle with a murderer and fail, he thought he heard himself saying sillily, "Lady Wallingford, if I may speak, wouldn't it be better if we talked about this another time? There's no need to murder the girl at once, is there? I mean, if Jonathan did something different, perhaps we could avoid it? or we might look at it—at the portrait—in a different light? and then you might see her in a different light? Sometimes a little attention . . ."

He was not quite sure how much of this he had actually said, but he stopped because Jonathan was speaking. Jonathan was speaking very angrily and very quickly, and he was talking of Betty's father the Air Marshal, and of his own aunt who would put Betty up for a few days, and how they would get married almost tomorrow, and how all the paintings and all the parents and all the prophets under heaven could not interfere. He spoke close above Betty's ear and several times he tried to get her to turn and look at him. But she did not; she had gone even paler than she had been before, and as Lady Wallingford took the first step towards the door she too began to turn towards it. She twisted herself suddenly out of Jonathan's arm and she said nothing in reply to the entreaties, persuasions and commands which he continued to address to her. Richard thought her face as she did so was very like another face he had seen; the identification of that other troubled him for a moment and then was suddenly present—it was Lester's when he had last seen it, Lester's when she was dead. The common likeness of the dead was greater than any difference between their living faces; they were both citizens of a remoter town than this London, and the other town was in this room. He saw beyond Betty, Lady Wallingford, who had walked across the room and was looking back at Betty from the door, and her face, though it was not that of the dead, was like a hard cliff in the world of the dead, or like a building, if the dead had buildings, a house or a temple of some different and disastrous stone. The whole ordinary room became only an imitation of a room; Jonathan and he were ghosts in a ghostly chamber, the realities were the man in the cleft of the rock and the rising beetles, and the dead face of Betty, and the living face—but in what way living?—of her tyrant. Even while he shivered in a sudden bleakness, Betty had disengaged herself from Jonathan and gone over to her mother. Lady Wallingford opened the door. She said to Betty, "We will go to Holborn." She motioned her daughter before her; they went out. The two men heard the shutting of the outer door.

They looked at each other. With that departure the room became again a room, and no more the outskirts of another world. Richard drew a breath and glanced again at the painting. It seemed to him now impossible to miss its actuality. Seen as human beings, those shapes had been motionless; seen as beetles, they were already in motion and on the point of flight. The painting lived, as the *Mona Lisa* does, in the moment of beginning, in the mathematical exactitude of beginning. Yet now Richard uncertainly felt more; there was an ambiguity in it, for the shapes might be either. That was its great, apparently unexpected, and certainly unwanted, success:

men who were beetles, beetles who were men; insects who had just been men, men who had just become insects. Metamorphosis was still in them. But could he then, he wondered, still gazing, think of them the other way, insects who had just become men, men who had just been insects? why not? Could humanity be living out of them?—some miracle in process? animality made newly rational? and their motion the rising into erect man? and the stretched arm the sign and power that called them?

He looked along the arm; his eyes rose to the face that ruled and called them? He saw it was impossible. That blank face could never work miracles; or if it could, then only miracles of lowering and loss. He could not persuade himself that it was growing into power; the metempsychosis there, if any had been, was done. The distance in the cleft behind, which he now clearly saw, as if the walls of it palely shone with their own light, held no promise of a lordlier change. There was no life there but that of rock—"*tutto di pietra di color ferrigno*—all iron-hued stone." What other life that stone might hold in itself, the life in the woman's face by the door, the life that had seemed to impinge on the room, could not be known by a face that had lost understanding. And then he remembered that this was but the backward-looking, the false, the devised face. What might the true face be that looked away down the cleft, between the walls, to the end of the corridor, if there was an end? That indeed might know more, much and very terribly more.

He made an effort and turned his eyes away. Jonathan was moving towards him; he said as he came, "What a mother!"

44

"But didn't you guess anything of this?" Richard asked, almost with curiosity.

"Oh I don't know," Jonathan answered irritably. "I thought perhaps while I was doing it that there was something odd about it, and then I thought there wasn't and that I was imagining things. One gets confused and can't judge. And I certainly thought she wouldn't notice it, or want to notice it. Nor would she, but she doesn't mean me to marry Betty."

Richard said, "But supposing to destroy it was the only way? Suppose Miss Wallingford asked you to?"

"Well, she hasn't," said Jonathan. "It'll be time enough, when she does. I don't know—probably I should. It'd be tiresome, but if it eased things . . . She doesn't care for this Simon herself; she only goes because her mother makes her."

"I'd like to see him for myself," Richard said. "Where is he? What was that remark about Holborn?"

"You go," said Jonathan. "It's a place just between Holborn and Red Lion Square—you'll easily find it. Go and hear him speak. He doesn't do it often, but you'll find out when he's going to. Go and see, and tell me the result."

"Well, I think I will," said Richard. "Tomorrow. I'm very sorry about all this. What do you think you'll do?"

"Just think first," Jonathan answered. "Shall I stick out or shall I try and come to terms? I don't believe Sir Bartholomew'll be much good, even when he does get back from Moscow, but at least I could see him, and it's going to be damned difficult to keep in touch with Betty. She might be a novice or a nun, the way her mother keeps her. I believe she even reads her letters and I'm

sure she watches her telephone calls. Come round tomorrow, will you, if it's not a bother? I shall want to talk
to you."

Richard promised and left. He came out into the
London streets about the time when everyone else was
also going home, and after a glance at the crowded transport he determined to walk. There was about the general hubbub something that eased and pleased him. He
relaxed his spirit a little as he moved among them. He
thought of Jonathan and Betty, and he thought also, "I
wish Lester were here; she'd know what to do and she
knows Betty." It would be very convenient now if Lester could call on Betty; he wished for Jonathan's sake
that she could. A little of Lester's energy and Lester's
style and even Lester's temper might be of a good deal
of use to Betty now.

It occurred to him, with a light surprise, that he was
thinking quite naturally of Lester. He was sincerely
sorry, for Jonathan's sake, that her strong femininity
was lost—for Jonathan's sake, not at that moment for his
own. It was what she was that was needed. What she was
—not what she was to him. It occurred to him then that
he had on the whole been in the habit of thinking of
Lester only in relation to himself. He saw suddenly in
her the power that waited for use, and he saw also that
he had not taken any trouble about that power; that
he had, in fact, been vaguely content to suppose it was
adequately used in attending to him. He said, almost
aloud, "Darling, did I neglect you?" It was no ordinary
neglect that he meant; of that certainly he had not been
guilty—and of this other perhaps she had been as guilty
as he. No—not as guilty; she knew more of him in him-

self than he had ever troubled to know of her in herself. It was why her comments on him, in gaiety or rage, always had such a tang of truth; whereas his were generally more like either cultured jesting or mere abuse. The infinite accuracy of a wife's intelligence stared out at him. He acknowledged what, in all his sincere passion, he had been unwilling to acknowledge, that she was often simply right, and the admission bound him to her the closer, dead though she might be. He thought how many chances he had missed of delighting in her entire veracity. instead of excusing, protesting, denying. The glowing splendor of her beauty rose, and it was a beauty charged with knowledge. It was that, among much else, that he had neglected. And now they all needed her and she was not there.

She was. It was along Holborn that he was walking, for he had half thought of going that night to look for Simon's hall or house or whatever it was. And there, on the very pavement, the other side of a crossing, she stood. He thought for the first second that there was someone with her. He was held by the appearance as motionless as in their early days he had thought he must be—though in fact in those early days he had never actually stopped. Now he did. It was as if that shock of her had at last compelled him to acknowledge it outwardly—at last, but as he had always almost believed he did, perhaps more in those days at the beginning when the strangeness was greater and the dear familiarity less. But the strangeness, for all the familiarity, had never quite gone, nor was it absent now; it was indeed, he felt, the greater, as well it might be. They stood on either side that Holborn by-way, and gazed.

He felt, as he gazed, more like a wraith than a man; against her vigor of existence he hung like a ghost and was fixed by it. He did not then remember the past hour in Jonathan's room, nor the tomb-like image of Lady Wallingford. Had he done so, he would have felt Lester's to be as much stronger than that woman's as hers had seemed stronger than his own. Lester was not smiling any recognition; the recognition was in her stillness. The passionate mouth was serious and the eyes deep with wonder and knowledge: of him? certainly of him. He thought almost he saw her suspire with a relief beyond joy. Never, never again would he neglect. The broken oaths renewed themselves in him. One hand of hers was raised and still almost as if it rested on some other arm, but the other had flown to her breast where it lay as if in some way it held him there. They made, for those few seconds, no movement, but their stillness was natural and not strange; it was not because she was a ghost but because she was she that he could not stir. This was their thousandth meeting, but yet more their first, a new first and yet the only first. More stable than rock, more transient in herself than rivers, more distant-bright than stars, more comfortable than happy sleep, more pleasant than wind, more dangerous than fire—all known things similies of her; and beyond all known things the unknown power of her. He could perhaps in a little have spoken; but before he could, she had passed. She left him precisely the sensation of seeing her go on; past him? no; up the by-way? no; but it was not disappearance or vanishing, for she had gone, as a hundred times she had, on her proper occasions, gone, kissing, laughing, waving. Now she neither kissed nor laughed nor waved, but that which was in all three lingered with him as he saw she was no longer there.

Lights were coming out in the houses; the confused sound of the City was in his ears. He was giddy with too much apprehension; he waited to recover; then he crossed the by-way and he too went on.

Chapter Three

CLERK SIMON

Jonathan spent the rest of the day in the abandoned studio. After the first hour he made three efforts to ring up Betty. He gave his own name the first time, but was told that Miss Wallingford was not in. The second time he gave Richard's name and for the third he invented a flight lieutenant. But neither was more successful. It was, of course, possible at first that the ladies had not returned from Holborn, but by half-past ten it seemed more likely that Lady Wallingford had simply secluded her daughter. He knew that if she had given orders that Miss Betty was not to be disturbed, it was very unlikely that anybody would disturb her. Between his two later calls he put in another. He knew that Sir Bartholomew had some small property in Hampshire, just as Lady Wallingford owned a house somewhere in Yorkshire, and he claimed to be speaking on behalf of the Hampshire County Council on some business of reconstruction. He asked if Sir Bartholomew had returned from Moscow or if not, when he was likely to return. The answer was that nothing could be said of Sir Bartholomew's movements. He suggested that Lady Wallingford might be asked. The answer was that that would be useless; instructions had been issued that no other answer could be given. Jonathan at last gave up the telephone and sat down to write letters.

He wrote to Betty; he wrote to Lady Wallingford. He offered, after a slight struggle with his admiration of himself, to suppress the picture; the admiration just managed to substitute "suppress" for "destroy." It was still worth while trying to save Betty and the picture too. But he knew that if he were driven far enough, he would consent to its destruction; though he could not quite avoid envisaging another picture in which something much more drastic should be deliberately done about Father Simon. He succeeded, however, in keeping this on the outskirts of his mind and even in mentioning to himself the word "dishonesty." His virtue, with some difficulty, maintained itself in the uncertain center of his mind. He told Betty he would be in his flat all the next day, in case she could ring up or indeed come. He proposed an aunt's house in Tunbridge Wells as a shelter for her. He told her that he would write to Sir Bartholomew through the War Office. He was perfectly well aware that Lady Wallingford would read the letter, but it told her nothing she could not have guessed, and it would at least make clear that he had other channels of communication with the Air Marshal.

He put off going to the post with these letters until almost midnight, in case by any wild chance Betty should ring up. But at last he gave up hope, took the letters, went to the door, and as he opened it switched out the light. At that moment the front door bell rang. He caught his breath and almost ran to it. He opened it; it was not she. In the dim light of the landing he saw a tall figure, apparently wrapped in some kind of cloak, and in his fierce disappointment he almost banged the door shut. But as his hand tightened on it, a voice said, "Mr. Drayton?"

"Yes?" Jonathan said morosely. The voice was urbane, a little husky, and had the very slightest foreign accent which Jonathan did not at once recognize. He peered forward a little to see the face, but it was not easy, even though the caller wore no hat. The voice continued. "Lady Wallingford has been with me tonight to tell me of a painting. I am Simon the Clerk."

"Oh!" said Jonathan, "yes. I see. . . . Look, won't you come in?" He had been quite unprepared for this, and as he ushered his visitor into the studio, his only feeling was one of extreme gratitude that in a moment of peevishness he had flung the covering again over the canvas. It would have been awkward to show Simon straight in at it. He could not quite think why he had come. It must, of course, be about the painting, but unless to see if he agreed with Lady Wallingford . . . and it would be odd to be as urgent as all that, especially as he disliked being painted. Still, it would come out. He was very much on his guard, but as he closed the door he said, as friendlily as he could, "Do sit down. Have a drink?"

"No, thank you," Simon answered. He remained standing with his eyes on the covered canvas. He was a tall man, with a smooth mass of gray—almost white— hair; his head was large; his face thin, almost emaciated. The face had about it a hint of the Jew—no more; so little indeed that Jonathan wondered if it were only Richard's account that caused him to think he saw it. But, considering more carefully, he saw it was there. The skin was dark and Jonathan saw with a thrill of satisfaction that he had got in his painting almost the exact kind of dead hue which it in fact possessed. The eyes were more deeply set than he had thought; otherwise he had been pretty accurate in detail. The only thing in which he had been wrong was in producing any appearance of bewilderment or imbecility. There was nothing at all of either in the Clerk's gaze. It was not exactly a noble face, nor a prophetic; priestly, rather. A remote sacerdotalism lived in it; the Clerk might have been some lonely hierarch out of a waste desert. He stood perfectly still, and Jonathan observed that he was indeed as near perfectly still as a man could be. There was no slightest visible motion, no faintest sound of breath. He was so quiet that quietness seemed to emanate from him. Jonathan felt his own disturbance quelled. It was in a softer voice than his usual one that he said, making what was almost an effort to move and speak at all, "Are you sure you won't have a drink? . . . Well, I think I will, if you'll excuse me." The other had very slightly shaken his head. Outside the room, the bells of the City began to chime midnight. Jonathan said to himself, as he had made a habit of doing since he had first met Betty whenever he was awake at midnight, as he often was, *"Benedicta sit, et benedicti omnes parvuli Tui."* He turned away and poured out his drink. With the glass in his hand, he came back. The hour was striking, near and far, wherever bells were still capable of sound, all over the wide reaches of London. Jonathan heard it through the new quiet. He said, "And now, Father Simon, Lady Wallingford?"

"Lady Wallingford was distressed about this painting," Simon answered.

"Distressed?" Jonathan said nastily. "Exhilarated was more the word, I should have thought." Then the sense of the quiet and of the other's presence made him ashamed of his petulance. He went on. "I beg your pardon. But I can't think she was altogether unhappy. She was very angry."

"Show it to me," the Clerk said. It was not perhaps quite a command, but very nearly; it almost sounded like a Marshal of the Air speaking to an official artist who ranked as a regular officer. Obedience was enforceable, though unenforced. Jonathan hesitated. If Simon took Lady Wallingford's view, he would be in a worse state than he was now. Was it possible that Simon would not take Lady Wallingford's view? In that case he might be very useful indeed; possibly he might persuade Lady Wallingford to alter her own. It was a great risk. The other saw the hesitation. The husky urbane voice said, "Come; you must not think I see things as she does."

"No," said Jonathan doubtfully. "Only . . . I mean she *has* talked to you. I don't know what she's told you, but she's so damned convinced and convincing that she'd even persuade me that a smudge of umber was a vermilion blot. Mind you, I think she's made up her mind to find something wrong with it, in order to interfere with Betty and me, so she wasn't disinterested."

"It doesn't matter what she told me," the other said. "I never see things with other people's eyes. If she's wrong—I might be of use."

"Yes," said Jonathan, moving to the easel. "If you could convince her, of course."

"She will think what I say," the Clerk said, and there was such a sudden contempt in his voice that Jonathan looked round.

"I say, you are sure of her!" he said.

"I'm quite sure of her," the Clerk answered, and waited. All this time he had not moved. The room itself, and it was large and by no means over-furnished, seemed almost full and busy beside him. Jonathan, as he threw back the cover, began to feel a warm attraction towards this unmoving figure which had the entire power to direct Lady Wallingford what to think. He determined, if by any chance Simon should pass this painting as harmless, to do him another about which there should be no doubt whatever. He stepped aside and for the third time that day the picture was exposed to study.

As Jonathan looked at it, he became extremely uneasy. The beetles, the blank gaze, the receding corridor, had not grown less striking since he had seen them last. If this was the Father, he could not think the Father would like himself. He wished again with all his heart that he had never begun to paint it. He knew exactly how he could have avoided it; he could have said he wasn't worthy. It would have been a lie, for being worthy was not a thing that came in with painting; painting had nothing to do with your personal merit. You could do it or you couldn't. But it would have been a convenient—and to that woman an easily credible—lie, and he wished he had told it, however difficult it would have been to say it convincingly. Betty, after all . . . He rather wondered if he could say now that he realized he wasn't worthy. But the Father did not look the sort of person who was taken in like that—anyhow, at the present stage, when he obviously had thought himself worthy. No, if things went wrong, he must argue again. By now he loathed and hated the entire painting; he would have cut it up or given it to the nation, if the nation had wanted it. He looked round.

Simon was still standing at gaze. The chimes rang a quarter-past twelve; otherwise the City was silent. Outside the large window beyond Simon the moon was high and cold. Her October chill interpenetrated the room. Jonathan shivered; something was colder—the atmosphere or his heart. Betty was far away, gone as lovers and wives do go, as Richard's wife had gone, gone to her deathbed. Betty's own bed was cold, even like her chastity. I would I were where Betty lies; no wedding garment except this fear, in the quiet, in the quiet, in the quiet, where a figure of another world stood. All things rose fluttering round it; beetles? too light for beetles: moths, bright light moths round a flame-formed dark; the cloak of the dark and the hunger in the dark. The high moon a moth, and he; only not Betty, Betty dead like Richard's wife, dead women in the streets of the City under the moon.

A distant husky voice with a strange accent broke the silence. It said, "That is I." Jonathan came to himself to see the Clerk staring. His head was a little forward; his eyes were fixed. He was so gratified that his voice let fall the words and ceased. The shock of them and of relief was so great that Jonathan felt a little lightheaded. He took a step or two back to get his vision into focus. He began to say something, but Simon was so clearly not listening that he gave it up and wandered away towards the window. But even as he did so he listened for what else that other should say which might give him hope, hope of Betty, hope of his work. He looked out into the moonlight, he saw in it, below him, on the other side of the road, two girls walking—they the only living in the night; and as his eyes took them in he heard again the voice behind him saying, but now in more than gratification, in low triumph: "That is I."

Jonathan turned. He said, "You like it?"

The other answered, "No one has painted me so well for a hundred years. Everything's there."

Jonathan went back. He did not quite see how to carry on the conversation; the allusion to "a hundred years" baffled him. At last he said doubtfully, "And Lady Wallingford?"

The Clerk slowly looked round at him as if he were recalled. He said and his face twitched slightly, "Lady Wallingford? What has she to do with it?"

"She was rather annoyed with it," said Jonathan. "In fact, she talked, as no doubt she told you, about insects and imbeciles."

The Clerk, still looking at him, said, "They aren't insects; they are something less. But insects is the nearest you can get. And as for imbecile, haven't you read *Sapientia adepti stultitia mundi?* That is why your work is so wonderful."

"Oh!" said Jonathan.

"That," the Clerk went on, turning his head again, "is what I am to these creatures, and Lady Wallingford (as you call her) is one of them. She thinks herself someone, but presently she'll find out. It's quite good for them to be hypnotized; they're much happier. But you—you are different; you are a genius. You must paint me often. Now you have shown me as I am to them and to myself, you must paint me often as I am in myself."

The chill sense of death was receding from Jonathan's heart. He began to feel that life was still possible, even life with Betty. He also wondered what his own painting of the face was like. He had first thought it was an ordinary portrait; then he had been uneasy about the bewilderment that seemed to show in it. Richard had agreed. Lady Wallingford had spoken of imbecility.

Now Simon seemed to see something else beyond that, something that was hidden in that and yet contradicted it. He might perhaps tell Lady Wallingford; he might make everything clear for him and Betty. In a second of silence Jonathan had married Betty, set up a house, painted Father Simon a stupendous portrait of himself without the beetles, painted several other shattering successes at the Peace Conferences and after, made a lot of money, become a father and an immortal at once, and was back again in the studio with the immediate necessity of explaining to Simon how all this was to be brought about. Better not go into further details of the painting; better get on with the main job.

He began, "Then you'll speak to——" but the other was already speaking. He was saying, "You must come with me, Mr. Drayton. I must have one or two people with me who are something more than these other creatures. The Doctrine is good for them; one gets nowhere by fighting it. All your books have it—the Koran, the New Testament, the Law. Hitler fought it; where is Hitler? There is nothing better, for those who need it. But you are an exception. You belong to yourself—and to me. Great art is apostolic. You must not lessen yourself. You are to be a master. I can do something to help you, but then you must have courage to paint the right things."

Jonathan listened to this with a certain warmth. He was a little shaken by great art being apostolic, but there was no doubt a sense in which it was true, though Sir Joshua's "common observation and plain understanding" pleased him better. He did think he was a remarkable painter and he did not care how often he was told so. But he did not lose sight of his main point. As soon as Simon paused, he said, "Then you'll speak to Lady Wallingford?"

Simon's voice had seemed to be closer and clearer. It receded again and grew huskier as he said, "What do you so want with Lady Wallingford?"

"I want to marry her daughter," Jonathan said.

The Clerk dropped his eyes to the ground. He said, after a moment, "I am not sure that you're wise. But it shall be as you like. I will talk to her—yes, in a few days, if you still wish. You shall have the girl if you want her. Show me something else."

"I haven't much here," Jonathan said. "The war paintings——"

"Oh the war!" the Clerk said. "The war, like Hitler, was a foolery. I am the one who is to come, not Hitler! Not the war; something else."

"Well, there's this thing of London," Jonathan said. "Wait, I'll turn it for you." He went round to the other easel, to the canvas on which he had not looked since the early afternoon because of all that had since happened, but now he did and saw it as he had seen it with Richard. He knew the validity of his own work—yet he knew also that he might so easily be wrong, as innumerable unfortunate bad painters had been. There was no way of being certain. But at least he believed that painting could be valid, could hold an experience related to the actuality of the world, and in itself valuable to mind and heart. He hoped this painting might be that; more he could not say. He saw beyond it the figure of the Clerk looming, and the window behind him, and it seemed almost as if he were now looking at the other painting made actual and released from canvas. The figure was there; the blank window behind; he could not at this distance and in this light see through it; it was but an opening into bleakness. And he himself the only other being there. He looked at the Clerk's face and it too hung blank as the window, empty of meaning. "I am being a fool," he thought, and looked, as he stepped back after turning the easel again, at the light on the canvas. He said, with the least flash of arrogance in his voice, "There! What do you think of that?"

The Clerk looked and flinched. Jonathan saw a quiver go through him; he shut his eyes and opened them. He said, "No, no; it's too bright. I can't see it properly. Move it."

Jonathan said coldly, "I'm sorry you don't like it. Myself, I think it's better than the other."

The Clerk said, "That is because you do not quite understand the meaning of your own work. This is a dream; that other is a fact. It is simply I who have come. I shall give all these little people peace because they believe in me. But these fancies of light would distract them. There is only one art and that is to show them their master. You had better—well, I know how you painters love even your mistakes and I will not say you should destroy it. But hide it for a year and come with me, and then look at it again and you will see it as I do."

Jonathan said cautiously, "Well, I'll see what Betty says. Anyhow I shan't have much time for views of the City during the next year or so." The words, and the tone, of mastery did not seem altogether unsuitable to the towering form; he himself was on the defensive. The very hint that there was much more in the other picture than he had supposed, that he painted more greatly than 'he knew, subtly soothed him. He was the more ready to owe Betty to a man who saw so deeply. He added, "You won't forget to speak to Lady Walling-ford?"

"Presently," the Clerk said. "But you must remember that you have a great work to do. When I am in union again, you shall paint me as I shall be. Soon."

Jonathan murmured something. The conversation was getting beyond him. He wished his visitor would go away before he said the wrong thing. The Clerk, almost as if he too felt that all had been said, turned. He said, "I'll come to you again, or else I'll send for you."

"I may be moved about," Jonathan said. "We of the Services, you know——"

"Your service is with me," the other answered. "I or —or Betty will let you know." His eyes stared out through the blank window. "What you shall paint! Trust me. I will make you . . . never mind. But put the other thing away. The color is wrong."

He gave Jonathan no opportunity for a reply. He went towards the door and Jonathan followed. At parting he raised his hand a little. He came out into the street and the moonlight and began to walk.

He went towards Highgate and he went easily though at great speed, and as he went the City seemed to dwindle around him. His mind was very earnestly set on himself. As he went the Jewish quality in his face seemed to deepen; the occasional policemen whom he passed thought they saw a Jew walking by night. Indeed that august race had reached in this being its second climax. Two thousand years of its history were drawing to a close; until this thing had happened it could not be free. Its priesthood—the priesthood of a nation—had been since Abraham determined to one End. But when, after other terrible wars had shaken the Roman peace, and armies had moved over Europe, and Caesar (being all that Caesar could be) had been stabbed in his own central place, when then that End had been born, they were not aware of that End. It had been proposed that their lofty tradition should be made almost unbearably august; that they should be made the blood companions of their Maker, the own peculiar house and family of its Incarnacy—no more than the Gentiles in the free equality of souls, but much more in the single hierarchy of kindred flesh. But deception had taken them; they had, bidding a scaffold for the blasphemer, destroyed their predestined conclusion, and the race which had been set for the salvation of the world became a judgment and even a curse to the world and to themselves. Yet the oaths sworn in heaven remained. It had been a Jewish girl who, at the command of the Voice which sounded in her ears, in her heart, along her blood and through the central cells of her body, had uttered everywhere in herself the perfect Tetragrammaton. What the high priest vicariously spoke among the secluded mysteries of the Temple, she substantially pronounced to God. Redeemed from all division in herself, whole and identical in body and soul and spirit, she uttered the Word and the Word became flesh in her. Could It have been received by her own people, the grand Judean gate would have been opened for all peoples. It could not. They remained alien—to It and to all, and all to them and—too much!—to It. The Gentiles, summoned by that other Jew of Tarsus, could not bear their vicarious office. Bragging themselves to be the new Israel, they slandered and slew the old, and the old despised and hated the bragging new. Till at last there rose in Europe something which was neither, and set itself to destroy both.

And when that had been thwarted, this also which was to happen had at last happened. Jew and Christian alike had waited for the man who now walked through the empty London streets. He had been born in Paris, in one of those hiding-places of necromancy which all the energy of the Fourteenth Louis had not quite stamped out. He was a child of the nobility, but he was hardly yet a boy when the Revolution had broken out. His family had moved safely through it, protected by wealth and cunning and in extremes by another kind of cunning learned in very ancient schools. His father had been to the world a scholar as well as a nobleman, one of the early philologists, but to a different circle and to his son his philology had been quite other. He knew sounds and the roots of sounds, almost the beginnings of sounds; the vibrations that overthrew and the vibrations that built up. The son followed his father.

He remembered now, as he walked, how he had come to know himself. It was not often he permitted himself the indulgence of memory, but that painted face which Jonathan had supposed to be blank of meaning yet in which he had read all he wished to read, seeing it full of power and portent—that artificiality had opened up recollection within him. He remembered how he had seen the crowds in Paris, their poverty, their need, their rage, and (so small as he was) understood how men need both comfort and control. And he had seen Napoleon rise and fall, but before that mastery was done his childish dreams of being king or emperor had been better instructed. He had learned three things from that small college of which his father was president—that there was another power to use, that there were ways of directing it, that many men would pay much to learn them. Could they be sold! but they could not be. They were private to those who had the right by nature, as all art is, but these especially to the high priestly race. Only a Jew could utter the Jewish, which was the final, word of power.

There were not in the circles where he grew up any of the mere obscenities of magic—no spectacular outrages of the Black Mass or profane sensualities of the Sabbath. There were certain bloody disciplines to test the postulant—it was all. The mass of men were at once despised and pitied by the chaste sorcerers. He learned to shelter, to feed, to console them, but at the same time that he was separate from them. He had watched a man starve, but he was not cruel; it was in his training. He was not lustful; only once in all his life had he lain with a woman, and that for a rational purpose. He had not been kept from talk with holy Rabbis and charitable priests; if he had chosen their way no one would have interfered with him unless he had become inconvenient to the great work. He did not so choose; he preferred his own.

He was not, in fact, much different from any man, but the possibilities slowly opened to him were more rare. There shaped itself gradually in his mind a fame beyond any poet's and a domination beyond any king's. But it was fame and domination that he desired, as they did. That his magical art extended where theirs could never reach was his luck. The understanding of his reach had come when he first assisted at a necromantic operation. As the dead body stood and spoke he felt the lordship of that other half of the world. Once, as he had learned the tale, the attempt at domination had been made and failed. The sorcerer who had attempted it had also been a Jew, a descendant of the house of David, who clothed in angelic brilliance had compelled a woman of the same house to utter the Name, and something more than mortal had been born. But in the end the operation had failed. Of the end of the sorcerer himself there were no records; Joseph ben David had vanished. The living thing that had been born of his feminine counterpart had perished miserably. It had been two thousand years before anyone had dared to risk the attempt again.

He came up towards Highgate, and as he came he let his memories fade. He put away the recollection of the painting; the time for his spiritual enthronement was not quite come. But he felt the City lessen—not only London, but all bodies and souls of men. He lifted his head; his face was lean and hungry under the moon. He felt himself walking alone among tiny houses among which men and women ran about under his protection and by his will. There waited him, in the house to which he was going, the means of another operation than his coming empery in this world; of which his child was the instrument. For a moment he thought of Jonathan and Jonathan's love. He smiled—or rather a sudden convulsion passed across his face, a kind of muscular spasm rather than a smile. It was not meant to be unkind; he did not dislike Jonathan, and he wished his genius to thrive and paint the grand master even more intensely. But Betty was for another purpose. Nor was he even aware that what had once been a smile was now a mere constriction. One cannot smile at no one, and there was no one at whom he could smile. He was alone. He went on, ignorantly grimacing.

Chapter Four

THE DREAM

In the house at Highgate Betty Wallingford was lying awake. She was wholly wretched. Her mother, after they had returned from that secret conversation in Holborn in which she had not been allowed to take part, had sent her to bed. She had wished to protest; she had wished to ring up Jonathan. But it would have been quite useless. She could not remember a time when it would not have been useless. If she had been Lady Wallingford's real daughter, she might have had a better chance, or so sometimes she thought. But since, years ago, Lady Wallingford had spoken of her adoption, she had always felt at a disadvantage. No allusion was ever made to it now. She had tried, once or twice, to ask Lady Wallingford about her real parents, but her adopted mother had only said, "We will not talk of that, Betty," and so of course they did not. As for Sir Bartholomew, she had been forbidden to mention it to him, and anyhow he was hardly ever at home and was only interested in air matters. So she only knew she was not what everyone thought she was.

Everyone in London, that is. There was in the north, in Yorkshire, a small house where she and Lady Wallingford sometimes went. They always went by themselves, and when they got there she was not even treated as a daughter. She was, purely and simply, the servant. It was supposed to be training for her, in case (as might happen, Lady Wallingford said) she ever had to earn her own living. She did the work; she showed in the Vicar or any other local visitor, and then she went back to her nice bright kitchen, where she had that morning's *Daily Sketch* (which Lady Wallingford took in for her) and her radio on which she was only allowed to listen to the most popular music (because, Lady Wallingford said, that was what girls of that class liked). She was called Bettina there. "Ridiculous names these girls have nowadays!" Lady Wallingford had once said to the Vicar as he was leaving; and the Vicar had said, "Not at all ridiculous! a very good name." But he had not looked very attentive and Lady Wallingford never let her go out alone, so there was no help there. And anyhow there was no need for help; what was there to help?

It had been going on for a long time, even before she had left school. She had always been in terror lest any of the other girls should pass and see her from a car. Or even, quite impossibly, call. She had tried to think what she would say, and to practice saying it. There would be nothing unusual in her mother and herself being there, but to be treated as a housemaid . . . She knew they would never believe anything she could say, and still more certainly that she could never say it. She used to lie awake by night thinking of it and wondering if the next day would bring them, but it never did; and presently the two of them always went back to London and then she was Betty Wallingford again—only of course she was no more Betty Wallingford than she was a housemaid. She was nothing and no one. Her mistress-mother, her mother-mistress, told her what to do; she and the man who sometimes came to see her, this Father Simon.

Of all the girls at school, two only now remained in her mind; indeed, she knew them a little still. She would have liked to be friends with Lester Grantham, who was now Lester Furnival, but it had never come about. At school Lester had never wanted to be bothered with her, though she had been in a vague way half-scornfully kind, and when she and Lady Wallingford met they had never got on very well. Lester had once or twice called with Evelyn Mercer, who was the other girl, but Betty did not like Evelyn. She might have borne Lester knowing about her being Bettina, but she would have been anguished by Evelyn's finding out, and Evelyn was the sort of person who did find things out. When Evelyn came to see her, she used to sit and talk to her; she had hunted her down at school sometimes just to talk to her. But it used to be horrible and she would cry, and even now Evelyn would ask so many questions and tell so many horrid stories that Betty felt she could not bear it. Of course, she had to, because Evelyn sat, eying her and talking. So that presently she became the very image of Betty's fear, more even than Lady Wallingford; and one of her worse nightmares was of running away from Evelyn, who was racing after her, calling, "Bettina! Bettina!" And other acquaintances she had none.

During the war she had thought she would have to do a job and perhaps go away from home. She had registered and she had been interviewed by a nice oldish woman. But nothing else had happened. She had been a little surprised and she had even spoken of it to Lady Wallingford, who had only said, "You're not strong enough—mentally strong enough, I mean." So she supposed—and she was right—that Lady Wallingford had taken steps. After that she had begun to worry over her mind, after that rather nice refugee had disappeared. During the little time she had known him, he had been rather comforting, but presently he had ceased to be about. And there was no one again.

Until there had been Jonathan Drayton. She could not remember how they had first met, and they had certainly not met often. If her mother had not wished to have a painting of Father Simon, they would have met less often. But even Lady Wallingford was sometimes compelled to allow one obstinacy to get in the way of another. She had been startled—though not much more startled than Betty—when Jonathan began to talk of an engagement. Betty remembered how she had clung to him the first time he had kissed her, and what he had said of her, but she tried not to remember that, for she had always known it would be no good, and now Lady Wallingford had chosen to be offended at his painting, and it was all ended. Very soon they would be in the country again. Lady Wallingford was always saying that, now the war was over, they would go there permanently —"and then you shall settle down. I shall have to go up sometimes, but you need never leave it again." Betty was beginning to look on it as a refuge; once there, she would be Bettina altogether and perhaps that would be peace.

But tonight it was no refuge. Jonathan was too near. He had sometimes talked to her about painting, and she had tried to understand and even ask questions, though her mistress—no, her adopted mother—had said, "Betty's rather backward," and repeated that she was mentally weak. But Jonathan had only said, "Thank God she's not cultured! and anyhow I'm not much more than adolescent myself," and gone on talking, and she had wanted to cry on his shoulder, as once or twice inex· plicably she had. She never would again. She would be taken to hear Father Simon speak on Love. In a way that was a relief. While he talked she sat in a kind of trance and forgot everything. That was in Holborn; when he came to Highgate it was different and not so peaceful. She had to do something. He was always saying to her, "Do not trouble yourself; only do as I say." She would; in that and the maid's kitchen were her only hope.

She lay, waking and waiting—waiting for her mind to grow weaker, waiting for her memory of Jonathan to cease, waiting for an end. She was afraid of Lady Walling- ford and desperately afraid of Evelyn. Evelyn would get everything about Jonathan out of her and would tell people—no, she would not, for Evelyn was dead. In her sheer rush of gratitude Betty sat up in bed. It was almost her only individual movement for years. She drew a deep breath. Something of horror had stopped for ever. Evelyn, Evelyn was dead. Of course. Lester was dead too; she was a little sorry about Lester, but Lester had never wanted her. That had been Lester's husband this after- noon; he looked nice. At the time of the wedding she had been in Yorkshire; not that she would have been asked anyhow. Yorkshire— Oh, well, Yorkshire; but Evelyn could never, never come to Yorkshire now. "Evelyn," she said to herself, clasping her knees, "Evelyn's *dead.*" In her entire joy, she even forgot Jonathan—in her sudden sense of a freedom she had not known. She had at least no consciousness of impropriety; she was mentally strong enough for joy. She said it again, draw- ing breath, hugging herself, savoring it: "Evelyn's dead."

The door opened. Lady Wallingford came in. She

switched on the light and saw Betty. Betty saw her and before a word could be spoken or a glance exchanged, she thought, "People die." Lady Wallingford said, "Why are you sitting up like that?" and Betty answered, because it was so important, "Evelyn's dead."

For once Lady Wallingford was taken aback. She had never had much interest in Evelyn, though she was not as hostile to her as she had been to Lester, for she knew Betty was afraid of Evelyn. She did not altogether wish Betty to lose this and she answered almost immediately—but there had been a second's pause, a moment in which Betty all but triumphed, "Yes. But remember that that means she is still alive." She did not give this time to settle; she was well assured that the thought would return. She went on. "But we can't think of it now. Our Father needs you."

"Oh not *now*——" Betty exclaimed. "I'm so tired. I can't—after this afternoon—Mother, I *can't.*" She spoke with more boldness than usual. The sense of freedom that Evelyn's death had given her was still strong, and an even larger sense that changes could happen which had risen in her mind when Lady Wallingford entered. People died. She looked at her mother almost as an equal; her mother would die. But she could not maintain her gaze. Lady Wallingford stared her down. As the girl's eyes fell, she said, "We are waiting. Dress and come down." She stayed for a moment, still staring; then she turned and went out.

Discouraged and miserably helpless, Betty got up and put on her clothes. She knew what would happen; it had happened before. She knew she went out, but where and with what result she did not know—only that afterwards she was again back in the house, and exhausted. Lady Wallingford always kept her in bed the next day. These occasions were known to the servants as "Miss Betty's turns." It was vaguely understood that Miss Betty was subject to something not quite nice. Something mental. Nor indeed were they far wrong, for the mind as well as the body suffered from those lonely excursions, and it was a question for her directors how long she would be able to bear them.

Her hands were trembling as she finished dressing. She had put on, and with difficulty fastened, a pair of outdoor shoes. If only, she thought, she did not have to leave the house! Or if she could know where she went and what she did! She might be braver then. It was this getting ready to go that frightened her, and the not knowing. Her tyrants never by any chance referred to her compulsory expeditions, except on the nights themselves. They would be waiting for her. She had forgotten Evelyn's death and Lady Wallingford was perpetual. She looked at the clock; it was half-past one. There was no use in delay. She went down.

They were waiting, as she had known, in the drawing-room. Lady Wallingford was sitting by a table. Simon was walking softly up and down. When she came in he stopped and scanned her. Then he pointed to a chair. He said, in that husky voice she dreaded, though it was never unkind, "I want you to go out."

She was without initiative. She went to the chair and sat down. She said, "Yes, Father."

He said, "You shall be at peace soon. You could be at peace now if you did not fight. In a moment you will not fight; then you will be in peace. Presently you will always be at peace. Let yourself be in my will. I can send you; I can bring you back; only take the peace. Be in peace and you will be in joy. Why do you—no, you will not fight; you are not fighting; you are dying into peace; why should you not die in peace? Peace. . . ."

The quiet husky soothing voice ran on, recapitulating the great words; bidding the sufficient maxims. She knew she would lose herself; now it did not seem so horrid; now she wondered she was not quicker to let go. She usually was. But tonight something interfered with the words. Her hands, quiet though they lay, were strangely warm, and the blood in them seemed to beat. Her body (though she did not then realize it) held a memory that her mind had forgotten. The strength of Jonathan's hands was still in her own and rose up her arms and stirred in her flesh. His voice, still subconditionally remembered in her ears, stirred in her corridors. She did not think of it but all her living body answered, "Jonathan!" and on that cry rose against the incantation that all but appeased her. The word *love*, when the Clerk uttered it, was only a dim sound of distant wind, but it said, "Jonathan"; the word *peace* was great waters on a gentle shore, but it murmured, "Jonathan!"; the word *joy* was an echo and no more, but it echoed: "Jonathan!" Even the afternoon, even the painting and all, had but made him more intense; as a man in sleep utters his love's name, so now, as she all but slept, her body sighed for its friend. She did not speak, but as she yielded to the spell, she moaned a little; she slept, though with waking eyes, and she did not sleep peaceably. The Clerk knew it. He came near her; he spoke over her—he had a very great courage—those august words: "peace, joy, love." He used them for what he needed, and they meant to him—and to her—what he chose.

Lady Wallingford covered her eyes. She could not quite bear to see the nullification of life in the intellectual center of life. She detested her daughter, and she wished to distress and pain her. But then she wished her, while she lived, to be still herself so that she should be distressed and pained. That other who stood over the girl who was his daughter also, did not wish her to be herself, or even that only for a purpose. He wished her to be an instrument only; *peace, joy, love,* were but names for the passivity of the instrument. He was unique; yet he was no more than any man—only raised to a high power and loosed in himself.

Presently Lady Wallingford heard his voice near her. It said, "You didn't tell me she was so enamored. It doesn't matter. I've found her in time." She moved her hand. He was standing by her, looking over to Betty where now she sat quietly in her chair, her eyes open, her body composed. He drew deep breaths; he said, so quietly that Lady Wallingford hardly heard, so strongly that the entranced girl rose at once to obey: "Go now and bring me the news."

She rose. Her eyes looked at him, simply, almost lingeringly. She gave him her attention, with a kind of delight. The last revolt had been abolished; a docile sweetness possessed her. Docility and sweetness were natural to her. In a quiet that might have been peace, in an attraction that might have been love, in a content that might have been joy, she turned from her director towards the door. Her exhaustion on the next day would come not only from what she was about to do, but from this surrender which would then have ceased. Yet every time her restoration was a little less; a day might come when this hypnotic quiescence would occupy her whole life. That day (the Clerk thought) would be soon. Then he would be able to send her forever into the world she could now only visit.

Betty went out of the room. The Clerk followed her, and Lady Wallingford, drawn by a desire she half dreaded, joined him and went with him. The house was warm and quiet. Sir Bartholomew was in Moscow; the servants were asleep in their rooms. Betty went to a lobby, took out a raincoat and a rough hat, and put them on. The two stood motionless, the tall man and the shorter woman, their arms hanging by their sides, their feet precisely together, their eyes fixed on the girl. They watched her go to the front door and open it wide. Beyond her lay the empty street, lit by the moon to a bluish pallor. The silence of it rushed in on them, a silence in which the quiet hall sounded as if, but a moment before, it had been noisy. Betty went out. The Clerk went quickly down the hall and almost closed the door, leaving it open but a chink. He stood by it, his head bent, intently listening. Lady Wallingford remained where she was, trembling a little. Hardly five minutes had passed when, in that perfect silence, deeper than any lull in any town, any stillness in any countryside, the faint sound of slow dragging feet was heard. They were literally dragging, each was pulled along the path. The Clerk let go the door and stood back. It was pushed open a little farther and through the crack Betty squeezed herself in. She was very pale, her eyes were almost shut, she drooped with the heaviness of her fatigue. She came in; she made a motion to push the door to; she stumbled forward and fell. The Clerk caught her; she lay against him. The clerk looked over his shoulder at Lady Wallingford, who as at a sudden call ran forward. She bent down and picked up her daughter's feet. Between them the two creatures carried the girl upstairs, their monstrous shadows rising against the walls. They took her to her room and laid her on her bed. They undressed her and got her into the bed, all in silence and with the softest and quickest movements. Then they drew up chairs and sat down, one on each side. Lady Wallingford took up a notebook and a pen. The Clerk leaned his head close to Betty's and said something in her ear. He moved his head so that his ear was close to Betty's mouth, and in a voice hardly to be heard, with broken phrases and long intervals, she began to speak. He repeated, in a voice harder than was usual with him, what she said. Lady Wallingford wrote down the words. It was almost morning before the triple labor was done. The Clerk stood up frowning. Lady Wallingford looked at him. He shook his head slowly and presently they both left the room, she to her own, he to the staircase and the hall.

Betty had gone out from the house into the street. She did not consciously remember what she had to do, and as she stood in the shadow of the porch she drew a deep breath or two. Something—if in the porch she had had a shadow, it would have been like her shadow, but it was not, and it was more solid—lay in the porch, against the door behind her. She did not notice it. She began to walk down the street, towards Highgate Hill and the City that lay below. She went lightly and gaily; these times were always happy and fortunate; she could not compare them with others, for she knew no others. All but these joyous hours were secluded from her. Ig- norant of what she obeyed, but in a perfect volition of obedience, she went along. She did not know through what spectral streets she moved; she knew roads and turnings and recognized her way, but she did not name them. She was not thinking of them, for now she did not think. All that was, for the time, done. She only knew. But she did not know that the silence was any but an earthly silence, nor that the sky above her was the sky under which Lester and Evelyn walked. Nor did she think of any insolidity; if for a moment the fronts of the houses looked unearthly, she unconsciously attributed this to the effects of the moon. The world was as familiar as this world, and to her less terrifying.

It lay there, as it always does—itself offering no barriers, open to be trodden, ghostly to this world and to heaven, and in its upper reaches ghostly also to those in its lower reaches where (if at all) hell lies. It is ours and not ours, for men and women were never meant to dwell there long; though it is held by some that certain unaccountable disappearances have been into that world, and that a few (even living) may linger there awhile. But mostly those streets are only for the passing through of the newly dead. It is not for human bodies, though it has known a few—"Enoch, Elijah, and the Lady"— though they not in London, but in the places where they died. It has certainly been thought, but the speculation is that of dreamers, that in the year of our great danger the grand attack of our enemies succeeded; that London and England perished; and that all we who then died entered it together and live there till we have wrought out our salvation—to enjoy (purgatorially) a freedom unpermitted on earth; and that our conquerors live on that earth, troubled and frenzy-driven by a mystical awareness of our presence. More justly, it is held by learned doctors that in times of much bloodshed that world draws closer (so to call a neighborhood we cannot define) to this, that chance entry for the living is easier, and that any who wish to drive others there for their own purposes find the deathly work lighter. One day perhaps it will indeed break through; it will undo our solidity, which belongs to earth and heaven, and all of us who are then alive will find ourselves in it and alone till we win through it to our own place. It is full enough of passengers, but mostly alone, though those who died together may have each other's companionship there, as Lester and Evelyn had, and a few more fortunate friendships and intimate loves.

Betty Wallingford knew nothing of this. She walked in peace and gay, in her seeming body. She had been compelled in her body, and in her body she had left the house. That actual body lay now crouched in the porch of the house, unconscious, waiting her return. Lester's and Evelyn's flesh no longer waited them so; they had to find another way to the reintegration of the great identity of flesh and soul. But the days that had passed since their death had not held more for them than the few minutes since she had left the house had for her. In that state there might be ignorance, but even ignorance and fear meant only definite pause or definite action. The vagueness, the dreaming, the doubtful hanging-about are permitted only on the borders of intellectual life, and in this world they were rare. Neither angels nor insects know them, but only bewildered man. Far below Betty, as she came down the Hill, Lester and Evelyn walked. The City about them had not changed, nor they. They were still troubled in their hearts by what did not at all trouble her.

She walked on. It was already morning; the day had rushed, in brightness and freshness, to meet her. It was a clear October morning—a little cold, with a few clouds, but agreeable to all her senses. She almost smelled it— a new pleasant smell mingling with the old London smell, but that itself (though heavier than the other) no longer unpleasant, if indeed it ever had been; the ground bass of the whole absorbed music with which the lighter sun and sky mingled. Indeed the same effect struck her in sound, for she heard, as on similar journeys she had done, the distant noise of the waking City. It always seemed to her at first strange and then not strange. In general its citizens hardly noticed it; they are a part of it and their ears are deafened by it. But her hearing was now cleared and fresh, and she knew that it was happy and that she was happily going to it. She had to find it, or rather something in it, something which helped to compose it. All the sounds and times which went to make it were not equally important to her now. It was a question of time; she would come to the right time, for she had been directed to it, but there was a way to it, a part to be gone through first, a part of the City, not exactly disagreeable but strange. It was as if she were going through a part of her own past, though it was not always the same part, nor the same past. She knew that she only remembered certain parts of it. Someone had once told her that her mind wasn't very strong, "and indeed it isn't," she thought gaily, "but it's quite strong enough to do what it's got to do, and what it hasn't got to do it needn't worry about not doing." Who was it who had so joyously teased her so? to whom she had so joyously replied?

She began, as she came to the bottom of the Hill, to remember more clearly what did happen at these times. She had—they were hardly waking dreams, but she could not think of another word. Sometimes she seemed to be in a shadowy house, with the street faintly visible through the wall; sometimes she saw herself going by in a car with her mother. One way or another she was always in the dreams, and of some of them she was a little ashamed because she seemed to be making a frightful fuss. In ordinary dreams, as far as she knew, you did not criticize yourself. You were doing something or other and you were just doing it, but you rarely thought you might have done it very much better. Her shame, however, did not do away with her enjoyment; there was an agreeable exhilaration in her severe comments on herself. She began to try and recollect one or other of her dreams, but it was difficult, for she was now coming into the busy streets, and there was color and sound and many people, and the sky was sparkling, and her heart swelled with mere delight. And in the midst of it all she was at King's Cross Station.

It was crowded but not unpleasantly. She knew at once what she had to do, or the first thing. She had to go and find that other self and say a kind encouraging word to it; she had to help herself. Cleverer people, no doubt, would help others, but she did not envy them, though she did admire. Helping herself was almost like helping another, and helping another was much like helping yourself. She made for the platform where the York train stood. The happy exhilaration of action was upon her. She remembered that you had to change at York for Palchester, and at Palchester for Laughton; and she remembered how that other she grew more and more distressed at each change and less and less capable of showing it. The reason, for the moment, evaded her, but it ought not to be so. "Be yourself, Betty," she said admonishingly, and saw herself on the platform outside a compartment. This, she knew at once, was her most recent journey. She and her mother had gone down in July, and this was July, and there was she and there was her mother. Her mother—she was in these dreams always surprised at her mother, for she definitely remembered her as domineering and powerful, but whenever she saw her in this world there seemed to be something lacking; she looked so blank and purposeless and even miserable. And there by her mother was the other Betty, quiet, wan, unhappy. The porters were calling out, "Grantham, Doncaster, York"; the passengers were getting in. Betty came to the compartment. The dream was very strong. There was herself, her sister, her twin. She laughed at her; she said, gaily and yet impatiently, "Oh don't *worry!* Isn't it all a game? Why can't you play it?"

She did not know why she was so sure of the game, nor how she knew that it was her mother's game, and only a courtesy, if she could, to play it well. She added, "It won't hurt you." The other Betty said, "It does hurt me." She answered, "Well, if you can't stand a pinch— Oh darling, laugh!" The other Betty stood wretched and mute. Lady Wallingford said, "Get in, Betty. You travel first class as far as Laughton, you know." She added to a porter, "This part is for York?" The porter having just called out, "Grantham, Doncaster, York," exercised a glorious self-restraint, and said, "Yes, lady." He spoke perhaps from habit, but here habit was full of all its past and all its patience, and its patience was the thunder of the passage of a god dominant, miraculous and yet recurrent. Golden-thighed Endurance, sun-shrouded Justice, were in him, and his face was the deep confluence of the City. He said again, "Yes, lady," and his voice was echoed in the recesses of the station and thrown out beyond it. It was held in the air and dropped, and some other phrase in turn caught up and held. There was no smallest point in all the place that was not redeemed into beauty and good—except Lady Wallingford's eyes and her young companion's white face. But the joyous face of that Betty who stood on the platform, whom her mother did not see, leaned towards her, and as the train began to move, cried out to her twin, "A game! only a game!" The girl in the train momentarily brightened and almost tried to smile.

Betty stood and watched it go. When it had disappeared—into a part, into a past, of this world—she turned. She paused, not quite knowing what she should do. Her exhilarated heart saddened a little; a touch of new gravity showed in her face. She felt as if she had delayed on an errand, yet she had been right to delay, for she had been directed by the City itself to this meeting. It had been given to her and enjoined on her, but it had been somehow for her personal sake; now she must do her business for some other. She tried to remember what she had been bidden, but she could not. That did not matter; in this blessed place it would be shown to her. She walked slowly up the platform, and as she went the whole air and appearance of the station changed. With every step she took, a vibration passed through the light; the people about her became shadowy; her own consciousness of them was withdrawn. She moved in something of a trance, unaware of the quickening of the process of time, or rather of her passage through time. The perfect composure of the City in which all the times of London existed took this wanderer into itself, and provided the means to fulfill her errand. When she had left her house, it had been late October; she had stood on the platform in the fullness of the preceding July; she walked now through the altering months, to every step a day, till when she came to the bookstall, some six months had gone by, and she stood by it on a dark morning in January, the January her mortal body in the porch of the house had not yet known, nor Simon the Clerk, nor any on earth. She had moved on into the thing happening, for here all things were happening at once. These were the precincts of felicity. The felicity of the City knew its own precincts, but as yet, while she was but a vagrant here, she could not know them as such. She was happy, yet as she came to the bookstall a vague contradiction of felicity rose in her heart and faded. It was right that she should do whatever it was she was about to do, yet she did not quite like it. She felt as if she were being a little vulgar, though she could not guess how. She was holding—how she could not guess; and the question hardly occurred to her—a few coins. Before her on the bookstall were the morning and weekly papers. Apologetically—she could not help feeling apologetic—she bought a number. She went into the waiting-room and sat down to read.

The reading had absolutely no meaning to her. Her eyes ran over, her memory took in, the printed lines. But for herself she neither understood nor remembered them. She was not doing it for herself but because she had been commanded. She read one paper, finished it, folded it, laid it down, took up another, and so through all. She read the future, but the future was not known to her; it was saved, by the redemption that worked in that place, for the master who had sent her there. Let him make his profit of it; her salvation was his peril. The activities and judgments of the world in that new January were recorded in her, but she, being magically commanded, was yet free. She lightly rose at last and left the papers lying. She went out of the waiting-room and of the station; she took her way again towards Highgate. By the time she had come into the street, she had moved again through receding time. It was again October and a fresh wind was blowing.

Her mind now was a little subdued from her earlier joy. She caught herself looking forward to a tiresomeness, some kind of dull conversation. There were people waiting for her who would want things repeated or explained. "And I'm not," Betty protested, "very good at explaining. I've been trying to explain something to my mother for a long time, but I've never got it over." She spoke aloud, but not to anyone present; indeed there were few people present; the streets were emptier and there was no one by or in front of her. She spoke almost to the City itself, not in defense or excuse, but as a fact. She heard no answer, except that the air seemed to heighten and the light in it to grow, as if it proposed to her something of encouragement and hope. If she had seen Jonathan's other picture she might have recognized the vibration of that light, though neither she nor anyone could have guessed why or how he had been permitted that understanding of a thing he had never known in itself. "And," she went on, "I shan't feel as good as this presently. I shall very likely have a headache too, which'll make it worse." The remark died into the air; she walked on, trying not to be peevish. She came—so quickly—to the bottom of the Hill, and as she saw it waiting to be climbed (so conscious did all the streets seem) she said, with the first touch of real distress, "It does seem a shame." It did—to leave this goodness for

84

the stupid business before her; she knew it would be stupid and she could feel the first symptoms of the headache. However, it could not be helped; someone had to do the job, and if it were she—— She became conscious that she was making something of a difficulty out of climbing the Hill, and quickened her steps. The dullness she expected would be but a game and she would play it well. But as she mounted, the sense that she was near to leaving the City grew on her. She turned once or twice and looked back. It lay, lovely and light before her, but away to the East it was already a little shadowed, and the West was already rose and crimson as the sun sank. She would not, she knew, be here when it did sink; the night in this City was not for her. Another night waited her. It seemed to her that never when she had walked here before, had she felt it so hard to return. Then the sadness and the pain had taken her suddenly at the end. Now there was preparation; they approached and she had become protestant, almost rebellious at their approach. Why leave? why leave? She was already on the edge of the shadow over the Hill's height, and all before her the sunset, over the City—another sunset, another sun—glowed not as if the light were going but as if the night were coming, a holier beauty, a richer mystery. She closed her hand at her side and it was warm as if she held another hand in hers, and that hand-holding surely belonged here. On the very junction of the two worlds—rather, in the very junction of them within her —the single goodness of the one precipitated itself into the other. She knew its name; she knew who it was who, in that, belonged to this. There someone was denying it; here it was native. She called aloud: "Jonathan!" On the edge of shadow, so near and so near the dark house that waited her, so near some power in which this bright self and joyous life would be again lost, she cried out on her lover. She stamped one small foot on the pavement. The demands of the other Betty were rising in her, but the energy of this was still with her. She just stopped herself saying, "I won't go!"; that would be silly, but she called, her very mildness mutinying, on the name of her only happiness, wishing to claim and clutch that happiness—she called again: "Jonathan! Jonathan!" Freely and fully her voice rang out, as never in all her young tormented life had her mortal mouth called. Immortal, she cried to immortality; and the immortal City let the word sound through it and gave it echo and greater meaning in the echo: "Jonathan! Jonathan!" Alone in the growing shadow, she looked down the Hill, and listened and waited. If he were there, perhaps she could be there; if not—— The night about her grew; she lingered still.

Far away, in London's mortal measurement, but brief time enough immortally, the two dead girls walked. It was not, to them, so very long since they had left the Park—a few days or even less. But Evelyn had reached what would have been on earth the point of exhaustion from tears; there was here no such exhaustion, but as if by a kind of reflexive action she stopped. She might begin again when she would have been capable of beginning again; at present she could not. She did not dare leave Lester, though she did not like Lester any the better for that. Lester still interfered with her chatter, and without her chatter this world was almost unbearable to her. She was afraid of losing that escape from its pressure, nor did she know how Lester could bear that pressure. And if Lester would not listen, there was no one else to do so. Her fright required of her that relief and she hated Lester for depriving her of it. Yet Lester still held her arm and in default of better she dare not lose that pressure. And sometimes Lester did say something and encourage her to answer—only generally about silly uninteresting things.

Once, as they had been coming along Holborn, Lester had stopped and looked in one of those curious windows which were no windows. She had said hesitantly to her companion, "Evelyn, look, can you see any difference?" Evelyn had looked, but she had not seen anything particular. It seemed to be a shop with electric lamps and fires displayed—all vague and unreal enough. But Lester was looking at them seriously. She said, "That's the kind I've always meant to get. Do you see, the one in the back row?" Evelyn did not even want to look. She said in a high strained voice, "Don't be silly, Lester. What's the good?" It gave her some pleasure to retaliate; besides, she never had been interested in such convenient details. She would complain if things went wrong, but she would take no care to have them go right. Lester almost smiled; it was a sad little smile, but it was her first unpremeditated smile. She said, "No. But they do somehow look more real. And we both meant to get one. Richard was going to try and get me one for my birthday. Do be interested, Evelyn." Evelyn said sullenly, "You wouldn't be interested in what I was saying," and pulled away.

Lester with a small sigh had turned with her. That shop had for a moment seemed less like a façade and more like a shop. It had held the sort of thing that had once concerned her—not only for her own convenience, or to improve on her neighbors, but for a pleasure in its own neatness and effectiveness. As she turned away, at a corner, Evelyn felt her stop so suddenly that she herself gave a little squeal of fright. The grip on her arm relaxed and then was so tightened that she squealed again in protest. But Lester had been rough and unkind. She had said, "Keep quiet——" and had choked and drawn a deep breath or two. Evelyn felt how unfair it was; first she was to talk and then not to talk, and how could anyone know? She felt herself beginning to cry and then they had gone on again in silence, up northward, till they had come out of all the parts of London she knew and were in some long sordid street. There was still no one else.

But suddenly there was another sound. High beyond and above them a voice called, piercing the air and shaking their hearts. Both girls abruptly stood still. It was a human voice, a girl's voice, crying high in the silence, with assurance and belief. Lester threw up her head; she did not recognize the voice but the note of it lifted her. It was a woman's call; and that was the way a woman should call in this City, the way she should call if she—if she too could dare. She thought of Richard as she had just now seen him in Holborn, and she opened her mouth to send his name also ringing over the streets, as this other name which she could not yet catch was ringing. She heard her voice, "as if hoarse with long disuse," say dully: "Richard!" The sound horrified her. Was this all she could do? She tried again. It was.

She made a third effort and again she heard from her own mouth only the flat voice of the dead. She was possessed by it. Death, it seemed, was not over; it had only just begun. She was dying further. She could not call; presently she would not be able to speak; then not to see—neither the high stars nor the meaningless lights

—yet still, though meaningless, faintly metropolitan. But she would find even this pale light too much, and presently would creep away from it towards one of those great open entrances that loomed here and there, for inside one of them she could hide from the light. Then she would go farther in, so as not to see even the entrance, in spite of the brick wall that stood before it; farther in, and a little way down the coiling stairs. If Richard came along the street then . . . no; perhaps she would wait at the entrance till he did, and then call him in this faint croak. She had pushed him away once, but now she would not push him away; she would call him and keep him; let him too find it—all the stairs, all the living dead. It was not the dead, as she had thought, it was the living who dwelled in those tunnels of earth—deep and O deep beyond any railways, in the tubes they themselves, thrusting and pushing, hollowed out for their shelter. Richard should no longer be pushed away; he should be there with her, prisoner with her, prisoner to her. If only he too would die, and come!

She saw all this in her mind for as long as it took that other voice to call once more. She saw it clearly—for an aeon; this was what she wanted; this was what she was. This was she, damned; yes, and she was damned; she, being that, was damned. There was no help, unless she could be something other, and there was no power in her to be anything other. As she stood in a trance of horror at herself or at hell, or at both, being one, a word pierced her brain. The word was "Jonathan!" The far voice was calling: "Jonathan!" She knew the word; it was the name of Richard's friend. She had not herself much interest in Jonathan, but she had asked him to dinner because Richard liked him, she had studied his paintings with good will because Richard liked him. She recognized the name, and the name struck through her vision of the Pit. She was not yet so; no, she was not yet there; she was in the streets and breathed still the open air and knew the calls of love. Something, in or out of her mind, said to her, "Would it be unfair?" She answered with the courage and good sense native to her, but with a new and holy shyness: "It would be perhaps extreme." "It would be your own extreme," the voice, if it were a voice, continued. She said, "Yes."

The unspoken dialogue ceased. The call from above had ceased. She seemed to have shut her eyes; she opened them. She saw Evelyn in front of her, running hard. She called, and even as she did so she realized that she could call Evelyn easily enough and that that was not surprising—she called: "Evelyn!" The silent running figure looked back over its shoulder and Evelyn's thin voice came to her clearly. It said, "That was Betty." It turned its head again and ran on.

Lester also began to run. The face that had looked back had startled her; it had been excited and pleased. She remembered Betty and she remembered that Evelyn had not been very nice to Betty. They had once all three run in this way through the grounds of their school by the sea; indeed, as she ran, the bushes of those grounds showed through the houses and shops. Betty had run away and Evelyn had run after Betty, and suddenly she herself had run after Evelyn. It had not been often she took the trouble, for Betty bored her and anyhow Evelyn never did anything to Betty; even then she had been calling, "I only want to talk to you." But something in the talk made Betty cry and for once Lester had interfered; and now, as then, they ran down the path; no, not down the path but up the street, towards Highgate, out to the bottom of the Hill. High above them a single figure watched them come.

Betty watched them; they were at first far away and she did not know them. While she had gone out on her appointed way, she had been free from pain. But the terrible laws of that place gave her what she wanted when she insisted on it. Her distress, and now the nearness of her distress, might excuse a rebellion; it could not modify its results. She had stamped on the pavement and (as in the old tales) the inhabitants of that place sprang at once into being. She had called on something she knew. But that something was more deeply engaged on its work in the world of the shadow behind her, and this world would not give her that. She saw at a distance the two running women, strange and remote as in a painting or a poem. She watched them curiously and the time went by, as long to her as to Evelyn racing up the slope or to Lester outdistanced behind. Lester lost ground; she did not know clearly why she went, but Evelyn did; therefore the one ran faster and the other slower, for still in the outer circles of that world a cruel purpose could outspeed a vague pity. But the cruelty could not reach its end. Betty waited till, halfway up the Hill, the first running figure lifted its head slightly, so that she saw the face and knew it for Evelyn's. She took a step or two back, and the night of this world into which she had hesitated to advance took her as she retreated. Her nightmare possessed her; now it was happening. She screamed and turned and fled.

Evelyn called, "Betty! Betty! Stop!" but to Betty's ears the name rang confused. It had been "Bettina!" in her dreams; it was "Bettina!" now. She ran. There was but a short street or two between her and the house; they were to her the natural streets, the sad unhappy streets of Highgate. She forgot her fear of the house in her fear of Evelyn. "Bettina! Bettina!" O lost, lost! but now nearer the house and the cold quiet thing that waited her in the porch. "Bettina! Bettina!" No—she was there, and she and the shape by the door were no longer separate. A great exhaustion fell on her; her eyes closed; her body failed; she pushed weakly at the door and stumbled through. She fell; someone caught her; she knew nothing more.

Outside the house Evelyn stopped. For her that other world had not changed. It was as quiet and empty, as earthly and unearthly as ever. It was not quite dark; it never yet had been quite dark. The soft, intense, and holy darkness of that City was not known to her. She stood, gently panting, as a girl might who has whole-heartedly run from and been pursued by a welcome lover: so, and yet not so, for that swift and generous animality was not hers. The kind of rage that was in her was the eager stirring of the second death. She had wanted Betty, and now she did not know what she wanted. The house was before her, but she was afraid to try to enter it.

At that moment Lester caught her up. She said with an imperious demand, "What are you doing, Evelyn? Can't you let her be?" and as she spoke she seemed to herself again to be saying something she had said before —away in those gardens by the sea, a great sea the sound of which, beyond her own voice, she could dimly hear as she had so often heard it in her bed at school. It was almost as if, behind her, the whole City moved. She half-lifted her hand to catch Evelyn by the shoulder, and that too she had once done; but she let it fall, for now the revolt in her flesh was too strong. Yet, as if she had been swung round by that once impetuous hand, Evelyn turned. She said, as she had said before, in that foolish slurred voice whose protestations provoked disbelief, "What do you mean? I wasn't doing anything."

The answer shocked Lester back into fuller consciousness. They were no longer schoolgirls; they were—what were they? Women; dead women; living women; women on whose lips such words could have no meaning. The excuse of a child in a garden by the sea might have been accepted, if it had not been repeated here. But here it became dreadful. In the Park Lester could have half smiled at it; she could not smile now. She spoke with a fuller and clearer voice than ever it had been in this world; she spoke as a woman, as Richard's wife, as something more than a vagrant, even if not yet a citizen; and she said, "Don't, my dear. It isn't worth it——" and as if by compulsion she added, "here."

Evelyn stopped, almost as if detaching herself from the other's hand, and took a step away. Lester looked up at the house. It seemed to her strange and awful. Betty had taken refuge in it, as once on a garden-seat among the bushes. Over it, close to it, a lone star hung. The other houses were shadowy and uncertain; this alone was solid and real. It stood out, and within its porch the entrance was as black as one of those other dark entrances which she feared. As she gazed, there came from the house a small human sound. It was someone crying. The half-suppressed unhappy sobs were the only noise that broke the silence. Evelyn's sobs and chattering teeth had broken it in the Park, but Evelyn was not crying now. It was Betty who was crying—among the bushes, in the house, without strength, without hope. Lester, with her own yearning in her bones, stirred restlessly, in an impatient refusal of her impatient impulse to go and tell her to stop. In those earlier days, she had not gone; she had hesitated a moment just so and then turned away. Betty must really learn to stand up for herself. "Must she indeed?" Lester's own voice said to her. She exclaimed, with the fervent habit of her mortality: "Hell!"

The word ran from her in all directions, as if a dozen small animals had been released and gone racing away. They fled up and down the street, beating out the echo of the word with their quick pattering feet, but the larger went for the house in front of them and disappeared into the porch. She saw them and was appalled; what new injury had she loosed? There was then no help. She too must go there. And Richard? She had thought that in this terrible London she had lost Richard, but now it seemed to her that this was the only place where she might meet Richard. She had seen him twice and the second time with some undeclared renewal of love. What might not be granted a third time? voice? a word? Ghosts had spoken; ghost as he was to her in those first appearances, he too might speak. To go into the house might be to lose him. The quiet crying, still shockingly suppressed, continued. Lester hung irresolute.

Behind her, Evelyn's voice said, "Oh come *away!*" At the words Lester, for the first time in her life, saw a temptation precisely as it is when it has ceased to tempt —repugnant, implausible, mean. She said nothing. She went forward and up the steps. She went on into Lady Wallingford's house.

Chapter Five

THE HALL BY HOLBORN

Richard Furnival was as wakeful that night in his manner as Betty in hers. Once he had again reached his flat —it was taking him a long time to get used to saying "my flat" instead of "our flat"—and as the night drew on, he found himself chilled and troubled. He knew of a score of easy phrases to explain his vision; none convinced him. Nor had he any conviction of metaphysics into which, retaining its own nature, it might easily pass. He thought of tales of ghosts; he even tried to pronounce the word; but the word was silly. A ghost was a wraith, a shadow; his vision had been of an actual Lester. The rooms were cold and empty—as empty as any boarding-house rooms where the beloved has been and from which (never to return) she has gone. The afternoon with Jonathan had, when he left, renewed in him the tide of masculine friendship. But that tide had always swelled against the high cliff of another element, on which a burning beacon had once stood—and now suddenly had again stood. The sound of deep waves was in his ears, and even then his eyes had again been filled with the ancient fiery light. He had not, since he had first met Lester, lost at all the sense of great Leviathans, disputes and laughter, things native and natural to the male, but beyond them, and shining towards them had been that other less natural, and as it were more archangelic figure

—remote however close, terrifying however sustaining, that which was his and not his, more intimate than all that was his, the shape of the woman and his wife. He had yet, for all his goodwill, so neglected her that he had been content to look at her so from his sea; he had never gone in and lived in that strange turret. He had admired, visited, used it. But not till this afternoon had he seen her as simply living. The noise of ocean faded; rhetoric ceased. This that he had seen had been in his actual house, and now it was not, and the house was cold and dark. He lit a fire to warm himself; he ate and drank; he went from room to room; he tried to read. But every book he opened thrust one message at him— from modern novels ("Aunt Rachel can't live much longer——") to old forgotten volumes ("The long habit of living indisposeth us for dying"; "But she is dead, she's dead . . ."). His teeth chattered; his body shook. He went to bed and dozed and woke and walked and again lay down, and so on. Till that night he had not known how very nearly he had loved her.

In the morning he made haste to leave. He was indeed on the point of doing so when Jonathan rang him up. Jonathan wanted to tell him about the Clerk's visit and the Clerk's approval of the painting. Richard did his best to pay attention and was a little arrested by the mere unexpectedness of the tale. He said, with a serious sympathy, "But that makes everything much simpler, doesn't it? He'll deal with Lady Wallingford, I suppose?"

"Yes," said Jonathan's voice, "yes. If I want him to. I don't believe I do want him to."

"But why not?" asked Richard.

"Because . . . The fact is, I don't like *him*. I don't

like the way he talks about Betty or the way he looks at paintings. You go and see him or hear him or whatever you can, and come on here and tell me. God knows I . . . well, never mind. I shall be here all day, unless Betty sends for me."

After this conversation, Richard was about to leave the flat when he paused and went back. He would not seem to run away; if, by any chance, that presence of his wife should again appear, he would not be without all he could accumulate from her environs with which to greet her. Nor would he now seem to fly. He walked through the rooms. He submitted to memory and in some poignant sense to a primitive remorse, for he was not yet spiritually old enough to repent. Then, quietly, he went out and (unable quite to control his uselessly expectant eyes) walked through the streets till he reached Holborn.

It did not take him long to find the place of which he was in search. Behind Holborn, close to Great James Street, in a short street undamaged by the raids, were three buildings, one the largest, of a round shape, in the middle with a house on each side. They were not marked by any board, but as Richard came to the farther house, he saw that the door was open. A small exquisite carving of a hand, so delicate as to be almost a woman's or a child's hand, was fastened to the door-post, its fingers pointing into the house. Richard had never seen any carving that so nearly achieved the color of flesh; he thought at the first glance that it was flesh, and that a real dismembered hand pointed him to the Clerk's lodging. He touched it cautiously with a finger as he went by and was a little ashamed of his relief when he found it was hard and artificial.

He walked on as far as the end of the street; then he walked back. It was a warm sunny morning for October, and as he paced it seemed to him that the air was full of the scent of flowers. The noise of the streets had died away; it was very quiet. He thought, as he paused before turning, how pleasant it was here. It was even pleasant in a way not to have anyone in his mind, or on his mind. People who were in your mind were so often on your mind and that was a slight weariness. One would, of course, rather have it so than not. He had never grudged Lester anything, but here, where the air was so fresh and yet so full of a scent he just did not recognize, and London was as silent as the wood in Berkshire where he and Lester had been for a few days after their marriage, it was almost pleasant to be for a moment without Lester. His eyes averted themselves from where she was not lest she should unexpectedly be there. It was sufficient now to remember her in that wood—and even so, eclectically, for she had one day been rather difficult even in that wood, when she had wanted to go into the nearest town to get a particular magazine, in case by the time they did go on their return, it should be sold out, and he had not, for (as he had rightly and rationally pointed out) she could at a pinch wait for it till they got to London. But she had insisted, and because he always wished to consider her and be as unselfish as possible, they had gone. He was surprised, as he stood there, to remember how much he had considered Lester. A score of examples rushed vividly through his mind, and each of those he remembered was actual and true. He really had considered her; he had been, in that sense, a very good husband. He almost wondered if he had been too indulgent, too kind. No; if it were to do again, he would do it. Now she was gone, he was content to remember it. But also now she was gone, he could attend to himself. Luxuriating—more than he knew—in the thought, he turned. Luxury stole gently out within him and in that warm air flowed about him; luxury, *luxuria,* the quiet distilled *luxuria* of his wishes and habits, the delicate sweet lechery of idleness, the tasting of unhallowed peace.

He remembered with equal distaste that he was on an errand and felt sorry that Jonathan was not doing his own errand. Jonathan could, just as well as not; after all, it was Jonathan who wanted to marry Betty. However, as he had promised, as he was committed . . . it would be more of a nuisance to explain to Jonathan—and to himself, but he did not add that—than to go in. He contemplated the carved hand with admiration, almost with affection; it really was the most exquisite thing. There was nothing of Jonathan's shouting colors about it. Jonathan was so *violent.* Art, he thought, should be persuasive. This, however, was too much even for his present state of dreaming luxury. He came to, or almost came to, and found himself in the hall.

It was a rather larger hall than he had expected. On his left hand were the stairs; before him the passage ran, with another ascending staircase farther on, to a kind of garden door. There was apparently another passage at the end turning off to the left. On his right was the door into the front room, which was open, and beyond it another door, which was shut. Richard hesitated and began to approach the open door. As he did so, a short rather fat man came out of it and said in a tone of much good humor, "Yes, sir?"

Richard said, "Oh good morning Is this Father Simon's place?"

The short man answered, "That's right, sir. Can I do anything for you?"

"I just wanted to get some particulars for a friend," Richard said. "Is there anyone I could see?"

"Come in here, sir," said the other, retreating into the room. "I'm here to answer, as you may say, the first questions. My name's Plankin; I'm a kind of doorkeeper. Come in, sir, and sit down. They all come to me first, sir, and no one knows better than I do what the Father's done. A tumor on the brain, sir; that's what he cured me of a year ago. And many another poor creature since."

"Did he?" said Richard, a little sceptically. He was in the front room by now. He had vaguely expected something like an office, but it was hardly that; a waiting-room perhaps. There was a table with a telephone, a few chairs, and that was all. Richard was maneuvered to a chair; the short man sat down on another by the table, put his hands on his knees and looked benevolently at the visitor. Richard saw that, beside the telephone, there was also on the table a large-sized album and a pot of paste. He thought, but he knew one could not judge, that it looked as if Plankin had an easy job. But after a tumor on the brain——! He said, "I wanted to ask about Father Simon's work. Does he——"

The short man, sitting quite still, began to speak. He said, "Yes, sir, a tumor. He put his blessed hands on my head and cured it. There isn't a man or woman in this house that he hasn't cured. I've never had a pain since, not of any kind. Nor they neither. We all carry his mark in our bodies, sir, and we're proud of it."

"Really?" said Richard. "Yes, you must be. Does he run some kind of clinic, then?"

"Oh no, sir," Plankin said. "He puts everything

right straight away. He took the paralysis away from Elsie Bookin who does the typing, and old Mrs. Morris who's the head cook—he cured her cancer. He does it all. I keep an album here, sir, and I stick in it everything the papers say about him. But it's not like knowing him, as we do."

"No," said Richard, "I suppose not. Do you have many inquiries?"

"Not so very many, for the Father wants to be quiet here," said Plankin. "He sends most of them away after he's seen them, to wait. But they come; oh yes, they come. And some go away and some even come to the Relaxations."

"The Relaxations?" Richard asked.

"Oh well, sir," said Plankin, "you'll hear about them if you stay. The Father gives us peace. He'll tell you about it." He nodded his head, swaying a little and saying, "Peace, peace."

"Can I see the Father then?" said Richard. Inside the room the warm air seemed again to be full of that attractive smell. He might have been in the very middle of the Berkshire wood again, without Lester, but with an agreeable memory of Lester. The green distemper on the walls of the room was gently moving as if the walls were walls of leaves, and glints of sunlight among them; and the short man opposite him no more than a tree stump. He could be content to sit here in the wood, where the dead did not matter and never returned—no more than if they had not been known, except for this extra exquisiteness of a happy dream. But presently some sort of surge went through the wood, and the tree stump stood up and said, "Ah now that'll be one of the ladies. She'll tell you better than I can." Richard came to himself and heard a step in the hall. He rose to his feet and as he did so Lady Wallingford appeared in the doorway.

She did not, when she saw him, seem pleased. She stood still and surveyed him. Except for the moment or two of introduction, he had not on the previous afternoon been face to face with her, and now he was struck by the force of her face. She looked at him and she said coldly, "What do you want here?"

The challenge completely restored Richard. He said, "Good morning, Lady Wallingford. I came to ask a few questions about Father Simon. After yesterday I was naturally interested."

Lady Wallingford said, "Are you sure this is a place for you?"

"Well," Richard answered, "I hope I'm not pig-headed, and I can quite believe that Jonathan may have been wrong." He remembered that morning's telephone conversation and added, "If his painting *was* what you thought it. I was wondering if I could meet—I don't want to intrude—meet Father Simon. He must be a very remarkable man. And if he had any public meetings— Knowledge is always useful."

"You run a certain risk," Lady Wallingford said. "But I've changed my mind a little about your friend's painting. Of course, there can be no nonsense about an engagement. I have quite other views for her. But if you really wish to learn——"

"Why not?" said Richard. "As for the engagement —that perhaps is hardly my business. I am only thinking of my own instruction." He began to feel that he was making progress. Jonathan was always apt to rush things. He took a step forward and went on engagingly. "I assure——" He stopped. Another figure had appeared behind Lady Wallingford.

She seemed to know it was there, for without looking round she moved out of the doorway, so as to leave room for it to enter. Richard knew at once who it was. He recognized the shape of the face from Jonathan's painting, yet his first thought was that, in this case, Jonathan's painting was quite ridiculously wrong. There was no bewilderment or imbecility about the face that looked at him; rather there was a highness, almost an arrogance, in it which abashed him. He knew that on his right Plankin had dropped on his knees; he had seen Lady Wallingford move. That the movements did not surprise him was the measure of his sense of sovereignty. He resisted an impulse to retreat; he himself became bewildered; he felt with a shock that Simon was between him and the door. He knew the door was there, but he could not focus it properly. The door was not behind Simon; it was Simon: all the ways from this room and in this wood went through Simon. Lady Wallingford was only a stupid old witch in a wood, but this was the god in the wood. Between the tree stump and the watching witch, he stood alone in the Berkshire wood; and Lester had gone away into the nearest town. He had not gone with her because he had not gone with her. He had gone please her, to consider her, which was not at all the same thing. So she had gone alone, and he was alone with the god in the wood and the witch and the tree stump. The god was the witch's husband and father, his father, everyone's father; he loomed in front of him and over him. Yet he was also a way of escape from the wood and from himself. The high emaciated face was at once a wall and a gate in the wall, but the gate was a very old gate, and no one had gone through it, except perhaps the witch, for many years——

Plankin stood up. Richard's head jerked. Simon was speaking. He said, "Mr. Furnival?" Richard answered, "Father Simon? How do you do?"

The Clerk came a pace into the room. He was wearing a black cassock, caught round the waist by a heavy gold chain. He did not offer his hand, but he said in a pleasant enough voice, "You've come to see us? That is kind." The faint huskiness of the voice reminded Richard of Lester's, which, clear enough at hand, always sounded slightly husky on the telephone. It had been, to him, one of her most agreeable characteristics. He had sometimes rung it up in order to hear that huskiness, carefully explaining the eroticism to himself, but undoubtedly enjoying it almost as happily as if he had not known it was eroticism. It had been in that voice that she had uttered the last thing he had ever heard her say—on the telephone, that too-fatal afternoon: "See you presently, darling." It leaped in his mind. He said, "Yes. Jonathan Drayton's painting made me interested. I hope it's permitted to call like this?"

A constriction passed across the Clerk's face. He answered, "It's free to everyone who cares. And any friend of Mr. Drayton's is especially welcome. He is a great man—only he must not paint foolish pictures of the City. London light is nothing like that. You must tell him so. What can we show you? We've no buildings, no relics, no curios. Only ourselves." He came farther into the room and Richard saw that there were others behind him. There was a man who looked like a lorry driver, another like a clerk, another who might have been just down from the University. With them there were several women whom he did not immediately take in. These perhaps were those whom Simon had helped. Their eyes were all on the Clerk; no wonder, and again no wonder. Here, in this warm place, there was no illness, no pain, no distress. Simon would have seen to that. Perhaps no death, no ruined body, no horrible memory to mingle with amusing memories.

Simon said again, "Ourselves," and Richard, almost as if he pushed open the gate of the god, said suddenly, "I wish you'd known my wife," and the god answered in that husky voice, as if it came from deeper in the wood, "Is she dead?"

The harsh word did not break the calm. Richard said, "Yes." The god's voice continued. "Well, we shall see. Most things are possible. If I send for her, she may come." He lifted a hand. "Come, all of you," he said. "Come into the Relaxation. Come, Mr. Furnival."

As he used the commonplace phrase, he became again Simon the Clerk, a man to whom Richard was talking. He turned, and everyone turned with him and made way for him. He went into the hall, and in the general movement Richard found himself surrounded and carried along in the small crush. He went necessarily but also voluntarily. Simon's words rang in his ears: "May come . . . may come. . . . If I send for her, she may come." Dead? may come? what was this hint of threat or promise? dead, and return? But she had come; he had seen her; not far from here he had seen her. The sudden recollection shocked him almost to a pause. Something touched his shoulder, lightly; fingers or antennae. He stepped forward again. They were going down the hall and turning into a narrow corridor, as if into a crack in the wall, insects passing into a crack; they were all passing through. They had come to another door, narrower than the passage, and here they went through one at a time, and the witch-woman who had been walking beside him stepped aside for him to pass through. It was Lady Wallingford and she smiled friendlily at him, and now he smiled back and went on. Something just brushed his cheek as he did so, a cobweb in the wood or something else. He came into a clearing, an old wooden building, a hole; he did not precisely know which it was, but there were chairs in it, so it must be a room of some kind—rather like an old round church, but not a church. There was one tall armed chair. Simon was going across to it. Opposite to it was the only window the room possessed—a low round window that seemed to be set in a very deep wall indeed, and yet it could not be, for he could see through it now and into nothing but a kind of empty yard. He hesitated; he did not quite know where to go, but a light small hand, as if it were the carved hand he had seen on the door-post of that house, crept into his arm, and guided him to a chair at one end of a rough half-circle, so that he could see at once the Clerk in his chair and the tunnel-like window opposite. He sat down. It was Lady Wallingford who had led him. She withdrew her hand and he almost thought that as she did so her fingers softly touched his cheek, light as cobweb or antennae. But she had gone right away now, to the other end of that half-moon of chairs, and was sitting down opposite him. Simon, he, Lady Wallingford, the window—four points in a circle; a circle—return and return; may come and may come. They were all sitting now and Simon began to speak.

Richard looked at him. He knew the derivation of the word "Clerk," and that the original Greek meant "inheritance." The clerks were the inheritors; that was the old wise meaning—men who gathered their inheritance as now, in that strange husky voice of his, the being on the throned seat was gathering his own. He was pronouncing great words in a foreign tongue; he seemed to exhort and explain, but then also he seemed to collect and receive. Was it a foreign tongue? it was almost English, but not quite English, and sometimes not at all English. Richard was rather good at languages, but this evaded him. It did not seem to evade the others; they were all sitting, listening and gazing. The voice itself indeed sounded more like a chorus of two or three than a single voice. They all died for a moment on a single English word; the word was *Love*.

The Clerk sat and spoke. His hands rested on the arms of his chair; his body was quite still; except that his head turned slightly as he surveyed the half-moon of his audience. The Jewish traits in his face were more marked. The language in which he spoke was ancient Hebrew, but he was pronouncing it in a way not common among men. He paused now and then to translate into English—or so it seemed, though only he knew if it was indeed so, and the English itself was strange and dull. A curious flatness was in his voice. He was practicing and increasing this, denying accents and stresses to his speech. Wise readers of verse do their best to submit their voices to the verse, letting the words have their own proper value, and endeavor to leave them to their precise proportion and rhythm. The Clerk was go͏ farther yet. He was removing meaning itself from words. They fought against him; man's vocabu fought against him. Man's art is perhaps worth l in the end, but it is at least worth its own present communication. All the poems and paintings may, like faith and hope, at last dissolve; but while faith and hope—and desperation—live, they live; while human communication remains, they remain. It was this that the Clerk was removing; he turned, or sought to turn, words into mere vibrations. The secret school in which he had grown up had studied to extend their power over vocal sounds beyond the normal capacities of man. Generations had put themselves to the work. The healing arts done in that house had depended on this power; the healer had by sympathy of sound breathed restoring relationship into the subrational components of flesh.

But there were sounds that had a much greater spell, sounds that could control not only the living but the dead—say, those other living who in another world still retained a kinship and in some sense an identity with this. Great pronouncements had established creation in its order; the reversal of those pronouncements could reverse the order. The Jew sat in his chair and spoke. Through the lesser spells, those that held the spirits of those that already carried his pronunciation in their bodies, that held them fascinated and adoring, he was drawing to the greater. He would come presently to the greatest—to the reversal of the final Jewish word of power, to the reversed Tetragrammaton itself. The energy of that most secret house of God, according to the degree in which it was spoken, meant an all but absolute control; he thought, an absolute. He did not mean it for the creatures before him. To loose it on them would be to destroy them at once; he must precipitate it beyond. The time was very near, if his studies were true, at which a certain great exchange should be achieved. He would draw one from that world, but there must be no impropriety of numbers, either there or here; he would send one to that world. He would have thus a double magical link with infinity. He would begin to be worshiped there. That was why he had brought Richard in. Unknowingly, Richard's mind might hold precisely that still vital junction and communion with the dead which might offer a mode of passage. The Clerk did not doubt his own capacity, sooner or later, to do all by himself, but he would not neglect any convenience. He stirred, by interspersed murmurs, Richard's slumbering mind to a recollection of sensuous love, love which had known that extra physical union, that extra intention of marriage, which is still called marriage.

His eyes ceased to wander and remained fixed on the round window opposite. It looked on a yard, but it looked also on that yard in its infinite relations. There the entry of spirit might be. He drew nearer to the pronunciation; and that strange double echo in his voice, of which Richard had been partly aware, now ceased, and his voice was single. He knew very well that, at that moment, those other appearances of himself in Russia and China had fallen into trance. The deathly formula could only be pronounced by the actual human voice of the single being. There was in that round building one other who knew something of this most secret thing; she sat there, away on his right, and (with all her will) believed. She too knew that the moment was near and that she too was engaged to it. But also she knew that her usefulness to him, save as one of these indistinguishable creatures who were his living spiritual food, was past.

In the early days of her knowledge of him, Sara Wallingford knew he had found her useful. It was different now. He did not need her, except for convenience of guarding their daughter; when he sent their daughter fully away, she would be—what would she be? A desertion greater than most human desertions would fall on her. The time was near. He had told her of it long since; she could not complain. The time was very near. When it came and his triplicity was ended, she would be—what that painting had revealed; one of those adoring imbecilities. He had not troubled to deny it.

She remembered the awful beginning of the triplicity. It had been in that house in the North, and he had come to her, as he sometimes did, along garden ways at night. It had been the night after the conception of Betty, and she had known already that she carried his child. It had not been she who desired it, nor (physically) he. But the child was to be to him an instrument she could not be. She hated it, before its conception, for that; and when she felt within her all the next day the first point of cold which grew and enlarged till after Betty's birth—"as cold as spring-water"—she hated it the more. And her hate did not grow less for what had happened on that second night.

She had known, as soon as she saw him, that he was bent on a magical operation. He did not now need, for the greater of his works, any of the lesser instruments— the wand, the sword, the lamps, the herbs, the robe. She had been in bed when he came. She was twenty-nine then and she had known him for eight years. He did not need now to tell her to believe in him or to help him; she had been committed to that all those eight years. But in some sense the night of the conception had brought a change. Ever since then, though her subordination to him had grown, his need of her had grown less. On that night, however, she had not yet understood.

She lay in her bed and watched him. He drew the curtains and put out the light. There were candles on the dressing-table, and her dressing-gown, with matches in its pocket, lay on a chair by the bed. She put out a hand to see that it was convenient.

He was standing between her bed and the great mirror. They had had that mirror put there for exactly such operations, and however dark the room there always seemed to be a faint gray light within the mirror, so that when she saw him in it, it was as if he himself and no mere image lived and moved there. He had put off his clothes, and he stood looking into the mirror, and suddenly the light in it disappeared and she could see nothing. But she could hear a heavy breathing, almost a panting, and almost animal, had it not been so measured and at times changed in measure. It grew and deepened, and presently it became so low a moan that the sweat broke out on her forehead and she bit her hand as she lay. But even that moan was not so much of pain as of compulsion. The temperature of the room grew hotter; a uterine warmth oppressed her. She sighed and threw the blankets back. And she prayed—to God? not to God; to him? certainly to him. She had given herself to his will to be the mother of the instrument of his dominion; she prayed to him now to be successful in this other act.

In the mirror a shape of gray light grew slowly visible; it was he, but it was he dimmed. There seemed to be two images of him in one, and they slid into and out of each other, so that she could not be certain which she saw. Both were faint, and there were no boundaries; the grayness itself faded into the darkness. The moaning had ceased; the room was full of a great tension; the heat grew; she lay sweating and willing what he willed. The light in the mirror went out. His voice cried aloud: "The candles!" She sprang from her bed and caught at her dressing-gown. She had it on in a moment and had hold of the matches; then she went very quickly, even in the dark, to the dressing-table, and was immediately striking a match and setting it to the candles. She did not quite take in, as she moved her hand from one to the other, what she saw in the oval glass between, and as they caught she blew out the match and whirled swiftly round.

She almost fell at what she saw. Between her and the mirror, and all reflected in the mirror, were three men. One was nearer her; the other two, one on each side of him, were closer to the mirror. From the mirror three identical faces looked out, staring. She felt madly that that nearest form was *he,* her master, whose child she bore; but then the other—things? men? lovers? The sextuple horror, back and front, stood absolutely still. These others were no shadows or ghostly emanations; they had solidity and shape. She stared; her hand clutched at the table; she swayed, crumpled and fell.

When she came to herself again he and she were alone. He had said a sentence or two to reassure her. It was (he said) indeed he who remained; the others were images and actual copies of him, magically multiplied, flesh out of flesh, and sent upon his business. The curtains were pulled back; the world was gray with dawn; and as she looked out over the moors she knew that somewhere there, through that dawn, those other beings went. The world was ready for them and they went to the world. He had left her then; and since that night there had been no physical intercourse between them.

She—even she—could not have endured it. She believed that the he she knew was he, yet sometimes she wondered. At moments, during the next one-and-twenty years, while she worked for him and did his will, she wondered if it was the original whom she obeyed, or only one of those shapes sustained at a distance by the real man. She put the thought away. She read sometimes during those years of the appearance of a great religious philosopher in China, a great patriot preacher in Russia, and she guessed—not who—there was in them no *who*— but what they were. The war had for a while hidden them, but now that the war was over they had reappeared, proclaiming everywhere peace and love, and the enthusiasm for them broke all bounds, and became national and more than national; so that the whole world seemed to be at the disposal of that triplicity. A triple energy of clamor and adoration answered it. There were demands that these three teachers should meet, should draft a gospel and a policy, should fully rule the worship they provoked. It had been so with him in America and would have been in England, had he not deliberately remained in seclusion. And she knew that in all the world only she, besides the Clerk who now sat before her in the throned seat, knew that these others were not true men at all, but derivations and automata, flesh of his flesh and bone of his bone, but without will and without soul.

She knew why he had kept himself in seclusion. He knew that, when he chose, that world was his for the taking. Rhetoric and hypnotic spells and healing powers would loose idolatry, but beyond all these was the secret and crafty appeal to every individual who came to him separately—the whisper, one way or another: "You are different; you are not under the law; you are particular."

He played on both nerves; he moved crowds, but also he moved souls. The susurration of those whispers moved even many who would not otherwise easily have adored. She knew it bitterly, for it was so that she herself had been caught; and indeed she had been fortunate, for she had been useful and she was the mother of his child. Would that ease abandonment? She knew it would not. Even when the deed was done for which Betty had been brought into the world, and their daughter dismissed into the spiritual places, she herself would be no nearer him. He was already almost spirit, except that he was not spirit. But soon he would have spirits for companions, and——

But before then, though he delayed his full public manifestation till that other work was done, it would have happened. When the communion with that other world was, through Betty, established, he would go (she thought) into middle Europe, or perhaps farther—to Persia or India; and there those other shapes would come, each known to adoring multitudes, and there would be in secret a mystery of reunion, and then all would be in his hand.

She turned her eyes from him, she alone conscious of herself and him in all that group, and saw the rest losing their knowledge before him. They were beginning to sway gently to and fro; their faces were losing meaning; their arms and hands were rising slowly towards him. They were much like the insects in that painting, but their faces were more like his own; she knew when she looked at the painting that Jonathan had given him the face she had so often seen in this house, the blank helpless imbecile gaze. It was why she had been so angry. But *he* had not seen it. She looked at

Richard, Jonathan's friend, and wondered if he too were beginning to sway and change.

In fact, if he were not, he was at least already in some danger of it. He had been thinking of love, and what love would mean if he had known someone who would love him perfectly. Lester was not always completely understanding. Something rhythmical in her did not always entirely correspond to him. He moved a little, as if expressing his own rhythm, forward-backward, backward-forward. His eyes opened a little wider, and as he did so they fell on the woman who sat opposite him. He saw her as he had seen her the previous afternoon, and suddenly he recollected Jonathan's paintings. He saw the insects and he saw them here. He knew he was being caught in something; he made an effort to sit back, to sit still, to recover. The edge of things was before him; he thrust back. He thought of Lester, but not of her glory or her passion; he thought of her in a moment of irritation. He heard, in those precincts of infinity, the voice he had heard in other precincts, on Westminster Bridge. Vivid in his ears, she exclaimed to him, "Why have you kept me waiting?" His mind sprang alert; if she were waiting, what was he doing here?

He was again himself—"a poor thing but his own," or at least not in the sway of the creature on the throne. His native intelligence returned. He looked round; his eyes fell on the window. He heard the Clerk's voice, which was still speaking but now with such a small strange sound that Richard hardly knew it to be a voice at all. It was more like the echo of a voice thrown down a corridor, but not magnified, only diminished, as if it were passing out through the deep round window in the thick wall. But it was not so deep after all, though it was round; it was a window on a yard; an empty yard? no; for someone was in it, someone was looking in. A woman, but not Lester. He was profoundly relieved to find it was not Lester, yet he felt she was connected with Lester. She was coming in; she was coming through the wall. She was smiling and as he saw the smile he recognized her. It was his wife's friend Evelyn, who had died with her. She was smiling at the Clerk, and as he looked back at the man on the throne he saw that constriction which was the Clerk's smile pass across his face. He heard, mingling with that echo of a human voice, another sound—a high piping sound, coming over distances, or falling as a bird's call from the sky, but this was no bird's call. Richard shut his eyes; still, through those shut eyes, he seemed to see the two smiling at each other. The exchanged smile, the mingled sound, was an outrage. He felt himself to be a witness of an unearthly meeting, of which the seeming friendliness was the most appalling thing. If he had known the word except as an oath, he would have felt that this was damnation. Yet there was only a smile—no pain, no outcry, no obscenity, except that something truly obscene was there. He saw, visibly before him, the breach of spiritual law. He saw a man sitting still and a woman standing just within the wall, a slight thing, and so full of vileness that he almost fainted.

He did not know how long it lasted; for presently they were all on their feet and he too was able to stand up, and then they were all going away.

Chapter Six

THE WISE WATER

It had been, earthly, about five that morning when Lester entered the house at Highgate. It had seemed only evening in the City she had left, for that other City was not bound either to correspondence or to sequence. Its inhabitants were where it chose they should be, as it engaged in its work of accommodating them to itself. They could not yet, or only occasionally, know contemporaneously. Lester still, in general, knew only one thing at a time, and knew them in a temporal order. There was indeed, nearer the center of its life, another way of knowing, open to its full freemen and officers, but it was beyond these souls, and human language could not express what only sovereign and redeemed human nature could bear. Lester was finding out but slowly the capacities of her present existence, and even those she understood after her old manner. She was young in death, and the earth and its habits were, for this brief time, even more precious to her than they had been.

She paused, or so it seemed to her, inside the hall. It shook her with a new astonishment, and yet indeed it was but ordinary, to think that, so to enter, she had simply passed through the door. It was behind her, and she had not opened it. She had not the kind of mind that easily considered the nature of her own appearance to herself; on earth she had not, nor did she now. The sense of her passage encouraged her. She had no very clear idea that anyone would want to prevent her getting to Betty, but if she could go where she would she was strengthened in her purpose. She could, now, hear no sobs, though they were fresh in her ears. She saw the hall was dark, with a natural healthy darkness in which at first she felt some pleasure. She was free from the pale illumination of the dead. But presently it became clear to her that, dark though it might be, she could see in the dark. The whole hall, with its furniture, became distinct; shapes, though not colors, were visible to her. She felt again a sharp pang of longing for her own familiar things; it was indeed that pang that taught her that she could see, as a waking man finds himself in a strange room and knows by his immediate longing how strange it is. She did not wish to look at Lady Wallingford's properties. But she could not help it. She was there; it was dark; she could see in the dark. She stood and listened and heard no sound.

In fact, above her, Betty was not then crying. Her directors had left her and she was lying exhausted—perhaps unconscious. Her mother had gone to her own room; there to copy out her notes of Betty's automatic speech. She had begun to do it years before, when the Clerk and she had begun their combined work, and now she could not bear to cease. She knew it was superfluous; he could keep the whole in his mind. At first he had sometimes forgotten a detail, but now never. He never even wished to read what she did; except as a kind of menial, he never used her. But she continued to work.

The Clerk had left Betty's room. He walked slowly to the head of the stairs. He was, for him, a little perplexed in his mind. For the first time now through several years, she had not, in her repetition of the world's rumors, mentioned his name. It was strange. It might be that some odd chance had kept him from the shouting columns of the daily records. It might be that she was growing too weak to report all. It might be that he himself—but that he could not visualize even to himself. Only he felt that the time for his precursor to be dispatched into the other world was very near. There she could see more clearly and universally; she could speak from her own knowledge and not from borrowed information and that information so limited. He had never been able yet to force her through more than a certain period—a few weeks only; if he attempted more she could only, when she returned, moan, "The rain! The rain!" Floods of water fell on her, it seemed, as if time itself changed to rain and drowned everything, or even swept everything away. When she was habituated to that world, it would be different. Then she would have no consciousness of return; then she could, slowly, grow into and through this rain, and learn what it hid. At present it seemed to threaten that in her which was still necessary to him. His face cleared; he came to the stairs and began to descend. The moon through the windows gave him light, though the hall was dark below. Halfway down he suddenly stopped. There was some living being below him.

He could not see in the dark as Lester could. No magic could give to him in himself the characteristics of the dead. Nothing but a direct shock of destruction, so sudden and immediate that even he could have no time to check it, could kill him, and he did not believe that that was at all possible. He had practiced very steadily the restoration of himself against the quickest harm; his servants had, at his will, attempted his death and he had foiled them. But so doing, he had refused all possibilities in death. He would not go to it, as that other child of a Jewish girl had done. That other had refused safeguard and miracle; he had refused the achievement of security. He had gone into death—and the Clerk supposed it his failure—as the rest of mankind go, ignorant and in pain. The Clerk had set himself to decline pain and ignorance. So that now he had not any capacities but those he could himself gain.

He saw two eyes shining. He should have known what it was; he did not. He could not even see that it was a woman, or the ghost of a woman. He had not called it and he did not expect it. But he did think that it was one of the lesser creatures of that other world. He had seen them sometimes in earlier rites, and once or twice something had followed Betty in, without her knowledge, as if drawn after her, and had lingered for a while in the hall. Such things had not come in human form, and he did not now expect human form. They came usually in the shapes of small monstrosities—things like rats or rabbits or monkeys or snakes, or even dwarfed vultures or large spiders and beetles. They were indeed none of these; they did not belong to animal nature. Had animal nature been capable of enduring the magical link, he would have used it for his purpose, but it was not. Once, long ago, he had tried it with a monkey, but the link had died with its own death; it had no rational soul, and if (after death) it lived at all, it was only its own happy past that lived; it could not grow into other communion. He supposed this to be a dim monstrosity of that ghostly kind. It awaited his will. It was useless to ask its name or kind; such beings were only confused and troubled by such questions and could not answer. They did not know what they were; they did sometimes—not always—know what they were about. He stood high above it, looking scornfully down, and he said, "Why are you here?"

Lester had seen him as he began to descend the stair. She had no idea who he was. Her first thought, as she looked up at that great cloaked figure, was that here at last was one of the native inhabitants of the new City; and that she had perhaps been encouraged into this house to meet him. Her second was that this was some-one for whom she had been waiting. A childish memory of a picture or a tale of angels mingled with something later—an adolescent dream of a man of power, a genius, a conqueror, a master. Lester, like certain other women of high vitality and discontented heart, had occasionally felt that what she really needed was someone great enough to govern her—but to do that, she innocently felt, he (or she—there was no sex differentiation) would have to be very great. The vague dream had disappeared when she had fallen in love. Obedience to a fabulous ruler of shadows was one thing; obedience to Richard was quite another. He certainly rarely seemed to suggest it; when he did, she was rarely in agreement with him. Suddenly now the old adolescent dream recurred. She looked up at the high emaciated face, gazing down, and felt as if it were more than that of a man.

When, however, he spoke, she hardly heard the question. The voice which was husky to Jonathan was thick to her. She was not surprised; so perhaps these god-like beings spoke; or so perhaps she, uneducated in this sound, heard them. But she did just catch the words, and she answered, as meekly as she had ever thought she would, "I'm Lester. I've come to see Betty."

The Clerk heard below him what sounded like the single word, "Betty." He did not hear more. He came down a step or two, peering. There was, he thought, a certain thickening of the darkness, a kind of molded shape. He was sure now that something had followed Betty, but he was a little perplexed that it should—unless indeed it was something useless to him, being hungry and spiritually carnivorous. It was not in the shape of rat or monkey; it was roughly human, like a low tree rudely cut into human form. He lifted his hand and made over it a twisted magical sign, meant to reduce the intruder to the will that was expressed in it. He said, "Why?"

The sign, so loaded, was not without its effect, but its effect was consistent with Lester's nature and her present intention. It would have dissolved or subdued such momentary vitalities as, for instance, had sprung from her oath outside the house, but what had brought her into the house was a true purpose of goodwill; of help? she might have put it so: indeed she now began to answer so. She said, "To help——" and stopped. The word sounded pompous, not only before this god, but even to describe her intention. She almost felt herself blushing, as she thought of Betty and the times when she had not helped Betty. It was upon those vague and unexplored memories that the magical sign had power. The hall became to her suddenly full of shadows. Betty was on all sides of her and so was she. She had no idea she had even seen Betty as many times as now she saw herself abandoning Betty. There were a mass of forms, moving, interpenetrating, and wherever her eyes saw a particular one it seemed to detach itself and harden and become actual. She saw herself ignoring Betty, snubbing Betty, despising Betty—in the gardens, in the dormitory, in the street, even in this hall. They were so vivid to her that she forgot the god on the stair; she was secluded from him in all this ghostly vehemence of her past, and the ghostliness of any apt to be truly more than ghost. She lost the images of herself; she saw only images of Betty—beginning to speak, putting out a timid hand, or only looking at her. She threw up her hand, in her old gesture, to keep them off. Her head spun; she seemed swirled among them on a kind of infernal merry-go-round. If only any of them were the real Betty, the present Betty, the Betty she was coming to, the Betty she—fool!—had been coming to help. Where she had once refused to help, she was now left to need help. But that refusal had been laziness and indifference rather than deliberate malice—original rather than actual sin. It was permitted to her to recognize it with tears. The spiritual ecstasy ravaged her; she thought no more of help either given or taken; she was only in great need of it. She threw out her hand, in an effort to grasp, here or there, Betty's half-outstretched hand, but (actual as the figure seemed) hers never reached it; as the fingers almost touched, hers found emptiness, and there was Betty running away from her, down a garden path, down a street, down the hall, infinitely down the hall. But the vague and impractical yet real sympathy she had once felt for Betty, the occasional interference she had bestowed, allowed her now a word of appeal. She cried out, pleading as she had never supposed she could or would plead: "Betty! please! Betty!"

As she spoke, she found herself alone. But she knew

exactly where Betty was and she knew she had no hope but there. Her dreams of a god had vanished among those too certain visions of a girl; she wholly forgot the appearance on the stairs in her desperate sense of Betty. She moved up the stairs, towards the help she needed, and in her movement she disappeared from the Clerk's own gaze. He was not aware that she passed him; to him it seemed that the roughly molded human form had dwindled and quivered and vanished, and the eyes had faded. It could not, he thought, this poor vagrant from the other world, this less than human or angelic monstrosity, bear the question which he had put to it, and it had fallen into nothingness below him. He was right enough in what, after his own manner, he had seen—the supernatural shaking of Lester's center; but the processes of redemption were hidden from him. At the moment when she drew nearer to the true life of that City, he thought her to be dissolved. He went on calmly down the stairs and opening the door passed into the earthly night.

But Lester, mounting, came to Betty's room, and opening no door passed on into it. This time indeed she knew she went through the door, but then the door, when she came to it, was no longer a serious barrier. It was still a door; it did not become thin or shadowy. But being a door, it was also in itself her quickest way. To open it would have been to go round by a longer path. She was growing capable of the movement proper to her state. She could not so have passed through the empty rooms or dim façades of her earlier experience; those shadowy images retained for her the properties of the world they imaged. But in this real world she could act according to her own reality. She went through the door.

There, before her, stretched motionless in her bed, was Betty. Lester saw her clearly in the dark. She went on till she came to the foot of the bed; then she stood still.

She had never seen anyone look so exhausted and wan. The living girl's eyes were shut; she hardly drew breath; she too might have been dead, except that now and then she was shaken by a sudden convulsion. The dead Lester gazed at the seemingly dead Betty. Her heart sank; what help for her was here? what power in that shaken corpse to hold its own images at bay? If it were a corpse, then she and Betty were parted perhaps for ever. She might have left this reconciliation also too late, as she had left Richard. She had pushed Richard away; she had not gathered Betty in. She was to be left with her choice. She thought: "It isn't fair. I didn't know," and immediately regretted it. She had known—not perhaps clearly about Richard, for those unions and conflicts were of a particular kind, and the justice which must solve them was more intimate than she could yet understand, but she had clearly known about Betty. She had been very young then. But her refusal had been as definite and cold as the body at which she looked was definite and cold. Death for death, death to death, death in death.

The curtains at the windows were drawn back. The sun was rising; the room grew slowly bright with day. Lester stood there because she had nothing else to do. No impulse was upon her and no wish. She had nowhere to go. Evelyn was not in her mind. She knew she could do nothing unless she had help and her only help lay useless before her. Presently she was aware of a step outside the room. There was a tap on the door; another. The door was gently opened, and a maid came in and paused. She looked at Betty; she looked round the room; she looked at Lester without seeing her. Lester looked back at her without interest; she was remote and irrelevant. It was not odd to be unseen; that, of course. Only Betty mattered and Betty lay without sign. The maid went away. The morning light increased.

Suddenly Betty's eyes had opened. They were looking at Lester. A small voice, hardly audible even to Lester, inaudible to mortal ears, said, "Lester!" Lester said, "Yes," and saw that the other had not heard. The eyes widened; the voice said, "Lester! . . . but you're dead. Evelyn and you are dead." It added, dying on the sentence, "I'm so glad Evelyn's dead." The eyes closed. Exhaustion swallowed her.

Lester heard the relief in the dying words. She had forgotten Evelyn, but, fresh from that ghostly world where Evelyn and she had wandered, she retained some sense of companionship, and the relief—which was hostility—filled her with fear. She felt—though indirectly—the terror and the despair of those of the dead who, passing from this world, leave only that just relief behind. That which should go with them—the good will of those they have known—does not. There are those who have been unjustly persecuted or slain; perhaps a greater joy waits them. But for the ordinary man or woman to go with no viaticum but this relief is a very terrible thing. Almost, for a moment, Lester felt the whole City —ghostly or earthly or both in its proper unity—draw that gentle sigh. Disburdened, it rejoiced: at Evelyn's death? at hers? Was this to be all Betty and earth could give? a sigh of joy that she was gone? The form on the bed held all the keys. If she could speak so of one, that other waiting spirit felt no surety that she too might not be excluded, by failing voice and closing eyes, from the consciousness on which so much depended. It was awful to think how much did depend—how much power for everlasting decision lay there. Verdict, judgment, execution of judgment, hid behind those closed eyelids. Lester's impetuosity swelled in her. She wished to wake Betty, to bully her, to compel her to speak, to force help out of her. But she knew all such impetuosity was vain; and however, in her past, she had wrangled in private with Richard—and that was different; yes, it was different, for it was within the nearest image to love that she had known; it might be better or worse, but it was different; it was less permissible and more excusable—however that might be, she did not brawl in public. And she was in public now, in the full publicity of the spiritual City, though no inhabitants of the City except Betty were there. She had waited; she must wait. It was pain and grief to her sudden rage. She waited. The house, earthly, warm, lightened by the great luminary planet, was still to her a part of the City while Betty was there. Everything depended on Betty, and Betty on—on nothing that Lester yet knew.

The door of the room again opened. Lady Wallingford came in. She went to the bed and bent over Betty. She peered into her eyes, felt temples and wrists, and rearranged the bedclothes. Then she crossed to the window and drew one of the curtains a little, so that the sunlight no longer fell on her daughter's face. In so moving, she had passed round the foot of the bed. Lester began to step back; then she checked herself. She knew it did not matter; she was becoming different—how or why she did not know; but coincidence no longer meant contact. She had a faint sense, as she had done when she passed through the door, of something brushing against her. Her eyes blinked and were clear. Lady Wallingford went through the space which Lester seemed to herself to occupy, and so returned; it was all that could be said. The same space was diversely occupied, but the two presences were separate still. Lady Wallingford, exactly like a competent nurse, looked round the room and went out. Body and visionary body were again alone together. Outside the house a car was heard to start up and move off. Lady Wallingford was on her way to Holborn. Thither Richard was now walking along Millbank, while Jonathan in his room waited, with a fantastic but failing hope, for some word of Betty. And beyond them all, three continents murmured of their great leaders, and the two vegetable images of the Clerk swayed by his single will such crowds as he could sway, and he himself prepared for the operation which is called "the sending out," its other name being murder.

As the car's sound died away, Betty sat up. Bright in the shadow her eyes opened on Lester, tender and full of laughter. She pushed the bedclothes back, swung out her legs and sat on the side of the bed. She said, "Hallo, Lester! What are you doing here?" The voice was full of a warm welcome; Lester heard it incredulously. Betty went on. "It's nice to see you anyway. How are you?"

Lester had waited for something, but hardly for this. She had not begun to expect it. But then she had never seen, face to face, the other Betty who had gone almost dancing through the City, nor guessed the pure freshness of joy natural to that place. She had heard only the high hill-call, and now (subdued as it might be to gay and friendly talk) she recognized the voice. She knew at once that a greater than she was here; it was no wonder she had been sent here for help. She looked at the girl sitting on the bed, whose voice was the only sound but Evelyn's that had pierced her nothing since she died, and she said, hoping that the other might also perhaps hear, "Not too frightfully well."

Betty had risen to her feet as Lester spoke. She showed signs of going across to the window, but on the other's words she paused. She said, "What's the matter? Can I do anything?"

Lester looked at her. There was no doubt that this was Betty—Betty gay, Betty joyous, Betty revitalized, but still Betty. This was no sorrowing impotence of misery, but an ardor of willingness to help. Yet to ask for help was not easy. The sense of fatal judgment was still present; the change in Betty had not altered that, and her glowing shape was vivid with it. The slightest movement of that hand, the slightest aversion of those eyes, would be still like any similar movement of those dead hands or that white face would have been, frightful with finality. To ask that this should be set aside, even to plead, was not natural to Lester. But her need was too great for her to delay. She said at once, "Yes, you can."

Betty smiled brilliantly at her. She answered, "Well, that's all right. Tell me about it."

Lester said, rather helplessly, "It's all those times ... those times at school and afterwards. I can't manage them without you."

Betty wrinkled her forehead. She said in some surprise, "Those times at school? But, Lester, I always liked you at school."

"Perhaps you did," said Lester. "But you may remember that I didn't behave as if I particularly liked you."

"Oh, didn't you?" Betty answered. "I know you didn't particularly want me, but why should you? I was so much younger than you and I expect I was something of a nuisance. As far as I can remember, you put up with me nobly. But I don't remember much about it. Need we? It's so lovely of you to come and see me now."

Lester realized that this was going to be worse than she had supposed. She had prepared herself to ask for forgiveness, but that, it seemed, was not enough. She must herself bring the truth to Betty's reluctant mind; nothing else than the truth would be any good. She would not be able entirely to escape from those swirling images of the past, if they were indeed images and not the very past itself, by any other means than by Betty's dismissal of them. They were not here, in this room, but they were there, outside the door, and if she left the room she would be caught again among them. She did not understand how this different Betty had come to be, but the City in which she moved did not allow her to waste time in common earthly bewilderment. The voice was the voice she had wanted to imitate, the voice of the hill in the City. If the Betty of that moment and of this moment were the same, then perhaps Betty would understand, though there was in fact nothing to understand except her own perverse indolence. She said—it was the most bitter thing she had ever done; she seemed to taste on her tongue the hard and bitter substance of that moment—she said, "Try and remember."

Betty's eyes had been again wandering towards the sunlight at the window. She brought them back to look attentively at Lester, and she said quickly and affectionately, "Lester, you've been crying!"

Lester answered in a voice from which, for all her

growing vision and springing charity, she could not keep a rigidity of exasperation, "I know I've been crying. I——"

Betty interrupted. "But of course I'll remember," she said. "It was only that I didn't understand. What is it exactly you want me to remember?" She smiled as she spoke, and all the tenderness her mortal life had desired and lacked was visible in her. Lester felt an impulse to run away, to hide, even at least to shut her eyes. She held herself still; it had to be done. She said, "You might remember how I did behave to you at school. And afterwards."

There was a long silence and in it Lester's new life felt the first dim beginnings of exalted peace. She was not less troubled nor less in fear of what might come. She was, and must be now, the victim of her victim. But also she was now, in that world, with someone she knew, with someone friendly and royally disposed to good, with someone native to her and to that world, easy and happy. The air she breathed was fresh with joy; the room was loaded with it. She knew it as a sick woman knows the summer. She herself was not yet happy, but this kind of happiness was new to her; only, even while she waited, she recollected that once or twice she had known something like it with Richard—one night when they had parted under a street-lamp, one day when they had met at Waterloo. They belonged here, those times; yet those times were as true as those other sinful times that danced without. Her heart was tranquil. If she must go, she must go; perhaps this hovering flicker of known joy might be permitted to go with her. All that was noble in her lifted itself in that moment. The small young figure before her was her judge; but it was also the center and source of the peace. She exclaimed, as if for Betty to know all was necessary to the fullness of the moment and to her own joy: "Oh remember! do remember!"

Betty stood attentive. The times of her happiness had been hitherto on the whole unclouded by her mortal life, except as she might sometimes vaguely remember an unpleasant dream. She set herself now to remember, since that, it seemed, was what was wanted, something she could lately have been contented to leave forgotten. It seemed to her also something of a waste on this glorious morning, with time happily before them, to spend it—however, she knew she wanted to remember. As soon as she knew that Lester wanted it, she too wanted it; so simple is love-in-paradise. She stood and thought. She was still smiling and she continued to smile, though presently her smile became a little grave. She said, "Oh well, how could you know?"

Lester said, "I knew quite enough."

Betty went on smiling, but presently the smile vanished. She said, more seriously, "I do think Evelyn was rather unkind. But I suppose if she liked that sort of thing—anyhow we're not thinking of her. Well, now, that's done."

Lester exclaimed, "You've remembered?" and Betty, now actually breaking into a gay laugh, answered, "Darling, how serious you are! Yes, I've remembered."

"Everything?" Lester persisted; and Betty, looking her full in the eyes, so that suddenly Lester dropped her own, answered, "Everything." She added, "It was lovely of you to ask me. I think perhaps I never quite wanted to remember—Oh all sorts of things—until you asked me, and then I just did, and now I shan't mind whatever else there is. Oh Lester, how good you are to me!"

The tears came into Lester's eyes, but this time they did not fall. Betty's figure swam indistinctly before her and then she blinked the tears away. They looked at each other and Betty laughed and Lester found herself beginning to laugh, but as she did so she exclaimed, "All the same——!" Betty put out her hand towards the other's lips, as if to hush her, but it did not reach them. Clear though they saw and heard each other, intimate as their hearts had become, and freely though they shared in that opening City a common good, still its proper definitions lay between them. The one was dead; the other not. The *Noli me tangere* of the City's own Lord Mayor was, in their small degree, imposed on them. Betty's hand dropped gently to her side. They half recognized the law and courteously yielded to it. Betty thought, "Of course, Lester was killed." She also thought, and she said aloud, "Oh but I was glad Evelyn was killed." Her voice was shocked; stricken, she looked at the other. She said, "How could I be?"

Lester had again forgotten Evelyn. She remembered. She became aware of Evelyn running, not now from her but towards her, towards them both. She herself now was at the other end of Evelyn's infinite haste; she shared with Betty the nature of the goal, and she felt at a distance Evelyn hurrying and almost there. She threw up her head, as she had thrown it up at the first call from the hill. She said—and now nothing deadened her speech; she said—in the voice that was to Richard her loveliest and lordliest, "I'll deal with Evelyn."

Betty answered, half-laughing and half-embarrassed. "I can't think why she scares me a little still. But I didn't mean to want her to be dead. Only she's all mixed up with *there*. I usen't to think of that much when I was here." There was no need to explain what she meant by "there" and "here." Their hearts, now in union, knew. "But lately I seem to have to sometimes. Now you've made me remember, I don't so much mind. Stay with me a little while, if you can; will you, Lester? I know you can't settle that; things happen. But while you *can* . . . I've a feeling that I've got to get through something disagreeable, and I don't want to make a fuss again."

"Of course I'll stay—if I may," said Lester. "But make a fuss—you!"

Betty sat down on the bed. She smiled again at Lester; then she began to talk, almost as if to herself, or as if she were telling a child a story to soothe it to sleep. She said, "I know I needn't—when I think of the lake; at least, I suppose it was a lake. If it was a river, it was very broad. I must have been very small indeed, because, you know, it always seems as if I'd only just floated up through the lake, which is nonsense. But sometimes I almost think I did, because deep down I can remember the fishes, though not so as to describe them, and none of them took any notice of me, except one with a kind of great horned head which was swimming round me and diving under me. It was quite clear there under the water and I didn't even know I was there. I mean I wasn't thinking of myself. And then presently the fish dived again and went below me, and I felt him lifting me up with his back, and then the water plunged under me and lifted me, and I came out on the surface. And there I lay; it was sunny and bright, and I drifted in the sun—it was almost as if I was lying on the sunlight itself—and presently I saw the shore—a few steps in a low cliff, and a woman standing there. I didn't know who she was, but I know now, since you made me remember—Lester, I do owe you such a lot

—it was a nurse I once had, but not for very long. She bent down and lifted me out of the water. I didn't want to leave it. But I liked her; it was almost as if she was my real mother, and she said: 'There, dearie, no one can undo that; bless God for it.' And then I went to sleep, and that's the earliest thing I can remember, and after that only some things that belonged to it: some of the times I've been through London, and the Thames, and the white gulls. They were all in that part and in the other part too, the part I'm only just beginning to remember. And so were you, Lester, a little."

"I!" said Lester bitterly. It did not seem to her likely that she could have belonged to that world of light and beauty. Yet even as she spoke she irrelevantly thought of Richard's eyes at the corner in Holborn—and before that —before that—before she was dead; and she remembered how Richard had come to meet her once and again, and how her heart had swelled for the glory and vigor of his coming. But Betty was speaking again.

"I see now that you were, and now it seems all right. That was why I ran after you—Oh how tiresome I must have been! but it doesn't matter. I'm afraid I did make a fuss; I know I did over the headaches—there were some places where I knew I was going to have headaches—and over Evelyn. It really was rather silly of Evelyn. And then there was this house——"

She stopped and yawned. She threw herself back on the pillow and swung up her legs. She went on: "But I'm too sleepy now to remember all that I ought to about this house.... And then there was Jonathan. Do you know Jonathan? he was very good to me. We might go and look at the Thames some time, you and I and Jonathan...." Her eyes closed; her hands felt vaguely about the bed. She said, in tones Lester could only just hear, "I'm so sorry. I just can't keep awake. Don't go. Jonathan will be coming.... Don't go unless you must. It's lovely having you here.... It was sweet of you to come ... Jonathan will ... dear Lester...." She made an uncertain movement to pull the bedclothes up over her; before the movement ended she was asleep.

Lester did not understand what she had been saying. In what strange way she had been known to Betty, more happily than ever she herself could have supposed, she did not know. Betty had been talking almost as if there had been two lives, each a kind of dream to the other. It would once have been easy to call the one life a fantasy, easy if this new, gay and vivid Betty had not precisely belonged to the fantasy. She felt both lives within her too sharply now to call either so. There had been something like two lives in her own single life—the gracious passionate life of beauty and delight, and the hard angry life of bitterness and hate. It was the recollection of that cold folly which perhaps now made Betty seem to her—no; it was not. Betty was changing; she was dying back; she was becoming what she had been. Color passed from her cheeks; the sweet innocence of sleep faded, and the pallor of exhaustion and the worn semblance of victimization spread. The hands twitched. She looked already, as men say, "near dead." Lester exclaimed: "Betty!" It had no effect. The change affected the room itself; the sunlight weakened; power everywhere departed. The girl who lay before Lester was the girl she had turned away from. The hands and head could no longer threaten judgment; they were too helpless. Yes, but also they had judged. What had been, in that other state, decided, remained fixed; once known, always known. She knew quite clearly that

Betty had—forgiven her. The smile, the warmth, the loveliness, were forgiveness. It was strange not to mind, but she did not mind. If she did not mind Betty, perhaps she would not mind Richard. She smiled. Mind Richard? mind being forgiven—forgiven so—by that difficult obnoxious adorable creature? Let him come to her in turn and she would show him what forgiveness was. Till now she had not really understood it; occasionally in the past each of them had "forgiven" the other, but the victim had not much liked it. But now—by high permission, yes. And if Richard and Betty, then others; if this permission which now directed her life allowed, others. "Thus"—how did it go?—"through all eternity I forgive you, you forgive me." Wine and bread, the poem had called it; wine and bread let it be. Meanwhile there was nothing to do but to wait till that happened which must happen. In some way she had now been left in charge of Betty. She must keep her charge. She must wait.

All this time, since first Lester had entered the house, the unhappy soul of Evelyn had also waited. At first it had almost followed Lester in, but it did not dare. Frightful as the empty appearance of the City was to it, to be enclosed in the house would be worse. She would be afraid of being shut up with Lester and Betty, certainly with Lester, almost with Betty. She hated the victim of her torment, but to be alone with her in that dark solid house— the thought ought to have been agreeable, but it was not at all agreeable. As for Lester, she hated Lester too. Lester had patronized her, but then Lester could. She had the power to be like that and she was. She hated being alone in this place with Lester, though since she had run after Betty, even though she had missed her, she felt better. The street down which she had run after she had turned off from the hill, this street in which she now stood, had seemed more close, more helpful. The air held some sense of gain. This was more like the London she had known. The house should have been the climax; could she go in, she thought, it would be. Only she dared not go in. Lester was not to be trusted; Lester and Betty might be plotting.

After all, she was rather glad she had not caught up with Betty. Lester might have come up behind her and then the two of them might have done things to her. Or they might have thought she would have run into the house, but she had not; she had been too clever for that —and for them. She walked a few steps away. It was no good standing too near; they would not come out—no, but if they should . . . She could almost see them talking in the house, smiling at each other. She walked a little farther away and turned her head over her shoulder as she went. On her face was the look which had shocked Lester when she had earlier seen that turned head. It was hate relieved from mortality, malice incapable of death. Within the house, Lester's own face had taken on a similar change; some element of alteration had disappeared. She herself did not, of course, know it; her attention had been taken up by the growing glory that was Betty. But even Betty's face had not that other lucidity. What had looked at Lester from Evelyn's eyes, what now showed in her own, was pure immortality. This was the seal of the City, its first gift to the dead who entered it. They had what they were and they had it (as it seemed) forever. With that in her eyes, Evelyn turned her head again and wandered slowly on.

She came on to the hill and drifted down it, for having no choice of ways and yet being oddly compelled to go on—if not into the house, then away from the house—she only retraced her steps, slowly going back, slowly going down. She was about a third of the way down when from far off the sound of the Name caught her. She could hardly there be said to have heard it; it was not so much a name or even a sound as an impulse. It had gone, that indrawing cry, where only it could go, for the eternal City into which it was inevitably loosed absorbed it into its proper place. It could not affect the solid houses of earth nor the millions of men and women toilfully attempting goodness; nor could it reach the paradisal places and their inhabitants. It sounded only through the void streets, the apparent façades, the shadowy rooms of the world of the newly dead. There it found its way. Other wanderers, as invisible to Evelyn as she to them, but of her kind, felt it—old men seeking lechery, young men seeking drunkenness, women making and believing malice, all harborers in a lie. The debased Tetragrammaton drew them with its spiritual suction; the syllables passed out, and swirled, and drawing their captives returned to their speaker. Some went a little way and fell; some farther and failed; of them all only she, at once the latest, the weakest, the nearest, the worst, was wholly caught. She did not recognize captivity; she thought herself free. She began to walk more quickly, to run, to run fast. As she ran, she began to hear the sound. It was not friendly; it was not likeable; but it was allied. She felt towards it as Lester had felt towards the cry on the hill. The souls in that place know their own proper sounds and hurry to them.

Something perhaps of fear entered her, to find herself running so fast. It was a steep road and it seemed much longer than when she had run up it of her own volition. She ran and she ran. She was running almost along the very cry itself, not touching the apparent pavement; it wailed louder below her. Her immortality was in her face; her spirituality in her feet; she was lifted and she ran.

She did not recognize the streets; she came at last round by King's Cross, on into the congeries of streets on the other side of the Euston Road, on towards Holborn. The cry grew quieter as she neared its source. What had been a wail in the more distant streets was a voice in the nearer. She still ran along it. At last, so running, she came through a small gate into a yard, and across it to a small low window. There she stopped and looked in. She saw a kind of hall, with people sitting on chairs, and away at the other end in a high chair, a man who was looking back at her. Or perhaps he was not actually looking back at her, but she knew he saw her. A dizziness of relief took her; here at last was someone else. She was so aware of him and of his sidelong knowledge of her, that she hardly noticed she was moving forward and through the wall. A film of spiders' webs brushed against her; she broke through it. She had come back; at the very sight of him she had been able to return into the world of men. She had escaped from the horrible vague City and here was he to welcome her.

He was smiling. She thought—as neither Jonathan nor Richard had done—that it was properly a smile, though again the smile was sidelong. He had reason, for when he saw her he knew that at last his writ ran in the spiritual City. He had known that it must be so, he being what he was. But that silence of Betty's about his future had almost troubled him. A deathly silence had seemed to hover round him, as if he had made an error in magic and could not recover himself. It was certainly time he sent out his messenger before him. But he knew now it was no error, for the silence had spoken. This was its first word—solitary, soon to be companioned. He would ride there presently upon their cries. He was overcoming that world.

The exchange of smiles—if that which had no thought of fair courtesy could be called exchange; at least some imitation of smiles—passed between them. Separately, each of them declined the nature of the City; which nevertheless held them. Each desired to breach the City; and either breach opened—directly and only—upon the other. Love to love, death to death, breach to breach; that was the ordering of the City, and its nature. It throve between Lester and Betty, between Richard and Jonathan, between Simon and Evelyn; that was its choice. How it throve was theirs. The noise of London, which was a part of it, rose at a distance outside the house—all its talk and traffic and turmoil. In the quiet of the hall the man said to the woman, "I shall want you soon." She said, "Take me out of it." And he, "Soon." He stood up; that was when Richard found himself going out of the hall.

Chapter Seven

THE MAGICAL SACRIFICE

An hour or so later Jonathan opened his door to Richard. He said, "I say, what's been happening? You look ghastly. Sit down; have a drink."

Richard was very white and unsteady. He dropped into a chair. Even the warm studio and Jonathan could not overcome the sense of that other thing which, ever since he had left the house in Holborn, had run cold in his blood. As Jonathan brought him the drink, he shuddered and looked rather wildly round. Jonathan said anxiously, "Here, drink this. Are you all right?"

Richard drank and sat for a little silent. Then he said, "I'd better tell you. Either I'm mad or . . . But I'm not just wrong. I'm either right or I'm mad. It's no good telling me I was taken in by seeing a barmaid in a yard——"

"No; all right," said Jonathan. "I won't. I shouldn't be very likely to anyhow. Tell me what you like and I'll believe it. Why not?"

Richard began. He spoke slowly. He took care to be exact. He modified his description of his own sensations and emotions; he was as impartial as he could be. Once or twice he made an effort to be defensively witty; it was unsuccessful and he dropped it. As he came to the end, he grew even more careful. Jonathan sat on his table and watched him.

"I saw her come in. They looked towards each other and they smiled. And all I can tell you is that I know now what blasphemy is. It's not attractive and it isn't thrilling. It's just bloodcurdling—literally. It's something peculiarly different and it's something which happens. It isn't talk; it happens. My eyes began to go dark with it, because I simply couldn't bear it. And then, before I went quite under, we were all standing up and going out —down that corridor. I don't know what would have happened if one of them had touched me then. We got into the hall, and there was a lot of shuffling and whispering, and then an ordinary voice or two, and then everyone had disappeared except the caretaker. I saw the front door and I went straight to it. I was just at it when he called me. I couldn't go back or turn round. I stood still—I don't know why; I suppose I was still in a nightmare. And outside I saw that filthy little hand pointing in behind me. He spoke over my shoulder in that damn husky voice of his, and he said——"

"Yes; all right," said Jonathan as Richard's voice went up a note or two. "Steady."

"Sorry!" said Richard, recovering. "He said: 'I won't keep you, Mr. Furnival. Come back presently. When you want me, I shall be ready. If you want your wife, I can bring her to you; if you don't want her, I can keep her away from you. Tell your friend I shall send for him soon. Goodbye.' So then I walked out."

He lifted his eyes and looked at Jonathan, who couldn't think of anything to say. Presently Richard went on, still more quietly. "And suppose he can?"

"Can what?" asked Jonathan gloomily.

"Can," said Richard carefully and explicitly, "do something to Lester. Leave off thinking of Betty for a moment; Betty's alive. Lester's dead, and suppose this man can do something to dead people? Don't forget I've seen one. I've seen that woman Mercer walk straight into his hall. I know she's dead; she looked dead. That's how I knew I saw her. No; not like a corpse. She was—fixed; as solid as you or me, but a deal more herself than either of us. If he made her come, can he make Lester come? If he can, I shall kill him."

Jonathan said, staring at the floor, "No, I wouldn't do that. If . . . if he *can* do anything of that kind, don't you see it mightn't make much difference if he *were* dead? I wouldn't kill him."

Richard got up. He said, "I see. No." He began to wander about the room. Presently he said, "I won't have him touch Lester." He added, "If I were to kill myself?"

Jonathan shook his head. "We don't know anything about it," he said. "You couldn't be sure of being with her. And anyhow it's a sin."

"Oh a sin!" said Richard peevishly and was silent. His friend was on the point of saying, "Well, if souls exist, sins may," but he thought it would be tiresome, and desisted. Presently his eyes fell on the painting of those sub-human souls, and after staring at it he said abruptly, "Richard, I don't believe it. He may be able to hypnotize these creatures, but Lester wasn't much like them, was she? I don't believe he could control her unless she let him, and I shouldn't think she was much likely to let him. She wasn't, as I remember her, the kind of woman who likes being controlled, was she?"

Richard stopped. The faintest of smiles came to his lips. He said, "No. God help Father Simon if he tries to control Lester. Still"—and his face darkened again—"the plane was too much for her, and he might be."

They stood side by side and looked at the cloud of rising backs. Evelyn Mercer was one of them; would Lester be? was Betty meant to be? Their ladies called to them from separate prisons, demanding help and salvation. The corridor of iron rock opened—surely not for those sacred heads? surely those royal backs could never incline below the imbecile face. But what to do? Richard's habitual agnosticism had so entirely disappeared with the first sight of Evelyn that he had already forgotten it. Jonathan was beginning to think of seeking out a priest. But their tale was a wild thing and he did not know what a priest could do. No priest could command Simon; nor exorcise Lester; nor enliven Betty. No; it was left to them.

He said, "Well, damn it, this isn't the only painting I've done. Let's look at the one Simon didn't like."

"I don't see what good that'll do," Richard said miserably, but he went round with his friend. He seemed to himself within himself to be standing alone among the insects, and he could not avoid the thought that perhaps now, somewhere, somehow, Lester was one of the insects —an irrational scuttling insect that would keep closer to him than any of the others would. That, if she were so, might still be left of their love, and that would be all. Their past would end in this, and this forever. Only he knew she would not—unless Simon had utterly and wholly changed her very nature. She would, insect or woman or some dreadful insect-woman, keep away from him; and as he knew it, he knew he did not want her to. If she were that, he wanted her—in spite of the horror; if he could bear the horror!—to be by him still. Or perhaps he might come to some agreement with Father Simon—perhaps he instead of her—she would be very angry indeed if he did; he knew very well it would be a contest between them, if such a chance could be; pride clashing with pride, but also love with love. It would be unfair to do it without her knowledge, yet with her knowledge it could never be done. The thought flickered through his mind before he realized of what he was really thinking. When he did, he could hardly think of it; the terrible metapsychosis gnawed at him and would not be seen. He stared in front of him and realized slowly that he was looking deeply into the light.

The massive radiance of that other painting flowed out towards him from the canvas; it had not surely, when he had seen it before, been as weighty as this? it had not so projected energy? He forgot Simon and the cluster of spiritual vermin; he forgot Lester, except that some changing detail of her hovered still in his mind—her hand, her forehead, her mouth, her eyes. The inscape of the painting became central. There, in the middle of this room, lay the City, ruined and renewed, submerged and gloriously re-emerging. It was not the sense of beauty but the sense of exploration that was greatest in him. He had but to take one step to be walking in that open space, with houses and streets around him. The very rubble in the foreground was organic and rising; not rising as the beetles were to some exterior compulsion but in proportion and to an interior plan. The whole subject—that is, the whole unity; shape and hue; rubble, houses, cathedral, sky and hidden sun, all and the light that was all and held all—advanced on him. It moved forward as that other painting retired. The imbecile master and his companions were being swallowed up in distance, but this was swallowing up distance. There was distance in it and yet it was all one. As a painting is.

He drew a deep breath. As he did so, a phrase from

the previous day came back to him. He turned on Jonathan; he said, but his eyes were still on the canvas, "With plain observation and common understanding?"

"Yes," said Jonathan. "I'll swear it was. I don't wonder Simon didn't like it."

Richard could not bear the glow. It bore in upon him even more than it did on Jonathan—partly because it was not his painting, partly because he was already, despite himself, by his sight of Lester, some way initiated into that spiritual world. He walked to the window and stood looking out. The gray October weather held nothing of the painting's glory, yet his eyes were so bedazzled with the glory that for a moment, however unillumined the houses were, their very mass was a kind of illumination. They were illustrious with being. The sun in the painting had not risen, but it had been on the point of rising, and the expectation that unrisen sun had aroused in him was so great that the actual sun, or some other and greater sun, seemed to be about to burst through the cloud that filled the natural sky. The world he could see from the window gaily mocked him with a promise of being an image of the painting, or of being the original of which the painting was but a painting.

As he looked, he heard in the silence behind him a small tinkle. Something had fallen. Before his brain had properly registered the sound, he felt the floor beneath him quiver, and the tinkle was followed by a faint echo in different parts of the room. Things shook and touched and settled. The earth had felt the slightest tremor and all its inhabitants felt it. It was for less than a moment, as if an infinitesimal alteration had taken place. Richard saw in the sky upon which his eyes were fixed a kind of eyelid-lifting, an opening and shutting of cloud. He caught no direct light, but the roofs and chimneys of the houses gleamed, whether from above or in themselves he could not tell. It passed and his heart lifted. He was suddenly certain of Lester—not for himself, but in herself; she lived newly in the light. She lived—that was all; and so, by God's mercy, he.

He thought the phrase, and though it was strange to him it was very familiar. But he did not, in that second, feel he had abandoned his agnosticism for what he knew to be Jonathan's belief. Rather his very agnosticism rose more sharply and healthily within him; he swung to a dance and he actually did swing round, so that he saw Jonathan planted before his canvas and frowning at it, and on the floor a silver pencil which had rolled from the table. He walked across and picked it up, playing lightly with it, and as he began to speak Jonathan forestalled him. He said, "Richard, it *is* different."

"Different?" asked Richard. "How different?"

"I'm very good," Jonathan went on, but so simply that there was no egotism in the remark, "but I'm nothing like as good as this. I simply am not. I could never, never paint this."

Richard looked at the painting. But his amateur's eye could not observe with certainty the difference of which Jonathan seemed to be speaking. He thought he could have been easily persuaded that the shapes were more definite, that the mass of color which had overwhelmed him before now organized itself more exactly, that the single unity was now also a multitudinous union—but he would not by himself have been certain. He said, "You're the master. How?"

Jonathan did not answer the question directly. He said, in a lower voice, almost as if he were shy of some-

148

thing in his own work, "I suppose, if things—if everything is like that, I suppose colors and paints might be. They must be what everything is, because everything is. Mightn't they become more themselves? mightn't they? It was what I wanted to do, because it was like that. And if the world is like that, then a painting of the world must be. But if it is . . ."

Richard went across to him. "If it is," he said, "we weren't done and can't be done. If it is, we aren't beetles and can't be beetles, however they grin at each other in their holes. By all possible plain observation and common understanding, we aren't. And as my own common understanding has told me on a number of occasions that Lester doesn't like being kept waiting, I'd better try not to keep her waiting."

"Is she waiting?" said Jonathan with a slow answering smile.

"I can't possibly tell you yet," said Richard. "But I shall try somehow to find out. Let's do something. Let's plainly observe. Let's go to Highgate and observe Betty. Let's persecute Lady Wallingford. Let's love Simon; he likes love. Come on, man." He stepped back and waved his hand towards Highgate. *"Ecrasez l'infame.* Give them the point, gentlemen. And no heeltaps. Come. Have you ever seen Lester in a rage? 'Oh what a deal of scorn looks beautiful . . .' but I don't want it to get too beautiful."

He caught up his hat. Jonathan said, "I feel like a bit of my own painting. All right; come on. Let's get a taxi and go to Highgate and tell them where they stop. I don't quite know how."

"No," said Richard, "but the sky will or the earth or something. Simon control Lester? Simon couldn't control a real beetle. Nor could I, if it comes to that, but I don't pretend to. Come."

When they ran together out of the house, it was already something more than an hour since the Clerk had re-entered Betty's room. He knew that the crisis was on him; he had come to direct it. Up to now he had been content to send his daughter on her ghostly journeys as his messenger and in some sense his substitute. He had begotten her for this and for more than this; since she had grown out of early childhood he had trained her in this. Now the time of more had come and the mystical rain which had defeated her should mock him no longer. The tale of the enchanters held a few masters—not many —who had done this. One of the earlier, another Simon, called the Magus, had slain a boy by magic and sent his soul into the spiritual places, there to be his servant. This Simon would make a stronger link, for he would send his child. But to establish that link properly, the physical body must be retained in its own proper shape, that in future all commands might be sent through it to its twin in the other air. The earlier Simon had kept the body of the boy in a casing of gold in his bedchamber, and (as it was said) angels and other powers of that air had visibly adored it, at the will of the magician laid upon them through the single living soul, and exposed all the future without the slow tricks that had otherwise to be used, and shown treasures and secrets of the past, until their lord became a pillar of the universe and about him the planetary heavens revolved. But in those days magicians had public honor; now for a little while a secret way was better. It was to be today no bloody sacrifice; only a compulsory dissolution of bonds between soul and body—a making forever all but two of what must be at bottom forever one; the last fact of known identity alone remaining. When the uncorrupting death was achieved, the body should be coffined for burial. After the burial it would be no less than natural that the distressed mother should go to her own house in the North to be quiet and recover; and no less than likely that she might take with her a not too great case—Betty was not large—of private effects. She could go, nowadays, by car. It would be easy, on the night before the funeral, to make from dust and air and impure water and a little pale fire a shape to be substituted for the true body. That should lay itself down in the coffin, clasping a corded brick or two to give it weight, for though magic could increase or decrease the weight of what already had weight, yet these magical bodies always lacked the mysterious burden of actual flesh. But it would serve for the short necessary time, and afterwards let earth go indeed to earth and dust to dust. The substitution made, and the true body laid in the chest, it could be conveyed away. It should lie in the lumber-room of the Northern cottage, and there serve him when he wished, until when he and his Types were united, and the world under him made one, he could house it becomingly to himself in his proper home.

The time had come. He could utterly pronounce the reversed Name—not that it was to him a Name, for his whole effort had been to deprive it of any real meaning, and he had necessarily succeeded in this for himself, so that it was to him no Name but vibrations only, which, directed as he chose, should fulfill what he chose. He had quite forgotten the original blasphemy of the reversal; the sin was lost, like so many common sins of common men, somewhere in his past. He did not now even think of there being any fact to which the Name was correspondent. He had, that very morning, aimed the vibrating and recessional power on the latest and the nearest of the dead—the wife of the man who had come foolishly inquiring. And though she had not come, yet her companion in death had come—one who was, it must have chanced, more responsive than she. He had his own intentions for her. But first a balance must be preserved; where one was drawn in one must go out. He had drawn back the other woman's soul to wait now outside the house; there she crouched till the act was finished. So prepared, he came into his daughter's room.

His mistress entered with him. In the eyes of the servants he was a foreign consulting doctor who had sometimes done Miss Betty good and was a friend of the family. For the law, there was an ordinary practitioner who was well acquainted with her sad case and could do all that was necessary. Both of them would find now that for Betty they could do nothing. The pretense was to last just this hour; therefore his mistress came. Yet bringing the living woman it was unfortunate for him that he had not brought in with him the dead woman also whom he had left to her own ghostly place. So wise and mighty as he was, his wisdom had failed there. Had he done so, that poor subservient soul might have conveyed to him some hint of what else was in that room. He could see those he called; not, those he did not. He did not see the form that waited by the bed; he did not see Lester. He knew, of course, nothing of the exchange of redeeming love that had taken place between those two—no more than of that gallant Betty who had risen once from the lake of wise water. And if he had known anything, of what conceivable importance could the memories of two schoolgirls be to him? even though the memories of those girls should be the acts of souls? Because it would have been, and was, so unimportant, he did not see in the pale and exhausted girl in the bed any of the sudden runnels of roseal light which Lester now saw, as if the blood itself were changed and richly glowing through the weary flesh. Lester saw them—the blood hiding something within itself, which yet it did not quite succeed in hiding from any who, in whatever shy efforts of new life, had sought and been granted love. Lester might not have believed it, but then she did not have to try. She looked and saw; in that state what was, was certain. There was no need for belief.

The Clerk and she were very close. Lester did not recognize the identity of the shape she had seen on the stairs, and otherwise she did not know him. But as his great form came slowly into the room, she felt him to be of the same nature as that other shape. He now, and that he on the stairs, were inhabitants of this world in which she was. Their appearance, first in night and then in day, was overwhelming to her. The great cloak was a wrapping up of power in itself; the ascetic face a declaration of power. Those appearances, and that of the laughing Betty, belonged to the same world, but these were its guardians and masters. Lester felt unusually shy and awkward as she stood there; had he commanded then, she would have obeyed. She knew that she went unseen by men and women, but as his eyes passed over her she felt rather that she had been seen and neglected than that she had not been seen.

The giant, for so he seemed to her to be, paused by the bed. Lester waited on his will. So, behind him, did Lady Wallingford. Betty switched a little, shifted restlessly and finally turned on her back, so that she lay facing the gaze of her master and father. He said to her mother,

"Lock the door." Lady Wallingford went back to the door, locked it, turned and stood with her hand on the handle. The Clerk said to her again, "Draw the curtains." She obeyed; she returned. The room lay in comparative darkness, shut off and shut in. The Clerk said, in a gentle voice, almost as if he were waking a child, "Betty, Betty, it's time to go." But he was not trying to wake her.

Lester listened with attention. She believed that the giant was laying some proper duty on Betty, some business which she did not understand, but the inflexibility of the voice troubled her. The friendship which had sprung in the time of their talk made her wish to spare the present Betty this austere task. Besides she herself wished, as soon as was possible, to have a place in this world, to be directed, to have something to do. She made —she so rash, so real, so unseen—a sudden movement. She began, "Let me——" and stopped, for Betty's eyes had opened and in fear and distress were looking up at the Clerk, and her fingers were picking at the bedclothes, as the fingers of the dying do. Lester years before had seen her father die; she knew the sign. Betty said, in a voice only just heard through the immense stillness of the room, "No; no."

The Clerk thrust his head forward and downward. Its leanness, and the cloak round him, turned him for Lester to some great bird of the eagle kind, hovering, waiting, about to thrust. He said, "To go," and the words sprang from him as if a beak had stabbed, and the body of Betty seemed to yield under the blow. Only the fact that no blood gushed between her breasts convinced Lester that it was not so. But again and once again, as if the wounding beak drove home, the Clerk said, "To go . . . to go." A faint sound came from the door; Lady Wallingford had drawn a sharp breath. Her eyes were bright; her hands were clenched; she was drawn upright as if she were treading something down; she said—the light word hung in the room like an echo: "Go."

Lester saw, though she was not directly looking. Her manner of awareness was altering. Touch was forbidden her; hers and Betty's hands had never met. Taste and smell she had no opportunity to exercise. But sight and hearing were enlarged. She could somehow see at once all that she had formerly been able to see only by turning her head; she could distinctly hear at once all sorts of sounds of which formerly one would deaden another. She was hardly aware of the change; it was so natural. She was less aware of herself except as a part of the world, and more aware of her friend. There was as yet no distrust of the grand shape opposite her, but the tiny vibrations of that single syllable spun within her. She saw Betty receding and she saw Betty struggling. She spoke with passion; and her voice, inaudible to those others, in the room, was audible enough to any of the myriad freemen of the City, to the alien but allied powers of heaven which traverse the City, to the past, present and future of the City, to its eternity and to That which everywhere holds and transfixes its eternity; audible to all these, clear among the innumerable mightier sounds of the creation, she exclaimed: "Betty!"

Her friend's eyes turned to her. They entreated silently, as years before they had entreated; they were dimming, but what consciousness they had still looked out—a girl's longing, a child's call, a baby's cry. A voice lower than Lady Wallingford's, so low that even the Clerk could not hear it, though he knew she had spoken, but perfectly audible to Lester and to any of that other company whose business it might be to hear, said: "Lester!" It was the same timid proffer of and appeal to friendship which Lester had once ignored. She answered at once. "All right, my dear. I'm here."

Betty's head lay towards her. The Clerk put out his hand to turn it again, so that his eyes might look into his daughter's eyes. Before it could touch her, the spiritual colloquy had gone on. Betty said, "I don't at all mind going, but I don't want him to send me." The voice was ever so slightly stronger; it had even a ripple of laughter in it, as if it were a little absurd to be so particular about a mere means. Lester said, "No, darling: why should he? Stay with me a little longer." Betty answered, "May I? Dear Lester!" and shut her eyes. The Clerk turned her head.

Lester had spoken on her spirit's instincts. But she did not at all know what she ought to do. She realized more than ever that she was parted from living men and women by a difference of existence, and realizing it she knew that the grand figure by the bed was not of her world but of that, and being of that and being so feared, might be hostile and might even be evil. She did not any longer squander power by trying to speak to him. She was not exactly content to wait, but she knew she must wait. She became conscious all at once of the delight of waiting —of the wide streets of London in which one could wait, of Westminster Bridge, of herself waiting for Richard on Westminster Bridge, as she had done—when? The day she was killed; the day before she was killed. Yes; on that previous day they had agreed to meet there, and he had been late, and she had been impatient; no wonder that, after death, she had been caught again to the scene of her impatience and played out again the sorry drama. Oh now she would wait and he would come. She seemed, bodiless though in truth she was and knew it more and more, to feel her body tingling with expectation of him, with expected delight. She had once walked (he would have told her) in a kind of militant glory; she stood so now, unknowing. Her militancy was not now to be wasted on absurdities; as indeed it never need have been; there had been enough in herself to use it on. Her eyes, or what were once her eyes, were brighter than Lady Wallingford's; her head was up; her strong and flexible hands moved at her sides; her foot tapped once and ceased. The seeming body which the energy of her spirit flung out in that air was more royal and real than the entire body of Lady Wallingford. She gave her attention to the Clerk.

He was speaking slowly, in a language she did not understand, and sternly, almost as if he were giving final instructions to a careless or lazy servant. He had laid his left hand on Betty's forehead, and Lester saw a kind of small pale light ooze out everywhere between his hand and Betty and flow over the forehead. Betty's eyes were open again, and they looked up, but now without sight, for Lester's own quickened sight saw that a film had been drawn over them. Betty was again receding. Lester said, "Betty, if you want me I'm here," and meant it with all her heart. The Clerk ceased to give instructions, paused, drew himself up, and began to intone.

All three women heard him, yet there was not a sound in the room. His lips moved, but they did not make the sound. The intonation was within him and the intonation moved his lips; his mouth obeyed the formula. Presently, however, something syllabic did emerge. Lady Wallingford abruptly turned her back and leaned her forehead against the door. The light on Betty's forehead expanded upward; in the dimness of the room it rose like a small pillar. Lester saw it. She was now incapable of any action except an unformulated putting of herself at Betty's disposal; she existed in that single act. It was then she became aware that the Clerk was speaking to her.

He did not think so. His intention and utterance were still limited to the woman on the bed. He was looking there and speaking there. He saw the almost dead face and the filmed eyes. But Lester saw a change. The eyes closed; the face relaxed. Betty slept, and slept almost happily. Lester felt the strange intoning call not to Betty but to her; it was she that was meant. Just as she realized it, she lost it. Her heart was so suddenly and violently racked that she thought she cried out. The intensity of the pain passed, but she was almost in a swoon from it, and all the sense of her physical body was in that swoon restored to her. She was not yet capable of the complex states of pain or delight which belong to the unbodied state, and indeed (though she must pass through those others) yet the final state was more like this world's in the renewal of the full identity of body and soul. She was unconscious for that time of the Clerk, of Betty, of the room, but she heard dimly sounds gathering at her feet; the intoning rose up her from below and touched her breasts and fell away. As she recovered, she looked down. She saw the bluish-green tinge of the death-light crawling round her ankles. She knew at once that that was what it was. She had not at all died till now; not when she tried to answer the voice from the hill and failed. Even that was but a preliminary to death, but this was dissolution. Better the vague unliving City than this, but she had come out of that City and this was what lay outside; this lapping pool which, as it rose into her, mingled itself with her, so that she saw her limbs changing with it. She thought, in a paroxysm of longing, of the empty streets, and she made an effort to keep that longing present to her. She fought against dissolution.

But the backward-intoned Tetragrammaton continued to rise. It flowed up not equally, but in waves or sudden tongues. It reached up to her knees. The appearance of her clothes which had so long accompanied her had disappeared; looking down, she saw in that swimming bluish-green nothing but herself. She could see nothing but that and she heard on all sides the intoning flow in on her.

Of one other thing she was conscious. She had been standing and now she was no longer standing. She was leaning back on something, some frame which from her buttocks to her head supported her; indeed she could have believed, but she was not sure, that her arms, flung out on each side held on to a part of the frame, as along a beam of wood. In her fighting and sinking consciousness, she seemed to be almost lying along it, as she might be on a bed, only it was slanting. Between standing and lying, she held and was held. If it gave, as at any moment it might give, she would fall into the small steady chant which, heard in her ears and seen along her thighs, was undoing her. Then she would be undone. She pressed herself against that sole support. So those greater than she had come—saints, martyrs, confessors—but they joyously, knowing that this was the first movement of their re-edification in the City, and that thus in that earliest world fashioned of their earthly fantasies began the raising of the true houses and streets. Neither her mind nor her morals had prepared her for this discovery, nor did she in the least guess what was happening. But what of integrity she possessed clung to that other integrity; her back pressed to it. It sustained her. The pale dissolving nothingness was moving more slowly, but it was still moving. It had not quite reached her thighs. Below them she felt nothing; above she rested on that invisible frame. She could not guess whether that frame could resist the nothingness, or whether she on it. If it did not, she would be absorbed, living, into all that was not. She shut her eyes; say rather, she ceased to see.

At the moment when the anti-Tetragrammaton was approaching that in her which her fastidious pride had kept secluded from all but Richard, Betty suddenly turned on her bed. She did so with a quick heaving movement and she spoke in her sleep. The Clerk had sunk on one knee, to bring his face and slow-moving lips nearer to hers. She had seemed to him already yielding to the spell, and at the unexpected energy of her turning, he started and threw back his head. He had been prepared, he thought, for any alteration in Betty, though he expected one particular alteration, but he was quite unprepared for this ordinary human outbreak of life. He threw back his head, as any close watcher might. But then, in his own mind, he was not supposed to be simply anyone. He missed, in the suddenness, the word which broke from the sleeping girl, as anyone might. But then he was certainly not simply anyone. The intoned vibrations, for less than a second, faltered; for a flicker of time the eyes of the master of magic were confused. He recovered at once, in poise and in speech and in sight. But what he saw there almost startled him again.

His books and divinations had told him, and the lesser necromantic spells he had before now practiced on the dead had half shown him, what he might expect to see. As he approached, after the graded repetitions, the greatest and most effective repetition—and the very center of that complex single sound—he expected, visibly before him, the double shape; the all but dead body, the all but free soul. They would be lying in the same space, yet clearly distinct, and with the final repetitions of the reversed Name they would become still more distinct, but both at his disposal and subject to his will. He would divide without disuniting, one to go and one to stay, the spiritual link between them only just not broken, but therefore permanent. In his other necromancies on dead bodies he could only do it spasmodically, and only on those lately dead, and only for a little. But this was to be different. He had expected a double vision and he had a double vision. He saw two shapes, Betty and another. But he had never seen the other before.

Had it been one of those odd creatures, such as that which he had almost seen in the hall, he would not have been taken by surprise, nor had it been any stranger inhabitant of the bodiless world. He knew that surprise does not become the magician and is indeed apt to be fatal, for in that momentary loss of guard any attack upon the adept may succeed. His courage was very high; he would not have been startled at any tracery of low or high, at cherub or cacodemon. Or so he believed and probably with truth. But he did not see cherub or cacodemon. He saw two sleeping girls—now one and now the other, and each glancing through the other; and they were totally unlike. Not only so, but as he sought to distinguish them, to hold that bewildering conjunction steady to the analysis and disposal of his will, he saw also that it was the strange sleeper who lay wanly still with closed eyes, and Betty who slept more healthily than ever he had seen her sleep—fresh, peaceful, almost smiling. She had spoken, but he had not heard what she said. Only now, as he renewed, with all his will, the pronunciation of the reversed Name, he heard, in the very center of the syllables, another single note.

Betty had indeed spoken a word, as a sleeper does, murmuring it. She had said, in a sleepy repetition of her last waking and loving thought: "Lester!" As the word left her lips, it was changed. It became—hardly the Name, but at least a tender mortal approximation to the Name. And when it had left her lips, it hung in the air, singing itself, prolonging and repeating itself. It was no louder than Betty's voice, and it had still some likeness to hers, as if it did not wish to lose too quickly the sense of the mortal voice by which it had come, and it retained still within it some likeness to the word "Lester," as if it would not too quickly abandon the mortal meaning by which it had come. But presently it let both likenesses pass, and became itself only, and at that rather a single note than sequent syllables, which joyously struck itself out again and again, precisely in the exact middle of every magical repetition, perfect and full and soft and low, as if (almost provocatively) it held just an equal balance, and made that exact balance a spectacular delight for any whose celestial concerns permitted them to behold the easy dancing grapple. The air around it quivered, and the room and all within it were lightly shaken; and beyond the room and the house, in all directions, through all the world, the light vibration passed. It touched, at a distance, London itself, and in Jonathan's flat Richard saw the eye-flicker of light in the roofs and heard the tinkle of his friend's pencil as it fell.

Lester, lying with closed eyes, felt the change. She

felt herself resting more quietly and more securely on her support; it might be said she trusted it more. Close beside her, she heard a quiet breathing, as if on some other bed near at hand a companion gently slumbered, friendly even in sleep. She did not see the tongue-thrusting Death lie still, or even here and there recoil, but she stretched out her legs, and felt them also to be resting on some support, and yawned as if she had just got into bed. She thought, in a drowsy happiness, "Well, that's saved her getting up," but she remembered no action of her own, only how once or twice, when she had been thirsty in the night, Richard had brought her a glass of water and saved her getting up; and in her drowsiness a kind of vista of innumerable someones doing such things for innumerable someones stretched before her, but it was not as if they were being kind, for it was not water that they were bringing but their own joy, or perhaps it was water and joy at once; and everything was altered, for no one had to be unselfish any more, so free they all were now from the receding death-light of earth. She thought, all the same, "Darling, darling Richard!"—because the fact that he was bringing her his own joy to drink before she sank again to the sleep that was her present joy (but then waking had been that too) was a deed of such excelling merit on his part that all the choirs of heaven and birds of earth could never properly sing its praise; though there was a word in her mind which would do it rightly, could her sleepiness remember it—a not very long word and very easy to say if someone would only tell her how. It was rather like a glass of water itself, for when all was said she did in her heart prefer water to wine, though it was blessed sometimes to drink wine with Richard, especially one kind of wine whose name she could never remember, but Richard could, Richard knew everything better than she, except the things about which he knew nothing at all, for the word which was both water and wine—and yet not in the least mixed—had cleared her mind, and she could be gay with Richard now among all those things that either knew and the other not; and both of them could drink that word in a great peace. Now she came to think of it, the word was like a name, and the name was something like *Richard*, and something like *Betty* and even not unlike her own, though that was certainly very astonishing, and she knew she did not deserve it; still there it was— and anyhow it was not in the least like any of them, though it had in it also the name of the child Richard and she would one day have for they never meant to wait too long, and it would be born in a bed like this, on which she could now from head to foot luxuriously stretch herself; nor could she think why she had once supposed it to be hard and like wood, for it was marvelously spring-livened; spring of the world, spring of the heart; joy of spring-water, joy.

Oblivion took her. The task was done, and repose is in the rhythm of that world, and some kind of knowledge of sleep, since as a baby the Divine Hero closed his astonishing eyes, and his mother by him, and the princely Joseph, their young protector. Lester had taken the shock of the curse—no less willingly or truly that she had not known what she was doing. She had suffered instead of Betty, as Betty had once suffered through her; but the endurance had been short and the restoration soon, so quickly had the Name which is the City sprung to the rescue of its own. When recollection came to her again, she was standing by the side of the bed, but all the pale light had faded, and on the bed Betty lay asleep, flushed with her proper beauty and breathing in her proper content.

On the other side the Clerk still knelt. As soon as he heard that interrupting note, he had put out still more energy; he thought he had used it already, but for him there was always more, until his end should come indeed. He managed to complete the repetition into which the note broke, but the effort was very great. The sweat was on his forehead as he continued with the spell. He could just utter his own word as he willed, but he could not banish from it the other song. He put out his hand towards his mistress and beckoned, that she might lay her will with his. It was his folly. There is no rule more wise in magic than that which bids the adept, if the operation go awry, break it off at once. In the circles of hell there is no room for any error; the only maxim is to break off and begin again. When the Clerk saw before him the two shapes, he should have made an end. There had been an intrusion of an alien kind. He would not; say rather, he could not; he could not consent to leave it undominated. He was compelled therefore to summon his minion. The false slippery descent was opening, the descent so many of his sort have followed, according to which the lordly enchanters drop to lesser and lesser helps—from themselves to their disciples, to servants, to hired help, to potions and knives, to wax images and muttered murderous spells. Simon was not yet there, but he was going, and quickly.

Sara Wallingford was still leaning with her forehead against the door and pressing it more closely. She knew, as far as she could, what the operation meant. But as the intoning had proceeded, her merely mortal hate got the better of her knowledge; she murmured: "Kill!

kill!" She did not care what became of Betty, so long as Betty was dead. When, dimly, she heard the ringing opposition of the Name, she felt only a fear that Betty might live. And while with all her force she rejected that fear lest it should weaken the effort, she felt her master beckon. If indeed they had been, with whatever subordination, allies, there would have been between them an image of a truth, however debased, which might have helped. There was not. They had never exchanged that joyous smile of equality which marks all happy human or celestial government, the lack of which had frightened Richard in Simon's own smile; that which has existed because first the Omnipotence withdrew its omnipotence and decreed that submission should be by living will, or perhaps because in the Omnipotence itself there is an equality which subordinates itself. The hierarchy of the abyss does not know anything of equality, nor of any lovely balance within itself, nor (if he indeed be) does the lord of that hierarchy ever look up, subordinate to his subordinates, and see above him and transcending him the glory of his household. So that never in all the myths, of Satan or Samael or Iblis or Ahriman, has there been any serious tale of that lord becoming flesh by human derivation; how could he be so supposed to submit, in bed or cradle? Simon himself, in the mystery of generation, had reserved something; he, like all his fellows, intended to dominate what he begot; therefore he and they always denied their purposes at the moment of achievement. "How shall Satan's kingdom stand, if it be divided against itself?" Messias asked, and the gloomy pedants to whom he spoke could not give the answer his shining eyes awaited: "Sir, it does not."

The man beckoned; the woman stood upright. She

had no choice; she was his instrument only; she must go and be used. But (more than she guessed) she was also the instrument of her own past. As she took a step away, there came a tap on the door. It was very gentle, but to those two it was shattering in the silence—a blasting summons from the ordinary world. All three of them heard it. Lester heard it; to her it sounded precisely what it was, clear and distinct. To say she might have been alive again is too little; it was more happily itself, more sweetly promising, than if she had been alive. It was a pure and perfect enjoyment. She knew she could, if she chose, exert herself now to see who waited on the other side of the door, but she did not choose. It was not worth while; let the exquisite disclosure come in its own way. The Clerk's face convulsed; he made a gesture of prohibition. He was too late. Lady Wallingford's past was in her and ruled her; all the times when she had thought about the servants now compelled her. She was the servant of her servants. The glorious maxim (sealed forever in the title of the Roman pontiff—*servus servorum Dei*) ruled her ingloriously. She was, for that second, oblivious of the Clerk. She put out her hand and switched on the light—there was no time to draw back the curtains; she unlocked and opened the door. She faced the parlormaid.

The maid said, "If you please, my lady, there are two gentlemen downstairs who say they must see you. The gentleman who spoke said he didn't think you'd know his name but the other is Mr. Drayton. They say it's very urgent and to do with Miss Betty." She was young, pleasant and inexperienced; her mildly surprised eyes surveyed the room and rested on Betty. She broke out, "Oh she *is* looking better, isn't she, my lady?'

The news of Jonathan's arrival might, in her state of passion, have enraged Lady Wallingford; the impertinence of a servant outraged her past. It pulled her past and her together; unfortunately it pulled her together in the opposite direction from what was then going on. All the rebukes she had ever delivered rose in her; she did not see them, as Lester had seen her own actions, but her voice shook with them. She said, "You forget yourself, Nina." She went on. "Tell Mr. Drayton's friend I can't see them. Send them away and see I'm not interrupted again."

The maid shrank. Lady Wallingford stared angrily at her. As she did so, a curious sensation passed through her. She felt rooted and all but fixed, clamped in some invisible machine. A board was pressed against her spine; wooden arms shut down on her arms; her feet were iron-fixed. She could do nothing but stare. She heard her last dictatorial word, "see I'm not interrupted again." Was she not to be? The maid took a step back, saying hastily, "Yes, my lady." Lady Wallingford, immovable to herself, stared after her. She could not pursue.

She was not, however, then left to that doom. As the maid turned, she exclaimed, "Oh!" and stepped back, almost into her mistress. There was a sudden swiftness of feet; two forms loomed in the corridor. The maid slipped to the other side of the doorway and as Lady Wallingford broke—or was allowed to break—from the wooden beams which had appeared to close on her, Richard and Jonathan had passed her and come into the room.

Richard was speaking as he came. He said, "You must forgive this intrusion, Lady Wallingford. We know—Jonathan and I—that we're behaving very badly.

But it's absolutely—I do mean *absolutely*—necessary for us to see Betty. If you believe in the Absolute. So we had to come." He added, across the room to Lester, without surprise, but with a rush of apology, and only he knew to whom he spoke, "Darling, have I kept you waiting? I'm so sorry."

Lester saw him. She felt, as he came, all her old self lifting in her; bodiless, she seemed to recall her body in the joy they exchanged. He saw her smile, and in the smile heaven was frank and she was shy. She said—and he only heard, and he rather knew than heard, but some sound of speech rang in the room, and the Clerk, now on his feet, looked round and up, wildly, as if to catch sight of the sound—she said, "I'll wait for you a million years." She felt a stir within her, as if life quickened; and she remembered with new joy that the deathly tide had never reached, even in appearance, to the physical house of life. If Richard or she went now, it would not much matter; their fulfillment was irrevocably promised them, in what manner so-ever they knew or were to know it.

Betty opened her eyes. She too saw Lester. She said, "Lester, you did stop! How sweet of you!" She looked round the room. Her eyes widened a little as she saw Richard; they passed unconcernedly over the Clerk and Lady Wallingford; they saw Jonathan. She cried out and sat up; she threw out her hands. He came to her and took them. He said, controlling the words, "You're looking better." He could not say more. Betty did not speak; she blushed a little and clung.

The Clerk looked down on her. The operation had failed; he did not doubt that he would yet succeed, but he must begin again. He did not permit himself any emotion towards whatever had interfered. It would waste his energy. These men were nothing. It had been in the other world that frustration had lain, and it should be seen to. Composing heart and features, he turned his head slowly towards Lady Wallingford. She took his will, and obeyed. She said, "We had better go downstairs. You can see, Mr. Drayton, that Betty is better; aren't you, Betty?"

"Much better," said Betty gaily. "Jonathan dear . . ." She paused; she went on, "I'll get up and dress. Go away for a few minutes and I'll be down."

Jonathan said, "I'd much rather not leave you."

"Nonsense," said Betty. "I'm completely all right. Look, I'll be very quick. Mother, do you mind?"

It was the one thing that Lady Wallingford now minded more than anything else. But even hell cannot prevent that law of the loss of the one thing. She was full of rage—much of her own; something of the Clerk's which he had dismissed for her to bear. She was the vessel of such human passion as remained to him. She said, "If you will come down——?" The Clerk made a gesture with his hand as if to direct the two young men to pass in front of him, and his sudden constriction passed across his face. He looked particularly at Richard. But Richard was no longer the Richard of the house behind Holborn. He had tasted the new life in Jonathan's flat; he had drunk of it in his wife's eyes. As, while Jonathan spoke to Betty, he gazed at her, she began to withdraw, or rather it was not so much that she withdrew as that something—perhaps only the air of earth—came between them. But in that second of her immortal greeting, her passion and her promise, he had been freed from any merely accidental domination by the Clerk. She vanished; and, still at ease, he turned to meet Simon's look and grinned back at him. He said, "You see, my dear Father, we had to make our own arrangements. But it was very kind of you to offer. No, no; after you. Lady Wallingford's waiting."

The unfortunate young maid had not known whether to go or stay. She had thought that Lady Wallingford might want the gentlemen shown out. She gathered, from the look Lady Wallingford gave her as she came through the door, that she had been wrong. The strange doctor followed; after him the two other visitors. Mr. Drayton paused to look back at Miss Betty; then he softly closed the door. The maid, even in her gloom, remembered that she had always said there was something between him and Miss Betty.

Chapter Eight

THE MAGICAL CREATION

All this while, Evelyn Mercer sat on the doorstep. It would once have seemed strange to her to think of herself sitting and hugging herself, as any old beggar-woman might, and she not old, though too much a beggar. She was acutely conscious of her beggary, ever since she had seen the man sitting in the chair. He had smiled and nodded at her, and she had expected and hoped he would speak. If he had only asked her a question, she could have told him everything—about her tiresome mother, and silly Betty, and cruel Lester. She did not expect him to talk, and all she wanted was for him to listen to her. She did not ask anything more; she was not the kind of girl that would. Lester was more like that, and even Betty.

In looking at him, she had become aware of her pain, which she had not been till then. It was not much more than a discomfort, a sense of pressure on her lungs. If she could talk, she would be able to appease it. He had sat nodding at her, as if he were telling her how right she was to come, and then he had stood up, and his nod as he did so had suddenly seemed to change. Instead of being a nod of welcome, it was now a nod of dismissal. She was to go; as she realized it, she yelped. She had not been able to help it. She had yelped rather like a lost cat, for she was frightened of being sent away, and the discomfort in her lungs had become immediately worse. But his head had still nodded dismissal. He was still smiling and the smile had a kind of promise. Her own smile, which was the smile with which she had run after Betty, had become oddly fixed; she felt her face harden. As, still looking over his shoulder, in that mingling of promise and dismissal, he began to move away towards the door of the hall, she found that she herself was no longer in the hall but in the yard without. She had receded as he receded. She was up against the window, staring through it, but outside it, and sniffing at something in the air. It vaguely reminded her of fish, but it was not fish. She remained sniffing for some time, hoping that the man would come back. The smell had something to do with him, and he with the pain in her lungs. Presently she slipped away from the window-sill which she had been clutching; for the smell caused her to follow it. It was the kind of smell Betty had when Betty had to listen to her, though she had never understood that before. She began to run, out of the yard and along the street. Her head was stretched out; her eyes were bright, though they saw nothing except the pavement before them. She ran a long while, or not so long. When at last she stopped, it was outside a door—the door of the house from which she had hurried. Now she had hurried back.

As the semi-bestiality of her movement ceased, her muddled and obsessed brain managed to point that out to her. It even managed to suggest that to run forever between those two points would be unsatisfactory. She had now made almost the same passage three times; and perhaps while she was in the streets that was all she could do. But how could she get out of the streets? She was not let go in there and she did not dare go in here. She went right up to the door—the smell was strongest there; it was fish, surely—and stood by it listening. Betty was inside; for all she knew, *he* also might be inside. She even put her hand on the door. It sank through; she began to pull it back and found it caught as if in a tangle of thorns. She felt a long sharp scratch before she got it loose. Tears came into her eyes. She was lonely and hurt. She looked at her hand through her tears, but it was a long time before she could see the scratch, almost as if neither scratch nor hand was there until she had found them. The hand itself was dim, because she had been crying; and dirty, because she had been leaning against the sill; and bleeding—at least, if she looked long enough it was bleeding. If the door was such a tangle of thorns, it was no use trying to go in. She went out of the porch and down the few steps. Her lungs were hurting her. She said aloud, "It isn't fair."

Lester had said the same thing, but as a rational judgment. This was not so much a rational judgment as a squeal. The squeal eased her lungs, and as she recognized this, she spoke again, saying, "Why won't anyone help me?" and found that her ease increased. She added, "I do think they might," and then the pain was no more than a slight discomfort. It seemed to her that the London air never had suited her, but she had never been able to agree with her mother where else they should live, so that somehow or other, because her mother had been inconsiderate, they had had to go on living in London. She was, at bottom, a little afraid that her mother too was in that dark house. Her mother didn't like fish; not that what she was waiting for was fish. It was the tall man who nodded his head.

She sat down on the bottom step, sideways, with her eyes on the door and her legs drawn up. She forgot about the scratch, except occasionally and resentfully because the door was a tangle of thorns. Whenever her lungs began to hurt her, she talked to herself aloud. Soon, though she did not realize it, she was keeping up a small continuous monologue. She did not talk of herself, but of others. The monologue was not (primarily) self-centered but mean. Men and women—all whom she had known— dwindled in it as she chattered. No one was courteous; no one was chaste; no one was tender. The morning—for it was morning with her too—grew darker and the street more sordid as she went on.

In the middle of some sentence of attribution of foulness she stopped abruptly. The door had opened; there he was. He looked at her and she scrambled to her feet. He had come away from the conflict within the house, for purposes of his own. He had said to Lady Wallingford, "Keep her here." But he would not wait, for he knew that he had now a spy in the spiritual places, who could, when he could talk to her, tell him of Betty and what had interfered with the great operation. He had left her where she was, holding her by that sympathy between them, by her instinctive obedience to the reversed Name, which had made itself known to her in the curious smell. She had lingered in it, as he knew she would. Now, as she rose, he lifted a finger. He was still in his own world and she in hers, but they were already visible to each other. He went so quickly that men did not see him, but behind him she was more truly invisible, as the actual streets of London were to her.

He came to the house behind Holborn and he passed down the corridor into the secret hall. He went to his chair and sat down. Evelyn did not quite like to follow him there; she waited just inside the door. Her lungs were beginning to hurt her again, but she did not dare to speak without his permission. But she hoped he would soon be kind and not as cruel as Lester. The fish smell was strong and the hall dim. It might have been in the depth of waters; waters of which the pressure lay on her lungs, and the distance was dark around her. As she stood there, she felt both light and lightheaded, except for that increased pressure. She was floating there, and beyond her he sat like the master of all water monsters, gazing away through the waters, and she must float and wait.

At the moment when the pain was becoming really troublesome, he turned his head. His eyes drew her; she ran forward and when she came to his seat, she sank on its steps as on the steps of the house. She had either to float or crouch; she could not easily stand. This did not astonish her; once she had been able to do something which now she could not do. The Clerk let her sit there; his eyes reverted to the distance. He said, "What do you know of that house?"

She began at once to chatter. After two sentences she found herself opening and shutting her mouth, but her voice had ceased. The pain was now really bad. She *must* speak, but she could only tell him what he wished to know. The tears again came into her eyes and ran down her face. That did not help. She choked and said— and immediately felt relief—"Betty was there and Lester had gone to her."

The name of the obstacle, of that first interference, of the other girl on the bed, was Lester. The Clerk frowned; he had thought Betty was, through all the worlds, secluded from any companionship. He knew that there must always be some chance that a strange life, in those depths, should loom up, but he had supposed he had certainly cut his daughter off from any human friendship, and this sounded human. He had now to deal with it. He said, "Who is—Lester?"

Evelyn answered, "She was at school with Betty and me, and whatever she pretends now she didn't have any use for Betty then. She never liked her. She was killed—when I was." The last three words had to be spoken, but she shook all over as she spoke. When the Clerk said, "Was she a friend of yours?" she answered, "Yes, she was, though she was always hateful and superior. We used to go about together. She ought to be with me now."

The Clerk considered. He knew of the fierce hunger for flesh, for their physical habitations, which sometimes assails the newly dead, even the greatest. He knew how that other sorcerer of his race, the son of Joseph, had by sheer power once for a while reanimated his body and held it again for some forty days, until at last on a mountainside it had dissolved into a bright cloud. What Jesus Bar-Joseph had not been able to resist, what he himself (if and when it was necessary) was prepared to do, he did not think it likely that this other creature, this Lester, would be able to resist. Especially if this other woman by him, her friend, drew her. He stretched out his hand over Evelyn's head, and she felt its weight where she crouched, though it was above her and did not touch her. He said, "What do you most want now?"

Evelyn answered, "To get back—or else to have someone to talk to. No one will listen to me."

The constriction which was his smile showed on the Clerk's face, in sudden contempt for this wretched being and for all those like her—how many millions!—who were willing to waste their powers so: talk of friends, talk of art, talk of religion, talk of love; all formulae and all facts dissolved in talk. No wonder they were hypnotically swayed by his deliberate talk. They swam and floated in vain talk, or sometimes they crouched in cruel talk. They fled and escaped from actuality. Unknowing, they spoke as he did, knowing; therefore they were his servants—until they dissolved and were lost. That might happen to this one. Let it, but before then perhaps she could be his auxiliary and draw that other shape from his daughter's bed.

It did not occur to him that he too was moving in the same direction. Sara Wallingford, Betty, Evelyn. Evelyn was a feebler instrument than Betty; even had there been no translucent Betty—and indeed for him there was none. But the helpless obedience of Betty was more exactly directed, more even of an accurate machine than this phantom in the worlds. There was indeed, even for her, a chance, could she have taken it. It lay precisely in her consenting not to talk, whether she succeeded or no. The time might be coming when she would have thrown that chance away, but for now she had it. She was looking up stealthily under his hand, that lay over her like a shadow on water; he was still gazing right away. But he said, "That might be done. I could give you a body—and as for talking, who would you most like to talk to?"

She knew that at once. In a voice stronger than she had hitherto been able to use in that world, she exclaimed, "Betty!"

He understood that. It seemed to him a poor and feeble wish, to be content to possess one other soul—to him who thought that numbers made a difference and even that quantity altered the very quality of an act, but he understood it. "The last infirmity of noble mind" can in fact make the mind so infirm that it becomes ignoble, as the divine Milton very well knew, or he would not have called it infirmity, nor caused Messias to reject it with such a high air; for paradise is regained not only by the refusal of sin but by the healing of infirmity. He looked down on her; she was touching her lips with her tongue. He said, "I could give you Betty."

She only looked up. He went on, "But first you must find her and this Lester. Then I will give her to you."

She said, "Always? Can I have her always?"

"Always," he said. As he spoke a hint of what he said was visible to them, a momentary sense of the infinite he named. The hall for each of them changed. It opened out for him; it closed in for her. He saw opening beyond it the leagues of the temporal world; he saw one of his Types exhorting crowds in a city of the Urals and another sitting in a chamber of Pekin and softly murmuring spells to learned men of China, and beyond them vague adoring shadows, the skies coalescing into shapes, and bowing themselves towards him. But for her the hall became a quite small room, which still seemed to grow smaller, where she and Betty sat, she talking and Betty trembling. Infinity of far and near lived together, for he had uttered one of the names of the City, and at once (in the way they wished) the City was there.

He dropped his hand nearer, and with a mortal it would have touched, but an infinity of division was between them (as between Betty and Lester), and it did not touch. He said, "You must get Lester away from her and

bring her here. Then you shall have Betty. Go and look
for them; look for them and tell me. Look and tell me;
then you shall talk to Betty. Look and tell me. Go and
find her; look and tell me. . . ."

She was willing to yield to his command; she did
yield. But she had not yet been dead long enough to
know and use the capacities of spirit; she could not in-
stantaneously pass through space, or be here and there at
once. But that was what he wished and his power was on
her. She was to be at once with Betty and with him, to
see and to speak. She was still aware of herself as having
the semblance of a body, though it was dimmer now,
and she still, as with the pain in her lungs or the words
she heard or uttered, understood her spiritual knowledge
in the sensations of the body. She was compelled now
to understand, in that method, the coincidence of two
places. She felt, by intolerable compulsion, her body and
her head slowly twisted round. She opened her mouth
to scream and a wind rushed into it and choked her. The
pain in her lungs was terrible. In her agony she floated
right up from the place where she sat; still sitting, she
rose in the air. This apparent floating was the nearest
she could get to the immaterial existence of spirit. She
thought she heard herself scream, and yet she knew
she did not; her torment was not to be so relieved. Presently she sank slowly down again on the steps of the
pseudo-throne, but now rigid—contorted, and sealed in
her contortion, staring. The Clerk had again lifted his
eyes from her; inattentive to her pain, he waited only for
tidings of that obstacle on whose removal he was set.

It was at this moment that Lester saw her. She had
known that she had been withdrawn from Richard. The
moment that had been given them was at once longer

and more intense than the previous moments had been, and she was more content to let it go. Dimly there moved in her, since her reconciliation with Betty, a sense that love was a union of having and not-having, or else something different and beyond both. It was a kind of way of knowledge, and that knowledge perfect in its satisfaction. She was beginning to live differently. She saw Richard look where she had been, and saw him also content. The men went out of the room with Lady Wallingford. The room, but for the dead girl and the living girl, was empty. They spoke to each other freely now across the division. Betty said, "Darling, what happened?"

"Nothing." Lester answered. "At least, very little. I think he tried to push you somewhere, and then . . . well, then he tried to push me."

"You're not hurt?" Betty asked, and Lester, with a rush of laughter, answered only, *"Here?"*

Betty did no more than smile; her gratitude possessed her. She stood and looked at her friend, and the charity between them doubled and redoubled, so that they became almost unbearable to each other, so shy and humble was each and each so mighty and glorious. Betty said, "I wouldn't have lost a moment, not a moment, of all that horrid time if it meant this."

Lester shook her head. She said, almost sadly, "But mightn't you have had this without the other? I wish you'd been happy then." She added, "I don't see why you couldn't have been. Need I have been so stupid? I don't mean only with you."

Betty said, "Perhaps we could go there sometime and see." But Lester was not immediately listening; she was laboring with the unaccustomed difficulties of thought, especially of this kind of thought. Her face was youthfully somber, so that it seemed to put on a kind of early majesty, as she went on. "Must we always wait centuries, and always know we waited, and needn't have waited, and that it all took so long and was so dreadful?"

Betty said, "I don't think I mind. I don't think, you know, we really did have to wait—in a way this was there all the time. I feel as if we might understand it was really all quite happy—if we lived it again."

Lester said, all but disdainfully, "Oh if we lived it again——"

Betty smiled. She said, "Lester, you look just like you used to sometimes—" and as Lester colored a little and smiled back, she went on quickly, "There, that's what I mean. If we were living the other times *now*—like this— Oh I don't know. I'm not clever at this sort of thing. But the lake or whatever it was—and then Jonathan—and now you. . . . I feel as if all of you had been there even when you weren't, and now perhaps we might find out how you were even when you weren't. Oh well," she added, with a sudden shake of her fair head that seemed to loose sparkles of gold about all the room, "it doesn't much matter. But I'd like to see my nurse again. I wonder if I could."

"I should think," said Lester, "you could almost do anything you wanted." She thought, as she spoke, of the City through which she had come. Were the other houses in it—the houses that had seemed to her so empty then— as full of joy as this? but then perhaps also of the danger of that other death? If now she returned to them, would she see them so? if she went out of this house and—— She broke in on Betty, who had now begun to dress with an exclamation: "Betty, I'd forgotten Evelyn."

Betty paused and blinked. She said, with a faint touch of reserve in her voice, "Oh Evelyn!"

Lester smiled again. "Yes," she said, "that may be all very well for you, my dear, and I shouldn't wonder if it was, but it's not at all the same thing for me. I made use of Evelyn."

Betty made a small face at herself and Lester in the mirror of her dressing-table. She said, "Think of the use she was trying to make of me!" and looked with a kind of celestial mischief over her shoulder at her friend.

"So I do," said Lester, "but it isn't the same thing at all, you must see. Betty, you do see! You're just being provoking."

"It's nice to provoke you a little," Betty murmured. "You're so much more *everything* than me that you oughtn't to mind. I might tempt you a little, on and off." Neither of them took the word seriously enough, nor needed to, to feel that this was what all temptations were—matter for dancing mockery and high exchange of laughter, things so impossible that they could be enjoyed as an added delight of love. But Betty swung round and went on seriously. "We *had* forgotten Evelyn. What shall we do?"

"I suppose I could go and look for her," Lester answered. "If she's still in those streets she'll be frightfully miserable. . . . She *will* be frightfully miserable. I must go." There rose in her the vague idea of giving Evelyn a drink, a cup of tea or a sherry or a glass of water—something of that material and liquid joy. And perhaps she ought to let Evelyn talk a little, and perhaps she herself ought to pay more serious attention to Evelyn's talk. Talk would not have checked the death-light, but if she could be a kind of frame for Evelyn, like the frame

to which she had held or by which she had been held—
perhaps Evelyn could rest there a little. Or perhaps—but
Evelyn had first to be found. The finding of Betty had
been like nothing she could ever have dreamed; might
not the finding of Evelyn be too? There was a word, if
she could only remember it for what she wanted—what
she was thinking—now. Richard would know; she would
ask Richard—after the million years. Compensation? no;
recovery? no; salvation—something of all that sort of
thing, for her and Betty and Evelyn, and all. She had
better get on with it first and think about it afterwards.

They were silent—so to call it—while Betty finished
dressing. Then Betty said, "Well now, shall I come with
you?"

"Certainly not," said Lester. "You go down to your
Jonathan. And if, by any chance, you should see Richard,
give him my love." The commonplace phrase was
weighted with meaning as it left her lips; in that air, it
signified no mere message but an actual deed—a rich gift
of another's love to another, a third party transaction in
which all parties were blessed even now in the foretaste.

Betty said, "I wish you could come. Are you sure
you wouldn't like *me* to? I shouldn't mind Evelyn a bit
now, if she wanted to talk to me."

"No," said Lester, "I don't suppose you would. But
I don't think it would be a terrifically good idea for
Evelyn—yet, anyhow. No; you go on. And don't forget
me, if you can help it."

Betty opened her eyes. She said, as Lester had said
earlier, the sweet reminders interchanging joy: "Here?"

"No," Lester said. "I know, but it's all a little new
still. And . . . *Oh!*"

The cry was startled out of her. Before Betty had

begun dressing, she had pulled the curtains and put out the light. Lester had so turned that she was now facing the window, and there, within or without, looking at her, was Evelyn—an Evelyn whom Lester hardly recognized. She knew rather than saw that it was the girl she had once called her friend. The staring eyes that met hers communicated that, but in those eyes was the same death-light that had crept about her own feet. It was indeed so; the torment of twisted space was but the sign and result of a soul that was driven to obey because it had no energy within itself, nor any choice of obedience. Lester was by her at once; the speed of her movement depended now chiefly on her will. She disappeared in that second from Betty's sight. She threw out her hands and caught Evelyn's arms; the dead and living could not touch, but the dead could still seem to touch the dead. She cried out, "Oh Evelyn, my dear!"

Evelyn was mouthing something, but Lester could not hear what she was saying. That however was because Evelyn was not talking to her at all, but to the Clerk. She was saying, "I can see Lester; she's got hold of me. I can't see Betty."

The Clerk said, "Speak to her. Ask her what she's doing. Ask her to come away with you."

"Evelyn!" Lester exclaimed. "Evelyn! What's happening? Come with me." She spoke without any clear intention; she had no idea what she could do, but the sense of belonging to some great whole was upon her, and she trusted to its direction. It could save this tortured form as it had saved her.

Evelyn answered, as she had been told, "Lester, what have you been doing?" But these words, instead of gaining significance, had lost it; they emerged almost imbecilely.

"I?" said Lester, astonished. "I've been——" She stopped. She could not possibly explain, if indeed she knew. She went on "—putting things straight with Betty. But I was coming to you, indeed I was. Come and speak to Betty." She was aware, by her sharpened sight, that Betty was no longer in the room, and added, "She'll be back soon."

Evelyn, her eyes wandering round the room, said gasping, "I don't want to stop. Come with me."

Lester hesitated. She was willing to do anything she could, but she never had trusted Evelyn's judgment on earth, and she did not feel any more inclined to trust it now. Nor, especially since she had seen Evelyn's face turned on her at the bottom of the hill and heard Evelyn's voice outside the house, did she altogether care to think into what holes and corners of the City Evelyn's taste might lead them. There was, she knew, in those streets someone who looked like a god and yet had loosed that death-light which had crept round her feet and now shone in Evelyn's eyes. She was not afraid, but she did not wish, unless she must, to be mixed up with obscenity. Her natural pride had lost itself, but a certain heavenly fastidiousness still characterized her. Even in paradise she preserved one note of goodness rather than another. Yet when she looked at that distressed face, her fastidi-ousness vanished. If she could be to Evelyn something of what Betty had been to her——? She said, "Do you want me?"

"Oh yes, yes!" the gasping voice said. "Only you. Do come."

Lester released her hold, but as she did so, two

grasping hands went up and fastened on hers. They gave a feeble jerk, which Lester easily resisted, or indeed hardly had to resist. She had once disliked coming into this house; now, at the moment of new choice, she disliked leaving it. Her only friend in the new life was in it. But she could not refuse the courtesies of this London to her acquaintance in an early London. She gave a small sigh and relaxed her will. She moved.

Her relaxed will took her where Evelyn would, but at her own speed and in her own manner. She was aware of the space she covered but not of the time, for she took no more time than Evelyn did to turn herself back on the steps of the Clerk's chair. Not only space but time spread out around her as she went. She saw a glowing and glimmering City, of which the life was visible as a roseal wonder within. The streets of it were first the streets of today, full of business of today—shops, transport, men and women, for she was now confirmed that not alone in the house she had left did that rich human life go on. It was truly there, even if (except through that house) she had no present concern with it. The dreadful silence she had known after death was no longer there; the faint sound of traffic, so common but oh so uncommon, came to her. It was London known again and anew. Then, gently opening, she saw among those streets other streets. She had seen them in pictures, but now she did not think of pictures, for these were certainly the streets themselves—another London, say—other Londons, into which her own London opened or with which it was intermingled. No thought of confusion crossed her mind; it was all very greatly ordered, and when down a long street she saw, beyond the affairs of today, the movement of sedan chairs and ancient dresses, and beyond them again, right in the distance and yet very close to her, the sun shining on armor, and sometimes a high battlemented gate, it was no phantasmagoria of a dream but precise actuality. She was (though she did not find the phrase) looking along time. Once or twice she thought she saw other streets, unrecognizable, with odd buildings and men and women in strange clothes. But these were rare glimpses and less clear, as if the future of that City only occasionally showed. Beyond all these streets, or sometimes for a moment seen in their midst, was forest and the gleam of marshland, and here and there a river, and once across one such river a rude bridge, and once again a village of huts and men in skins. As she came down towards what was to her day the center of the City, there was indeed a moment when all houses and streets vanished, and the forests rose all round her, and she was going down a rough causeway among the trees, for this was the place of London before London had begun to be, or perhaps after its long and noble history had ceased to be, and the trees grew over it, and a few late tribes still trod what remained of the old roads. That great town in this spiritual exposition of its glory did not omit any circumstances of its building in time and space—not even the very site upon which its blessed tale was sufficiently reared.

It was not for her yet to know the greater mystery. That waited her growth in grace, and the enlargement of her proper faculties in due time. Yet all she saw, and did not quite wonder at seeing, was but a small part of the whole. There around her lay not only London, but all cities—coincident yet each distinct; or else, in another mode, lying by each other as the districts of one city lie. She could, had the time and her occasions permitted, have gone to any she chose—any time and place that men had occupied or would occupy. There was no huge metropolis in which she would have been lost, and no single village which would itself have been lost in all that contemporaneous mass. In this City lay all—London and New York, Athens and Chicago, Paris and Rome and Jerusalem; it was that to which they led in the lives of their citizens. When her time came, she would know what lay behind the high empty façades of her early experience of death; it was necessary that she should first have been compelled to linger among those façades, for till she had waited there and till she had known the first grace of a past redeemed into love, she could not bear even a passing glimpse of that civil vitality. For here citizenship meant relationship and knew it; its citizens lived new acts or lived the old at will. What on earth is only in the happiest moments of friendship or love was now normal. Lester's new friendship with Betty was but the merest flicker, but it was that flicker which now carried her soul.

The passage ended. Lester, exhilarated by the swiftness and the spectacle of the journey, stood in the yard, outside the hall. And Evelyn, on the steps of the chair, had been able to turn and felt the agonized rigor relax. The cramps of her spirit were eased. She stood up; she ran very fast, under the eyes of her master and under the shadow of his lifted hand, and came to Lester who, coming by an easier and longer way, became again aware of her, as she had not been on the way. Evelyn's face was still a little set, but the hard glaring misery was gone. Evelyn smiled at her; at least her face jerked; she, like the other inhabitants of that house, bore Simon's mark in her body. Lester looked away; it seemed to her more courteous not to meet what she privately regarded as an unspeakable grimace. But then Lester's standard for smiles had been, that day, considerably raised.

She said, looking round her at the yard and then through the window, and speaking more pleasantly than ever in this world she had spoken to Evelyn, but firmly: "What do you want me to do here? If," she added, still pleasantly, "you do want me to do anything."

Evelyn said, *"He* does. Come in." Her voice was stronger and more urgent; she tried again to pull Lester on. She had no power on the other; her pull was no more than a poor indication of what she wanted. Lester, having come so far, consented. She moved forward with Evelyn through the wall. She saw Simon and recognized him at once. He was no more a portent to her; the falling away of the death-light had taken from him something of his apparent majesty, and a kind of need and even peevishness showed in his face. He himself did not see her now—not even her eyes as he had done in the hall of the house. But Evelyn's manner told him that she was there. The link between them was Evelyn; on her depended the abolition of that obstacle.

But there was only one way of action. Had the Clerk himself been able to enter that other world of pattern and equipoise, of swift principles as of tender means, he might conceivably have been able to use better means. But he never had done, and there remained now the necessity of setting up a permanent earthly and magical link which he could control. He supposed, since he thought in those terms, that the coming of this Lester with Evelyn meant that Evelyn had some sort of hold on Lester, and not at all that Lester had merely come. He who babbled of love knew nothing of love. It was why he had never known anything of the Betty who had sprung from the lake, if lake it was, that lay in the midst of that great City, as if in the picture which Jonathan had painted the shadow of the cathedral had looked rather like water than mass, and yet (as always) light rather than water. It lay there, mysterious and hidden; only, as if from sources in that world as in this, the Thames and all rivers rose and flowed and fell to the sea, and the sea itself spread and on it vessels passed, and the traffic of continents carried news of mightier hidden continents; no ship laden in foreign ports or carrying merchandise to foreign ports but exhibited passage and the principle of passage, since passage was first decreed to the creation. Simon to turn that passage back upon itself? to turn back speech which was another form of that passage? let him first master the words of three girls and drive them as he would.

He heard Evelyn say, as she came into the hall, "Here she is." He knew what had to be done and set himself to do it—to erect the material trap and magical link between himself and one dead girl that she might drag the other in. Let both be caught! The destroying anti-Tetragrammaton was not to be used for that, but there were lesser spells which deflected primeval currents. He stood upright; he set his deep fierce eyes on Evelyn; he began almost inaudibly to hum. The unseen motes in the air—and lesser points of matter than they—responded. After he had hummed awhile, he ceased and spat. The spittle lay on the floor at Evelyn's apparent feet and was immediately covered by a film of almost invisible dust. The motes were drawn to it. Faint but real, a small cloud gathered against the floor.

He sighed. He drew in air, and bending towards the

cloud which now stood up like a tiny pyramid he exhaled the air towards it. He reached his hands down towards the dust and in the midst of his sighs he spat
again. As his spittle fell on the dust, the pyramid thick-
ened and became more solid. With a curious small whistling sound, as of air rushing through a narrow channel,
the heap of dust enlarged and grew. There hung above
it in that hall another sound as small as the whistling—
the echo of a longing voice. It said, "Oh! Oh! a place for
me?" and the Clerk's voice—was it a voice? to Lester, as
now she heard the faint exchange, it seemed no more
than a mere lifting wave of the moon when the thinnest
cloud obscures and reveals it—answered: "For you; for
you." She herself was not permitted, or did not desire,
then to speak; she was troubled faintly in her heart as
that lifting wave came to her. Her own sins had not
been of that kind; disordered in love, she had still always known that love was only love. She did not understand what was going on; only there was something disagreeable in that sign and countersign of agreement—
"For me?" "For you." The Clerk stretched down his
hands again, but now as if he sheltered the early flicker
of a fire, and immediately the fire was there.

It came from his palms. It was not fire but an imitation of fire. The palms themselves gave no sign of it and
even though the seeming flames showed no reddening
from the heat. The fire itself was pallid; it had no
strength, but the flames darted down and hovered round
the dust. They ran over it and clung to it, and as he encouraged them with mimetic movements of his hands,
they sank deeper and were absorbed. As if their movement was communicated, the dust itself rose in sudden
gushes and fell again, but each time the heap was larger

than before. It was now about six inches high and had grown more like a column than a pyramid. It was waving to and fro, as a single unbranched plant might, and the whistling came from it, as if a dying man were trying to breathe. The whistling was thin, but so was the plant, if it were a plant, which it was not, for it was still dust, even if organic dust. It was vaguely swaying and waving itself about, as if in search of something it had no means of finding, and the pallid fire played about it as it sought. Simon's heavy sighs exhaled above it and his hands shielded it, though (to Lester's apprehension) there was a great, almost an infinite, distance between those palms and it, as if she saw something of a different kind that was without relation to the place in which it stood. Suddenly for the third time the Clerk spat on it and this time it grew at once higher by almost another six inches, and its movement became more defined though no more successful. It was now certainly feeling out with its summit—with what would have been its head, but it had no head. The fire was absorbed into it and disappeared; and as it did so the whole small column from being dust became a kind of sponge-like substance, an underwater growth. It began to try and keep a difficult balance, for it seemed to be slipping and sliding on the floor and by throwing itself one way and another just not falling. The thin whistling grew spasmodic, as if it had got some of its channels free, and was only here and there obstructed; and as the whistling ceased, so did the heavy breathing of the Clerk. He began to rise slowly from the position in which, like a witch-doctor, he had been half crouching; but he did so in sudden jerks, and as he did so the spongy growth in sudden jerks followed him and grew.

With its first jerk there came another change. For the jerk was not only an upward movement, adding perhaps another three inches to its height, but also interior, as if the sponge shook itself and settled. It now stood more firmly, and with the next one or two similar movements it took on the appearance of a rudimentary human body. It was developing from its center, for its feet and head were not visible, but only a something against its sides that might have been arms, and a division that might have been between its upper legs, and two faint swellings that might have been breasts. Soon, however, the arms did move outward, though they immediately fell, and below the center the thing split into two stumps, on which, each in turn, it soundlessly stamped. It was now throwing its upper end violently about, as if to free itself from its own heaviness, but it failed and subsided into a continual tremor. With this tremor, its sponginess began in patches to disappear, and give place to some sort of smooth pale-yellowish substance, which presently had spread so far that it was the sponginess which grew on it in patches. Thus there stood now on the floor the rough form of a woman, a little under two feet high and with the head gradually forming. The face, as far as it emerged, had no character; the whole thing was more like a living india-rubber doll than anything else, but then it did live. It was breathing and moving, and it had hair of a sort, though at present (as with such a doll) rather part of the formation of its head. It lifted its hands, as if to look at them, but its eyes were not yet formed and it dropped them again; and then it seemed to listen, but though its ears were almost there, it could not hear—and indeed the only sound it could have heard was Simon's breathing and that would only just have been audible even to a human ear.

Lester, as she watched, was a little surprised to find that the living doll was not more disgusting to her. It was faintly repellent, as an actual doll might be if it were peculiarly deformed or ugly. She disliked the spongy patches and the deadness of the apparent skin, but she could not feel strongly about it; not so strongly as Jonathan would have felt about a bad painting. She had a mild impulse to pick it up and put it right—pull and pat and order it, but she did not wish to touch it; and anyhow she did not know why it was there, nor why beside her she was aware that Evelyn was looking at it with such intensity and even giving what seemed little squeals of pleasure as it grew. Indeed, Evelyn presently gave a quick forward movement, as if she were about to rush to the doll. She was checked by the Clerk's voice.

He said, "Wait. It's too cold." The fire was still pallid in the interior of his hands, and now he breathed on them as if to blow it into life and it grew round each hand as if he had put on gloves of pale light, a light more like that of the false Tetragrammaton but not so deathly. With his hands thus encased, he took up the manikin between them and handled and dandled and warmed and seemed to encourage it, whispering to it, and once or twice holding it up above his head, as a father might his child, and as it turned its head, now grown, and looked over its shoulder, the girls saw that its eyes were open and bright, though meaningless. They saw also that it was longer and now nearly three feet in height, but it seemed to have no more weight, for still he cherished and caressed it, and held it out standing on one hand, as if it were no more than a shell. But that ended his play with it. He sat it again on the floor, struck his hands together—as if to break the fire from them, and indeed the pale fire flew in sparks around him and about the hall, and his hands were clear of it. He looked at Evelyn, and said, "That is for you and your friend."

Evelyn's answer was heard both by him and Lester. She said, "*Both* of us?"

Simon answered, "You'll find the sharing of it better than most things. It's something for you to get into. It'll grow when you do and you can go about in it. It will shelter you, and you will find presently you'll be able to talk to it, and it will understand better than anyone else and answer you as you want. It won't need food or drink or sleep unless you choose. If I call you out of it sometimes, I'll always send you back, and if I call you it will be to get the woman you want."

Evelyn said, "Can't I have it for myself?" The Clerk slowly shook his head. He looked sideways at the motionless Lester. In what now seemed a dim air, Lester was not easily seen; unless the truth was that, even then, even in her attention, she was already farther away. Emboldened by that remoteness, Evelyn said, in what was meant to be a whisper and came out as a croak, almost as if the dwarf-woman (could she yet speak) might have spoken, in a subhuman voice, "*Must* she come?"

The Clerk said, "If you are to go, she must." But the hall grew colder as he spoke, so that Evelyn felt it and shivered and turned to Lester with a desperate and yet feeble ferocity. The dwarf-woman seemed to her now her only hope, a refuge from the emptiness and the threats, a shelter from enmity and cold, and if presently she could get Betty into it to be victimized, she would be, she thought, content. So she tried to catch at Lester's hand and succeeded, for Lester left it to her. She had, half-unconsciously, withdrawn herself from that short dialogue with a pure and grave disdain; whatever these others were talking of she refused to overhear. Had the hand that now clutched at her held any friendship or love, she would have felt it in her spirit and responded, or to any need. But this was rather greed than need, and yet its touch was now not even inconvenient to her. The beginnings of heaven are not so troubled. Only with the touch, she knew at once what Evelyn wanted, and she said gently, "I wouldn't go, Evelyn."

Evelyn said, "Oh I *must*. Do come, Lester. It can't hurt you."

Lester unexpectedly laughed. It was years since anyone had laughed in that hall and now the sound, though low, was so rich and free, it so ran and filled the hall, that Evelyn gave a small scream, and the Clerk turned his head sharply this way and that, and even the dwarf-woman seemed to gaze more intently before her, with unseeing eyes. "No," Lester said, "I don't think it can. But it mayn't be too good for you."

Evelyn answered peevishly, "I wish you wouldn't laugh like that! And I want it. *Do* come. I've done enough things because you wanted them; you might just do this. Lester, *please!* I won't ask you for anything else. I swear I won't."

The echo of the laughter, which still seemed to sound, was cut off suddenly, as if in a sudden silence all there and all beyond heard her oath. The Clerk's constriction showed in his face and Lester, though she did not altogether realize that the silly human phrase was now taken at its precise meaning, shuddered. If it had been but silliness, it might not have passed beyond the visionary façades of the City, but it was not. It was greed and clamorous demand, and it swept into the City's courts and high places and was sealed with its own desire. Lester said, almost as if, unknowing, she tried to forestall that sealing: "Come back with me. Come to Betty or your mother. Let's——" She saw the fixed immortality in Evelyn's eyes and ceased.

Evelyn pulled at her, and looked back at Simon, as if she were asking him to help. He did what he could. He knew he had no direct power on this alien spiritual thing until he could get into contact with it; and that, since he had been checked in the previous clash, he could only do now by a plausibility. He said, as if uttering some maxim of great wisdom: "Love is the fulfilling of the law." Lester heard him. At that moment, doubtful of her duty, the maxim was greater than the speaker. She was not particularly aware of loving Evelyn, but she acknowledged her duty. The inconvenience of plunging with Evelyn wherever Evelyn wished to plunge was a little tiresome—no more. She felt as Betty had done when Lester insisted on recalling the past—that it was a pity to waste so much time. The lifting lightness of her new life looked ruefully at the magical shape of the dwarf-woman; her fledgling energy desired a freer scope. But there seemed to be no other way. She thought of Richard; she thought of Betty; she sighed—a small sigh, but a sigh. She thought of Evelyn's tormented face and the sigh ceased. She said suddenly, with one of those bursts of inspiration which are apt to possess noble and passionate hearts: "You'd be wiser to say that the fulfilling of the law is love." She had spoken, as it were, into the void, but then she went on to Evelyn, "Very well, if you want me to. But you'd be wiser—I'm sure you'd be wiser—to come away."

Evelyn did not answer. There was a pause of suspension in the whole hall. Then the dwarf-woman took a step forward. Under the Clerk's eyes, she began again to grow. She shook herself into shape as she did so, putting up her hands and settling her neck and head. There grew out of her smooth dead skin, into which the sponginess had now been wholly absorbed, fresh streaks and patches, ash-colored, which spread and came together and presently covered her and grew loose and wrapped itself round her like a dull dress. The dwarf pulled it into shape. There stood facing the Clerk, a short rather heavy-looking middle-aged woman, slightly deformed, with one shoulder a little higher than the other and one foot dragging a little, but undoubtedly, to all human eyes, a woman. Her eyes were brighter now and she seemed both to see and hear.

The Clerk lifted a finger and she stood still. He bent his knee slowly, lowering himself till his face was on a level with hers. He was muttering something as he did so. He put his hands on her thighs and from her thighs he passed them all over her. When he had finished, he leaned forward and very deliberately kissed her on the mouth. He sealed, so far as he could, a prison for those spirits, who had entered it by their own choice; and he judged he could do it well, for he knew the power that flesh—even impure and magical flesh—has on human souls, especially while they are still unused to that great schism in identity which is death. At first strangers in that other world, they may forget their bodies, but their bodies are their past and part of them and will not be forgotten. So that, sooner or later, these spiritual beings again strongly desire to be healed of their loss and whole. But this they cannot be until the whole of time is known to be redeemed, and when the hunger comes on them the blessed ones endure it smiling and easily, having such good manners that the time is no more to them than an unexpected delay before dinner at a friend's house.

He believed therefore that as, by proper magical means, a soul could within certain limits of time, be recalled to its body, so this false body might for a time ensnare and hold that other soul which was his enemy. He would have much preferred to operate necromantically on Lester's own proper body, and if Richard had remained under his influence he would have obtained through him some possession of hers which would have served for the first faint magical link with that body, and so set up a relation between them which might have brought her now corrupting flesh—or perhaps the scattered ashes of her cremated body—into this very hall. But Richard had failed him and he had no time to take more subtle ways; the danger to his domination of Betty now arising from Jonathan and from Lester was too great. He knew that the government of this world would be driven by popular pressure to make some approach to him, and that in no very long period the fatal meeting with his Types would be forced on him—fatal because though at a distance they might be energized and driven by his will, yet when the three met they must dwindle and fade beside him. And first he must have sent his daughter into the spiritual world. He must be forever before he could be now. So that altogether time was against him; the first condition of the universe was against him. He was hurried; he had to make haste.

Therefore the magical trap; therefore its tossing, as he now proposed, into the ordinariness of earth.

He whispered into the ear of the dwarf-woman, still pressing his hands on it. He and it were now alone in the hall. It could not be said to hear him, but it received his breath. He was now separated from those two other children of earth, and they from him, unless he deliberately called them. He knew that their awareness must be now of and through the body they in some sense inhabited; not that they lived in it as in a place, but that they only knew through it. There was no limit to the number of spiritual beings who could know in that way through one body, for there was not between any of them and it any organic relation. The singleness of true incarnation must always be a mystery to the masters of magic; of that it may be said that the more advanced the magic, the deeper the mystery, for the very nature of magic is opposed to it. Powerful as the lie may be, it is still a lie. Birth and death are alike unknown to it; there is only conjunction and division. But the lie has its own laws. Once even Lester had assented to that manner of knowledge, she must enter the City so. It remained to discover what she could do there.

In the front office of the house, the caretaker Plankin was standing by the door. He saw coming along from the side-passage a middle-aged woman. She was short and slightly deformed. Her eyes were fixed in front of her, and in spite of a dragging foot she was walking at a fair speed. She went by Plankin without noticing him and on into the street. He thought as he watched her, "Ah, the Father hasn't healed her yet. But he will; he will. He'll put his mark in her body."

Chapter Nine

TELEPHONE CONVERSATIONS

Lady Wallingford sat in her drawing-room. Jonathan and Richard were with her, but she did not ask them to sit down. Jonathan leaned on the back of a chair, watching the door. Richard paced up and down. Had Jonathan painted the scene, he might have shown a wilderness, with a small lump of that iron-gray rock in the center, and near it a couched lion and a pacing leopard. It would have been a vision of principles, and so (even then) Jonathan, at least as the others appeared, took it in. He wondered, as he looked at Lady Wallingford, if she would ever move again; he wondered with what expectation Richard stepped and turned.

Yet it was the memory of something hardly more than an accident which chiefly held the woman rock-rigid in her chair. She knew what Simon proposed, though she did not know how he meant to fulfill his purpose. He had in mind a simpler and cruder thing than any magical dissolution. That had failed; there remained simple murder. She knew that that was what the night was to bring. But she was now only remotely aware of it, for though she no longer felt her body clamped in that frame which had shut on her in the bedroom, yet her anger was almost equally strong and imprisoned her from within. The maid's words, "Oh she *is* looking better, isn't she, my lady?" held her. She was furious that Betty should look better; she was almost more furious that the maid, even deferentially, should comment on it. The obnoxious fact was emphasized in the most obnoxious manner. It is the nature of things intensely felt as obnoxious so as to emphasize themselves. She sat raging—immobile in her wilderness.

The maid herself was hovering in the hall. She did not like to stay, in case Lady Wallingford came out and saw her, or to go, in case Lady Wallingford rang for her, in which case the sooner she was there the better for her. She drifted uneasily about the foot of the stairs. Presently she heard above her a door shut. She looked up. Miss Betty was coming down the stairs.

Miss Betty was looking very much better. The maid lingered in admiration. Betty smiled gaily down at her and the girl smiled shyly back. She ventured to say, with a sense of obscure justification, "You *are* better, aren't you, Miss Betty?"

"Much, thank you," said Betty, and added remorsefully, "I expect I've given you a lot of extra work, Nina."

"Oh *no*, Miss Betty," Nina said. "Besides, I'd have liked it. My grandmother used to be with Sir Bartholomew's mother, so in a way we're in the family. She was your nurse, Miss Betty."

Betty stopped on the third stair; then in a leap she was down them, and had caught hold of the girl's arm. Her face was alight; she exclaimed, "Your grandmother my nurse! Is she alive? where's she living? Do tell me, Nina."

Nina, surprised but pleased by this interest, said, "Why, she's living in London, over in Tooting. I go and see her most weeks."

Betty drew a deep breath. She said, "Isn't that marvelous? *I* want to see her. Can I? can I now?"

"She'd be very pleased if you did, Miss Betty," Nina said. "Only," she added more doubtfully, "I don't know if my lady would like it. I think there was some trouble between grandmother and my lady. She was sent away, I know, but Sir Bartholomew helped her. It's all a long time ago."

"Yes," said Betty—"when I was born and before you were. That'll be all right. Tell me the address; I'll explain to my mother."

"It's 59 Upper Clapham Lane," Nina answered. "It was once her own boarding-house, and then my brother and his wife took it over, only he's in Austria now. But my grandmother still lives there."

Betty said, "I shall go today. Thank you, Nina. I'll see you when I come back." She released the girl and went on into the drawing-room. She entered it, Jonathan thought, like water with the sun on it; the desert blossomed with the rose. The wild beasts in it were no less dangerous, but she was among them in the friendship and joy of a child. She slipped her hand in Jonathan's arm and she said, smiling at them all, "Mother, I've just found out where my old nurse lives and I'm going to see her. Isn't it marvelous? I've so often wanted to."

"You had better," said Lady Wallingford's dead voice, "have lunch here first."

"Oh need we?" Betty said. "Jonathan, won't you take me to lunch somewhere and we could go on?"

"You were going to lunch with me anyhow," Jonathan said. "We can go anywhere you like afterwards."

"Do you mind, Mother?" Betty asked. "You see I really am absolutely all right."

As if the rock itself shifted, Lady Wallingford got to her feet. She would, under her paramour's instruction and for his sake, have put friendliness into her voice, had it been possible. It was not. She could neither command nor beguile. She said, "When will you be back?"

"Oh to dinner," said Betty. "May I bring Jonathan back?"

"No, thank you very much," Jonathan said hastily. "I couldn't tonight. Besides, you're dining with me and after that we'll see. Let's go."

"All right," said Betty. "I'll ring you up, Mother, and tell you what we decide."

Jonathan looked at Richard. "What are you doing?" he asked.

Richard came lightly forward. He said to Lady Wallingford, "I've intruded quite long enough. It's been quite unforgivable, and I don't suppose you mean to forgive me, which would save us both trouble. Goodbye, and thank you so much. I'm glad that Betty is better and that Sir Bartholomew will soon be back."

Betty exclaimed and Lady Wallingford, still in that dead voice, said, "How do you know?"

"Oh the Foreign Office!" Richard said vaguely. "One can pick things up. Goodbye, Lady Wallingford, and thank you again. Come, children, or we shall get no lunch."

But once outside the house, he disengaged himself. He sent off the two lovers and himself went on his way to his own flat. They, after the parting, went to lunch and the exchange of histories. Time was before them, and they had no need to hurry their understanding. After lunch they set out on their way to discover 59 Upper Clapham Lane. It was a largish respectable house, in reasonably good condition. Jonathan, as they looked at it, said, "*Is* everything brighter? or is it only being with you that makes me think so?—even than it was this morning?"

Betty pressed his arm. She said, "Everything's always as bright as it can be and yet everything's getting brighter. Unless, of course, it's dark."

Jonathan shook his head. "Why," he said, "you should be able to see better than I—why you should have more plain observation and common understanding than I—well, never mind! Let's ring."

Presently they found themselves in Mrs. Plumstead's suite; she made it seem that by the way she welcomed them. She was a charming old lady, who was extremely touched and pleased by the unexpected appearance of Betty. She managed to treat it as at once an honor conferred and a matter of course, and made no allusion to the long separation. She did, however, with an awful aloofness once or twice allude to the parting between herself and Lady Wallingford, saying with an iciness equal to Lady Wallingford's, "I didn't suit my lady." Jonathan said, in answer, "You seem to have suited Betty very well, Mrs. Plumstead," and added ambiguously, "Without you she couldn't have been what she is."

Mrs. Plumstead, sitting upright, said, "No; my lady and me—we did not suit. But there's a thing that's been on my mind, my dear, all these years, and I think I ought to tell you. I'm free to say that I was younger then and apt to take things on myself, which I wouldn't do now, for I don't think it was quite proper. Her ladyship and I did not see eye to eye, but after all she was your mother, my dear, and no doubt meant you well. And if it was to be done again, perhaps I would not do it."

Jonathan thought that Mrs. Plumstead at that moment might have passed for Queen Elizabeth pronouncing upon the execution of Mary Queen of Scots. And then he forgot such literary fancies in the recollection of Betty's other life and of the lake of which at lunch she had told him, and the high sky and the wise water and all the lordly dream, if it were a dream. Betty was leaning forward now and gazing intently at the old lady. She said, "Yes, nurse?"

"Well, my dear," the old nurse went on and ever so faintly blushed, "as I say, I was younger then, and in a way I was in charge of you, and I was a little too fond of my own way and very obstinate in some things. And now I do not think it right. But you were such a dear little thing and I did once mention it to my lady, but she was very putting-off and only said, 'Pray, nurse, do not interfere'—her ladyship and I *never* suited—and I ought to have left it at that, I do think now, but I was obstinate, and then you were such a dear little thing, and it did seem such a shame, and so—" the old nurse said, unaware of the intensity of the silence in the room —"well, I christened you myself."

Betty's voice, like the rush of some waterfall in a river, answered, "It was sweet of you, nurse."

"No; it wasn't right," Mrs. Plumstead said. "But there it is. For I thought then that harm it couldn't do you and good it might—besides getting back on her ladyship: Oh I was a wicked woman—and one afternoon in the nursery, I got the water and I prayed God to bless it, though I don't know now how I dared, and I marked you with it, and said the Holy Name, and I thought, 'Well, I can't get the poor dear godfathers and godmothers, but the Holy Ghost'll be her godfather and I'll do what I can.' And so I would have done, only soon after her ladyship and I didn't suit. But that's what happened, and you ought to know now you're a grown woman and likely to be married and have babies of your own."

Betty said, "So it was you who lifted me out of the lake!"

Jonathan thought that Lady Wallingford's behavior to her servants had been, on the whole, unfortunate. She had never credited the nurse she employed with such piety, decision and courage (or obstinacy, if you preferred the word). And now as in some tales Merlin had by the same Rite issued from the womb in which he had been mysteriously conceived, so this child of magic had been after birth saved from magic by a mystery, beyond magic. The natural affection of this woman and her granddaughter had in fact dispelled the shadows of giant schemes. And this then was what that strange Rite called baptism was—a state of being of which water was the material identity, a life rippling and translucent with joy.

Betty had stood up and was kissing her nurse. She said, "Goodbye, nurse. We'll come again soon, Jon and I. And never be sorry; some day I'll tell you how fortunate it was." She added, quite naturally, "Bless me, now."

"God bless you, my dear," the old woman said. "And Mr. Drayton too, if I may take the liberty. And make you both very happy. And thank you for saying it was all right."

When they were outside the house, Betty said, "So that's how it was! But . . . Jon, you must tell me about it—what it's supposed to be."

Jonathan said grimly, "I don't know that you'll be much better off for my explaining. After all, it's you that are happening. I'm not sure that I'm not a little scared of you, darling."

"I'm not sure that I'm not a little scared myself," said Betty seriously. "Not badly, but a little. It's mixed up with discovering that you're really you—wonderful, darling, but rather terrifying. Let's go and look at your pictures, shall we? I've never yet looked at any of them properly and yesterday I was shaking with fear of my mother. I don't mind her now at all."

"Anything," said Jonathan, "that pleases you pleases me. And God send that that shall be true until we die —and perhaps he will. Let's take a taxi. That's one great advantage of being engaged—one always has a perfectly good reason for taking taxis. All these things are added to one."

They spent some time in his room looking at various paintings, before Betty allowed herself to look at those two which still stood on their respective easels. She lingered for a long time before that of the City-in-light and Jonathan saw her eyes fill with tears. He caught her hand and kissed it. She went close to him. She said, "I *am* a little scared, dearest. I'm not ready for it yet."

Jonathan said, holding her, "You're ready for much more than a painting . . . even if the colors have really become colors."

"It's terribly like a fact," Betty said. "I love it. I love you. But I'm *not* very intelligent, and I've got a lot to learn. Jon, you must help me."

Jonathan said only, "I'll paint you next. By the lake. Or no—I'll paint you and all the lake living in you. It shall be quite fathomless and these"—he kissed her hands again—"are its shores. Everything I've done is only prentice work—even these things. I don't much want to keep them any more."

"I'd just as soon you didn't keep the other one," Betty said. "Could you bear not to? I don't really mind, but it's rather horrid to have about—now."

"I could quite easily bear to get rid of it," Jonathan answered. "What shall we do with it? Give it to the nation? as from Mr. and Mrs. Jonathan Drayton on their wedding. Publicity and all that."

"Ye-es," said Betty doubtfully. "I don't think I want the nation to have it. It seems rather rude to give the nation what we don't want."

"What you don't want," Jonathan corrected. "Myself, I think it's one of the better examples of my Early Middle Period. You must learn to think in terms of your husband's biography, darling. But if we're not to keep it and not to give it to the nation, what shall we do with it? Give it to Simon?"

Betty looked at him, a little startled; then, as they gazed, they each began to smile and Jonathan went on. "Well, why not? He's the only one who's really liked it. Your mother certainly doesn't, and you don't, and I don't, and Richard doesn't. That's what we'll do. We'll take it down to Holborn and leave it for him. Betty, you won't go back to Highgate tonight?"

"Not if you don't want me to," said Betty. "Only

I've got nothing with me, so I don't see how I can go to a hotel, even if we could find a room. And I don't at all mind going back."

"No, but I mind," Jonathan said, seriously. "To be honest, I don't think Simon's going to leave it at this. I'm not particularly bothered at the moment, because after what's happened I don't believe he's a chance. I think Almighty God has him in hand. But I'd like, as a personal concession, to have you under my eye. There's my aunt at Godalming. Or there's here. Or, of course, there's Richard's place. That's an idea, if he didn't mind; it's more fitted out for a woman."

Betty said, "It would be very nice of Lester." She did not know what Lester was now doing, but in that young and heavenly hero-worship which in heaven is always prejustified by fact and is one mode of the communion of saints, she was convinced that Lester was engaged on some great and good work. She was even willing in a modest candor to presume on Lester's good will. But instinctively she put forward her own. She said, "And anyhow, Jon, I was going to ask if we mightn't get Richard to come with us to dinner somewhere."

"I'd thought of that myself," said Jonathan. "We might; we most certainly might. I'd hardly met his wife, but she seemed a good sort—even before all that you told me."

"Oh she's a marvel," Betty exclaimed. "She's . . . she's like the light in that picture—and very nearly like you."

Jonathan looked at the City on the canvas. He said, "If I'm going to start serious work, and if we're giving Simon his picture, and if you feel like that about her—and if Richard would care for it, do you think we might offer him this? Unless you'd prefer to keep it?—as, of course, I should."

Betty opened her eyes. She said, "I think it's a marvelous idea. Jon, would you? I'd always wanted to give Lester something, but I never could, and if you'd give them this, it'd be perfect. If they'd take it."

"If they—!" said Jonathan. "My girl, do you happen to realize that this is, to date, my best work? Are you suggesting that any decent celestialness wouldn't be respectful?"

Betty and all the air about her laughed. She said demurely, "She mightn't know much about paintings and she mightn't think them important—even yours."

"I'm not so sure that you do yourself," Jonathan said. But his lady protested anxiously, "Oh I do, Jon; well, in a way I do. Of course, I shall understand better presently."

Jonathan abruptly interrupted. "You're entirely right," he said. "But as and while I'm here, it's my job. We *will* ask Richard if he'd like it, and we'll ask him to dinner so as to ask him, and then we'll ask him if we can all sleep at his place—and on the way there we'll drop the other thing in on Simon. Come and help me telephone."

When he left the others Richard had returned to his flat. There he just managed to get to bed before he went to sleep. It was well into the afternoon before he woke, and woke more refreshed and serene than, as he lay there pleasantly aware of it, he could ever remember having felt in his life before, or at least not since he had been a very small child. This freshness and energy reminded him of that. He had no sense of nostalgia; he did not in the least wish to be small again and a child, but he could almost have believed he was now as happy as he remembered he had sometimes been then. An arch of happiness joined the then and the now, an arch he ought to have known all the time, under which or even in which he ought to have lived. It was somehow his fault that he had not and yet it had never been there or but rarely. If this was life, he had somehow missed life, in spite of the fact that he had on the whole had a very pleasant and agreeable life. There was a great difference between what he had known and what he ought to have known. And yet he did not see how he could have known it.

When he got up, he found himself amused and touched by his own physical resilience. As he moved about the room, he misquoted to himself, "And I might almost say my body thought"; and then his mind turned to that other body which had meant so much to him, and he drifted aloud into other lines:

Whose speech Truth knows not from her thought
Nor Love her body from her soul.

He had never before so clearly understood that sense of Lester as now when that second line must be rationally untrue. But his sleep had restored to him something he had once had and had lost—something deeper even than Lester, something that lay at the root of all magic, that the body was itself integral to spirit. He had in his time talked a good deal about anthropomorphism and now he realized that anthropomorphism was but one dialect of divine truth. The high thing which was now in his mind, the body that had walked and lain by his, was itself celestial and divine. Body? it was no more merely body than soul was merely soul; it was only visible Lester.

His mind turned again to that house by Holborn. He thought of it, after his sleep, as a nightmare to which he need not return unless, for any reason, he chose. In the sleep from which he had come there could be no nightmares. They were possible only to his waking life and sometimes from that cast back into the joy of sleep. He drew a deep breath. Simon was only an accident of a life that had not learned to live under that arch of happiness. It was astonishing how, this way, Simon dwindled. That last moment when something disagreeable had floated in at the window of the hall, some remote frigid exchange between imbeciles, was still repugnant to him. But now it was at a distance; it did not even distress him. What did distress him, as it crept back into his mind, was a memory of himself in the street outside the house, of his indulgent self. This unfortunately was no nightmare. He had, in that distant Berkshire wood, been just so; he had been kind to his wife. She (whatever her faults) had never been like that to him; she had never been dispassionately considerate. But he—he undoubtedly had. His new serenity all but vanished and he all but threw his hairbrush at his face in the mirror, as he thought of it. But his new energy compelled him to refrain and to confront the face, which, as he looked at it, seemed to bear the impress of love behaving itself very unseemly. Her love had never borne that mark. Rash, violent, angry, as she might have been, egotistic in her nature as he, yet her love had been sealed always to another and not to herself. She was never the slave of the false luxuria.

214

When she had served him—how often!—she had not
done it from kindness or unselfishness; it had been because she wished what he wished and was his servant
to what he desired. Kindness, patience, forbearance,
were not enough; he had had them, but she had had
love. He must find what she had—another kind of life.
All these years, since he had been that eager child, he
had grown the wrong way, in the wrong kind of life.
Yet how to have done other? how to have learned, as
she had learned, the language without which he could
not, except for a conceded moment, speak to the im-
perial otherness of her glory? He must, it seemed, be
born all over again.

A vague impression that he had heard some such
phrase somewhere before passed through him. But it was
lost, for as he dwelled on the strange notion of this
necessary fact, it was swamped by the recollection of
Simon. Not that he was now afraid of Simon's having
any power over Lester. But if there was that newly
visioned life, there was also—he had seen it—a creeping
death that was abroad in the world. There was something that was not Lester, nor at all like her, issuing
from that hideous little hall. Those who lay in that
house, once sick, had been healed. Had they? He did
not like to think of that healing. He would almost
rather have remained unhealed; yes, but then he did
not need healing. He thought uneasily of those who,
themselves reasonably secure, urge the poor to prefer
freedom rather than security. How could he have done
it himself—have lived in pain? have perished miserably?
Yet the cost of avoiding that was to be lost in the hypnotic mystery of the creeping death: an intolerable, an
unforgivable choice! And perhaps, unless someone in-

terfered, Simon would spread his miasma over the world: the nations swaying as he had seen men swaying. If even now—

The telephone interrupted him. Answering, he found at the other end a colleague of his at the Foreign Office, who began by asking whether Richard were (as he had said) coming back the next day. Richard said that he was. His colleague intimated that there was a particular reason and (pressed to say more) asked whether Richard were not acquainted with the activities of a certain Simon the Clerk. Richard began to take an interest.

"Well—no and yes," he said. "I know of him and as it happens since this morning I may be said to know him. Why?"

"Since you've been away," his friend said, "it's become rather urgent to get into touch with him—unofficially, of course. It's more and more felt here that if the allied discussions could—could infiltrate through him and the other popular leaders there might be a better chance of . . . of——"

"Of peace," said Richard.

"Well, yes," his colleague agreed. "They must, all three of them, be remarkable men to have such followings and there don't seem, where they go, to be any minorities. . . . What did you say?"

"Nothing, nothing," said Richard. "No minorities?"

"No—or practically none. And it'll be in the best interests of the new World Plan that there should be no minorities. So that it's been hinted that if a kind of—well, not a conference exactly but a sort of meeting could be adumbrated . . . Someone here thought you knew Simon."

"I do," said Richard. "And you want me to——"

"Well, since you know him," his colleague answered, "it'd be easy for you to ask him indefinitely, as it were. Could you manage it, d'you think? You can see the kind of thing we want. The fact is that there's a sort of pressure. Even the Russians are feeling it—and we hear a couple of Chinese armies have gone over complete to their own prophet. So the Government thinks it would rather deal with the three of them together than separately. If we could sound them——"

Richard was silent. This language was one he very well knew, but now it had a deeper sound than his colleague's voice could give it. The Foreign Office did not mean badly; it was no more full of "darkness and cruel habitations" than the rest of the world; and when Oxenstierna had complained of the little wisdom with which the world was governed, he had not clearly suggested how anyone was to get more. But if the official governments were beginning to yield to pressure, to take unofficial notice of these world leaders, then those healed bodies behind Holborn must be only a few of a very great number, and those swaying shoulders the heralds of great multitudes of devotion: devotion to what? to the man who had smiled at the dead woman, and claimed to hold Lester at disposal, and knelt in some obscure effort by Betty's bed, the man to whom the wicked little carved hand pointed. He himself might have been among the worshipers; he owed his salvation to his wife, for it was precisely the irreconcilability of his wife with Simon which had preserved him—and he most unworthy, given up to the social virtues, needing rebirth.

He did not know how great the multitudes were who followed those unreal Two; nor how unreal the

Two were. He knew only the reports in the papers, and Simon. He seemed to feel again the light antennae-like touch on his cheek; he saw again the strange painting of the prophet preaching to insects: what insects? His colleague's voice went on. "Furnival, are you still there? You'd better know that Bodge"—Bodge was the Foreign Secretary—"is giving it his personal attention. He isn't here today, but he will be tomorrow. Couldn't you just sound this Father Simon by then?"

Bodge—the Cabinet room—the swaying shoulders and the lifted faces, the backs of the English ministers rising in the air, the corridor down which the nations could go, the window through which the dead had come. He said abruptly, "I don't know; I can't say. I'll be in tomorrow to report. . . . Yes; all right, I'll see. . . . Oh yes, I understand how urgent it is. . . . No; I don't promise anything. I'll come tomorrow. Unless," he added with a sudden absurd lightening of heart, "unless my wife interferes."

The magical shape walked slowly along the Embankment. Hours had passed since it had emerged from the hidden place of its making into the streets of London; it had come out not by its own wish, for it could have no wish of its own, but under the compulsion of its lord in his last word, merely going, and anywhere. A poorly dressed, somewhat deformed woman went along the pavement. At first, following its maker's preoccupation, it had gone northward towards the Highgate house. But as that preoccupation grew distant and was slowly lost, since he gave it no further guidance, it presently faltered and stood still and then began to turn westward. It could not return, for that would be to disobey him;

it could not go directly on, for that would be to stress his influence too far. It swung therefore in a wide arc, going always against the sun and passing so down street after street and alley after alley. Sometimes, but not often, it faulted by taking a blind turning and had to retrace its steps, but in general, as if it sniffed its way through the lower air, it was wonderfully accurate. But when, in its southward course, it came to the river, it hesitated and did not cross and abruptly turned off towards the east along its own side, and so on, until somewhere by Blackfriars it could see (could it indeed have seen anything at all) the still-lifted cross of St. Paul's. And there, a little way along Victoria Street, it ceased again and stood still.

It could not, for it was sensitive enough to some things, easily enter within the weight of those charged precincts. It avoided them precisely at the point where, had it been living woman, it might by sight or any other sense, have become conscious of them. So also those departed spirits who were now sealed to it were aware of its surroundings through what would have been its or their senses, had it or they lived. One of them had settled, almost happily, to such an existence. Evelyn (to give that spirit still the old name) was content merely to be again generally aware of earth; she did not care about the details. She was listening for its voice, even though at first that voice could only echo her own inaudible soliloquy. Perhaps afterwards it might even answer, and she and it would become an everlasting colloquy, but at the moment it did not. Those who passed it heard a kind of low croak coming from it, but not what it said. What it croaked to itself was a mass of comments and complaints: "But you would think, wouldn't you?" or "It's not as if I were asking much" or "I did think you'd understand" or "After all, fair is fair" or "She might" or "He needn't" or "They could at least" . . . and so on and on through all the sinful and silly imbecilities by which the miserable soul protects itself against fact. If this was Evelyn's pleasure, this was the pleasure she could have.

But Lester also, for the first time since her death, was aware of what we call the normal world. At first she was conscious of this body as a man is of his own; it was not hers, but it was in that way she knew the dragging foot, the dank palms, the purblind eyes. She knew the spasmodic croakings, as a man may hear his own exclamations. She disliked its neighborhood, but there was no help for that, and by it alone she was aware of the material universe. So understood, that universe was agreeable to her. She knew and liked the feel of the pavement under the feet; she enjoyed through dim eyes the dull October day, and the heavy sky, and the people, and all the traffic. She seemed to be almost living again, for a little and by no insistence of her own, in the world she had left.

At first she had not seemed, and had hardly desired, to control this body as it went on its way. She was passive to its haste. But as that haste dwindled and as it began to circle round its center, she felt a sense of power. She saw still, as from above, the false body swinging round and it seemed improper that she herself should be so swung. The full sense of this came to her at almost the moment when that body hesitated by the river under the golden cross of the cathedral. As if from the height of the cross, Lester saw its circling path. There seemed—she almost thought it in human words—

no sense in circling round and round Simon; he was no such attractive center. Indeed, from the height at which she looked down he was no center at all, except indeed that here and there in the streets she discerned a few forms engaged on precisely that wheeling worship. She knew them by their odd likeness to large beetles walking on their back legs. By an almost unconscious decision she checked the dwarf-woman just as it was about to move forward again. She said—and she just had to say, or at least to think, "No, no; the other way!" The shape tottered, twisted and was reluctantly forced round. It began, jerkingly and slowly, but certainly, to retrace its steps along the Embankment. It went as if against a high wind, for it was going with the sun and against all the customs of Goetia. Had it been a living witch of that low kind, it would have resisted more strongly; being what it was, it did but find difficulty in going. But it went on, plodding, croaking, jerking, back towards Westminster.

Of Evelyn, Lester was no longer immediately conscious. The magical form which united them also separated; through it they co-hered to each other but could not co-inhere. Lester had joined herself to this form for the sake of Evelyn, and Evelyn (so far as she could know) had been promptly removed. In fact, Evelyn no longer wanted her, for Evelyn was concerned only with her own refuge in this false shape, and with her own comfort in it. She did not much care whether it stayed or went, or how or where it went; she cared only that there should be, somewhere in the universe, a voice which, at first repeating, might presently come to respond to, her own. Lester was not unaware of the croaking voice and justly attributed it to Evelyn, but she saw no reason to stop it.

Sounds now came to her through a new kind of silence, a sweet stillness which they did not seem to break; of all the London noises none came so near to breaking it as that croak, but the silence, or perhaps she herself, withdrew a little and the noise went about below it, as the dwarf-woman plodded below the clouds.

The clouds indeed were heavy in the sky. The river ran equally heavily with the weight of its murk. A few boats rode on it; the Thames traffic, at this height of its course, had not renewed itself. Lester's attention turned to it, and the dwarf, folding her arms, paused conformably and leaned on the parapet. The Thames was dirty and messy. Twigs, bits of paper and wood, cords, old boxes drifted on it. Yet to the new-eyed Lester it was not a depressing sight. The dirtiness of the water was, at that particular point, what it should be and therefore pleasant enough. The evacuations of the City had their place in the City; how else could the City be the City? Corruption (so to call it) was tolerable, even adequate and proper, even glorious. These things also were facts. They could not be forgotten or lost in fantasy; all that had been, was; all that was, was. A sodden mass of cardboard and paper drifted by, but the soddenness was itself a joy, for this was what happened, and all that happened, in this great material world, was good. The very heaviness of the heavy sky was a wonder, and the unutilitarian expectation of rain a delight.

The river flowed steadily on. Lester saw it, as if through the dwarf's eyes, and rejoiced. But she was aware that she was at the same time seeing some other movement, within or below it. She was looking down at it also. A single gull, flying wildly up beyond Blackfriars, swooped, wheeled, rose and was off again downstream.

London was great, but that gull's flight meant the sea. The sea was something other than London or than the Thames. Under the rush of the bird's flight—seen as once by another river other watchers had seen a dove's motion skirr and vanish—Lester, looking down, saw in the river the subsurface currents and streams. Below the exquisitely colored and moving and busy surface, the river by infinitesimal variations became lucid. On earth men see through lucidity to density, but to her it was as easy to see through density to lucidity. To her now all states of being were beginning to be of their own proper kind, each in itself and in its relationships, and not hampering the vision of others. So the Thames was still the Thames, but within it the infinite gradations of clarity deepened to something else. That other flow sustained and carried the layers of water above it; and as Lester saw it she felt a great desire to discover its source, and even that was mingled with the sudden human recollection that she and Richard had intended one day to set out to find for themselves the first springs of the Thames. So that even here she felt a high, new, strange and almost bitter longing mingle still with the definite purposes of her past.

She looked—but now no longer from a height above the seagull, but only from her instrument's eyes on the Embankment—she looked up the river. But now she could not see past the great buildings of the Houses and the Abbey; and even those instituted masses seemed to her to float on that current of liquid beauty. As she looked at them the premonition of a pang took her; a sense of division, as if it was at that point that the lucid river flowed into the earthly river, so that beyond that point the way divided, and the source of the Thames was one thing and the springs of the sustaining tributary another. At that point or indeed at any; but always the same division at each. She was suddenly afraid. The strong current below the surface scared her. It flowed from under the bridge, cold and frightening, worse than death. The bridge above it where she and Richard had met this time and that was so frail. They had met above the surface Thames, but they had not guessed what truly flowed below—this which was different from and refused all earthly meetings, and all meetings colored or overlooked by earth. Oh vain, all the meetings vain! "A million years?" not one moment; it had been the cry of a child. Her spiritual consciousness knew and shuddered. She could never exclaim so again; however long she waited, she only waited to be separated, to lose, in the end. The under-river sang as it flowed; all the streets of London were full of that sweet inflexible note—the single note she had heard in Betty's room, the bed on which she had safely lain. This was it—bed and note and river, the small cold piercing pain of immortal separation.

It passed. The time was not yet, though it was quite certain. The cruel clarity flowed by. She was left with a sense that she had better make the most of the present moment. She had thought she might be of use to Evelyn, but clearly she was not being; all she knew of Evelyn were these spasmodic croaks. What then? something she must do. Betty? Richard? Richard—with this body? She made herself aware of it. It would be revolting to him; it was almost revolting to her, even now, to think of going to her lover in this disguise. Yet if she could—? if they could speak? The shape was not so revolting, for what was it, after all? nothing. Before that great separation came, to take and give pardon and courage . . . if . . .

She was not clear how far she was responsible for what followed. Certainly she acted, but there was a pure precision about the process which surprised and delighted her, so that, had Betty or Richard been there, she could have laughed. She turned in herself again to the contemporary City, and the dwarf-woman, starting up, began again to walk. It came presently opposite Charing Cross Tube Station. There it stopped and turned and looked. Lester knew herself anxious to forewarn, to prepare, her husband; and she thought, not unnaturally, of the telephone. Matter to matter; might not this earthly shape use the things of earth? She did not dichotomize; mechanics were not separate from spirit, nor invention from imagination, nor that from passion. Only not even passion of spirit could create the necessary two pennies. She might be (she thought in a flash) immortally on her way to glory, but she had not got two pennies. She recollected the Good Samaritan who had, and with laughter in her heart she tossed a hand towards that sudden vivid image. She was not like Simon; she could not make two pennies. If she were to have them, someone would have to give them to her. She remembered, but not as a claim, that she too had given pennies in her time.

The dwarf in that pause had leaned again against the parapet. The ordinary traffic of London was going on, but as if Lester's pause had affected it, there came at the moment a lull and a silence. Through it there toddled slowly along an elderly gentleman, peering through his glasses at an evening paper. Lester, shyly and daringly, moved towards him. She meant to say, "I beg your pardon, but could you possibly spare me two pennies for the telephone?" But she had not yet control of that false voice and the croak in which she spoke sounded more like "twopence as a loan." The elderly gentleman looked up, saw a poor shabby deformed creature staring glassily at him, heard the mumble and hastily felt in his pocket. He said—and it was mercifully permitted him by the Omnipotence to be on this occasion entirely truthful, "It's all the change I've got." He raised his hat, in some faint tradition of "brave and ancient things," and toddled on. The magical body stood holding the pennies in its pseudo-hand, and Lester felt in her that something of a stir in glory which she had felt in seeing Richard's movements or Betty's smile. She was made free of adoration.

The dwarf, under her impulse, crossed the road and went into a telephone box. She put the two pennies in the slot and dialed a number. Lester was aware that there was no reply; Richard apparently was not at home. She felt a small pang at the thought of their empty flat; the desolation seemed to be approaching. It was most likely that he was at Jonathan's. She compelled her instrument to try again. A voice said, "Jonathan Drayton speaking." She caused her instrument to press the button. She said—and now her power was moving so easily in these conditions that something of her own voice dominated the croaking spasms and rang down the telephone. "Mr. Drayton, is Richard there?"

"Hold on," said Jonathan. "Richard!" For soon after Richard's conversation with the Foreign Office he had been rung up by Jonathan and so warmly invited by both the lovers to join them that he had yielded and gone. Presently they were all to go and dine, but until then they had sat together talking and gradually, as far as possible, making clear to each other the mystery in which they moved. Betty showed an ever-quickened desire to get rid of the painting of the Clerk and his congregation; and both she and Jonathan had so pressed the other canvas on Richard that at last he had accepted it. He did so gratefully, for now, after all that he had seen, he found himself even more moved by it, so that at any moment he half expected to find that he had missed the figure of Lester walking in the midst of it—if that swift and planetary carriage of hers could be called a walk—and even that he himself might find himself not without but within it and meeting her there. And the three of them in the room had begun, uncertainly and with difficulty—even Betty—to speak of the true nature of the streets there represented, when the telephone had rung.

At Jonathan's call Richard went across and took the receiver. He said, "Richard Furnival," and then, to his amazement, but not much to his amazement, he heard Lester's voice. It was interrupted by some kind of croak which he took to be a fault in the instrument, but he heard it say, "Richard!" and at the noble fascination of that familiar sound he answered, not as unsteadily as he feared, "Is it you, darling?" At the other end the dwarf leaned against the side of the box; nothing at either end, to any who saw, seemed in the least unusual. Along the wires the unearthly and earthly voice continued. "Listen, dearest. Presently someone is coming to see you; it's a short and rather unpleasant woman—at least, that's what it looks like. But I shall be with her, I hope—I do so hope. Will you be as sweet to me as you can, even if you don't like it?"

Richard said, "I've been all kinds of a fool, I know.

But I'll do anything with you, if I possibly can. Jonathan and Betty are here."

"That's all right," the voice said. It added, "Once more. Before I go, before I give you up. Oh my sweet!"

The voice was so full of serene grief that Richard went cold. He said, "Nothing shall make me give you up. I've only just begun to find you."

"But you will, even if nothing makes you," the voice said. "It'll have to be like that. But I'll come first. Don't be too distressed about anything. And ask Jonathan to let me in; I'll speak to you inside. Goodbye. I do love you, Richard."

A kind of hubbub broke out on the telephone—another voice and the mechanic croaking—and then Lester's voice, dominating all, "Wait for us. Goodbye," and he heard the click of the receiver. He held his own a full minute before he slowly put it down. His two friends watched him coming back to them across the room. He said, "Something is coming here—a kind of woman. And Lester. I don't know anything more. She says she'll be with it."

"But—Lester . . ." Jonathan began.

"If that wasn't Lester," Richard said, "you're not looking at Betty now."

They both looked at her. She was standing by the window and beyond her the October darkness was closing in. She said seriously, "Did she sound—disturbed?"

"Not about that," said Richard. He was silent; then he broke out, "Why isn't one taught how to *be* loved? Why isn't one taught anything?"

Betty said, "Don't worry, Richard; we can't be taught till we can learn. I wish Jonathan was going to get as good a wife as yours is. She wasn't like us; she hardly had to find out how to learn. Jon, take that thing off the easel, won't you? We'll get rid of it tonight. Tonight."

She sounded almost impatient, but only because they had not already acted and the preaching horror was still in the room where they were and Lester was to come. Jonathan went and lifted the canvas. As he laid it face downwards on the table, he said, "Do you know what tonight is? All Hallows' Eve."

"A good night," said Richard, "for anything that has to be done."

"And a good night," Betty added, "for Lester to come to us here."

They fell into silence and for the time that followed they remained mostly silent. Once Jonathan, muttering something about food, moved, and he and Betty spread a rough meal of bread and cheese and cold scraps and wine. There was not much, but there was enough, and they ate and drank standing, as Israel did while the angels of the Omnipotence were at their work in Egypt. The night was heavy without and the sound of rain. The sense of the crisis was sharp in them and the expectation of that which came.

Presently the bell rang. They looked at each other. Richard said, "You go, Jonathan; she asked you to." Jonathan went to the street door and opened it. He saw in the night a short pale-faced woman and stood aside for her to come in. As it did so, he saw how blank its eyes were, how dead-dull its flesh. Yet he could have believed that, like a paralytic, it tried to recognize him and almost to smile. Neither of them spoke; it knew its way and went before him into the room where the others were.

They watched it come right in; they hardly watched but they heard Jonathan close the room door. Then Betty said, in a low voice of welcome, "Lester!" She saw, as the others did not, the form of her friend beside this other thing; and yet what she saw, she saw less clearly than before. They were growing away from each other. Lester was bound to pass more wholly into that other world which cannot catch its true and perfect union with this until the resurrection of all the past; the occasional resurrection which then obtained for her was rather purgatorial than paradisal, though sometimes the two were simply one. But Betty also was changing. That free and (as it were) immaculate self which had been by high disposition granted her was bound now to take on the conditions of its earthly place and natural heredity. The miracle that had preserved her was over and she too must be subjected to the tribulations and temptations of common life. As she so drew apart her vision faded. One evening yet remained and even now the other form and face were full of cloud.

But she saw her. Richard and Jonathan did not. They looked at that uncouth visitor, its blank struggling gaze, its lank hair, its dropped shoulder, its heavy hanging hands, its dragging foot, its dead flesh, its flopping dress, and could not speak. What had this to do with Lester? Lester herself, could she have felt regret, would in that moment have regretted that she had come. She did not. The Acts that were about to take place saw to that. They would, when the time came, see that she spoke what she had to speak, for she was already assenting to their will. It was why they had, since she had driven her present vehicle away from Charing Cross on the long walk to Jonathan's flat, quickened their purging. Up Villiers Street, along the Strand and Fleet Street, up Ludgate Hill, along the Old Bailey, they had worked on her. As the magical shape plodded on, its steps growing slower and heavier, through the rain and the dark, they troubled her with a sense of the physical body she had left. At first indeed, as the walk began, she had endured only a great wish that she had again the body as well as the soul of Lester, the body that Richard had loved and for which she had herself felt a small admiration. She wished, if she were to be thus materially before her husband, to give again the hand she had given, to speak to him with the mouth he had kissed. She had no physical desires except to be in his eyes her own physical self. But as she thought of it, she grew disturbed. Her faults, on the whole, had not been physical. Her body had carried no past of fornication or adultery, nor had she therefore mystically to free it from those avenging unions. She had not to disengage her flesh from those other bodies, or to re-engage her flesh so that its unions should be redeemed, approved and holy. Nor had she been given to the other luxurious commitments of the flesh. She had not been particularly lazy or greedy; as bodies go, hers was reasonably pure. As bodies go— but even then? More and more disliking this body to which she was transitorily bound, she more and more came to consider her dealings with her own. All through that long walk, she relived them and always she ended with this other false disrelish. She again and again began by being conscious of her looks, her energy, her swiftness; again and again she would (except for mere fastidiousness, which was of no account) have tempted others with it, though not to commit herself; again and again she melted to delicate pleasures and grew dependent on them, and as she did so, she woke to find herself in the end one with this other. It was this false deformed death of which she was proud, with which she tempted, in which she took her delight. Hers was this, or at least no more than this; unless, for again and again in the end the sudden impulse sprang—unless she could still let it be what it had been ordained to be, worthy in its whole physical glory of Betty, of Richard, of the City she felt about her, of all that was unfamiliar to her in the name of God. Her past went with her all that walk; and by the end of the walk her past had taught her this.

Yet, having so thought of herself in humility and serious repentance all the way, it was, when at last she came into Jonathan's room, of Richard that she thought. She was agonized for what she felt must be his horror if, seeming to be in this shape, she spoke. Betty's cry of welcome went unnoticed; she was here to speak and now how could she—how could she—speak? He was staring at —her? no; but at this; and he was her husband; how could she treat her husband so? All the coldnesses and all the angers were but delirium and bitterness of love; she could have helped them perhaps, but now this she could not help and this was worst of all. She had for a moment a terrible fear that this was they; even that this was she and that he—Oh he by whom alone in that world she lived—would know that this was she. The silence became a fearful burden to them all. It was Betty who saved them. She broke into action; she dashed across the room; she caught Jonathan's and Richard's hands. She cried out, "Come over here!"

The relief of her action released them; uncertainly, they obeyed. She pulled them across to the window; she said, "Turn round, both of you; look out there." She nodded her golden head at the darkness and to Jonathan it seemed as if a rain of gold drove through the night and vanished. They obeyed her still; one hand on the nearer shoulder of each she held them there. She turned her head over her shoulder; she exclaimed, "Lester, say something to us." Lester, in a rush of gratitude, did so. She said, it is true, no more than "Hullo!" but the voice was undoubtedly her voice, and (though no louder than on earth) it filled the room. Jonathan, hearing it, jumped a little. Richard did not; there was, in all the universe, no place in which that voice was not recognizable and good. He answered, with the immediate instinct of something that might yet be love, "Hullo, darling!"

Lester, dallying with peace and half-forgetful of the others, said, "Have I been very long? I'm so sorry." "Sorry" is a word that means many things; there is in general a friendliness about it and now it meant all friendliness. "We took such a time." Her laugh sounded in their ears. "Have you been waiting?"

Betty took her hand off Richard's shoulder. In the intimacy of those two, her hand was a solecism. Lester's voice went on. "But I've been tiresome so often, darling. I've been beastly to you. I——"

He said, "You've never been tiresome," and she, "No; speak true now, my own. I——"

He said, "Very well; you have. And what in all the heavens and hells, and here too, does it matter? Do we keep accounts about each other? If it's the last word I speak I shall still say you were too good for me."

"And——?" she said, and her laughter was more than laughter; it was the speech of pure joy. "Go on, blessing—if it's our last word."

"And I'm too good for you," Richard said. "Let me

turn round now. It's all right; I promise you it's all right."

"Do, darling," she said.

He turned, and the others with him. They saw the long room, and at the other end the painting of the City that dominated the room as if it and not the wall behind it were the true end of the room, as if the room precisely opened there on that space and those streets; and as if some unseen nature present there united both room and painting, the light in it was within the room also and vibrated there. The table with the remnants of the meal, the wine still in the glasses, the back of the other canvas lying on the table—all these were massive with the light. Between them and the table stood the dwarf-woman, but somehow it did not matter to any of them. The full and lovely voice said, almost as if a rich darkness spoke within the light, "It's nice to see you all again."

Betty said, "It's blessed to see you. But what *is* this, my dear?" She nodded at the dwarf.

Lester said, "It was made by—I don't even know who he is, but by the man in your room."

Richard said, "He's called Simon, and sometimes the Clerk, and he thinks himself no end of a fellow. Has he hurt you?"

"Not a bit," said Lester. "I've been with it of my own choice. But now I've seen you, I know what to do—before I go away. It must be taken back to him."

So much was suddenly clear to her. She was here—and Richard and Betty, and Jonathan too, were here for this purpose. It was time the magical dwarf was driven back to Simon. It had come from him; it must go to him. The Acts of the City were in operation; she felt their direction. She only could compel this movement; she only return to the false maker the thing he had falsely made. It was full time.

Betty said, "We were going to take him that other thing—the painting Jon did of him. You haven't seen it; but that doesn't matter. It's very good, but it'd be much better if he had it altogether. So Jon's being a saint and giving it to him. . . . Lester, there's someone else with you!"

It was fortunate that the Acts of the City had allowed the three those minutes to become accustomed to the voice and to the shape. For now the shape took a quick step forward and there broke from it a sudden confused noise. Neither Richard nor Jonathan at all recognized the human voice that was mixed with that croaking and cackling, but Betty recognized it. She had feared it too much and too often not to know. She did not step backwards, but she flinched, as if the noise had struck her. She exclaimed, "Evelyn!"

The noise ceased abruptly. Jonathan took a step forward, but Betty caught his arm. She said, "No, really, Jon; it's too silly. I'm not afraid; I know perfectly well I'm not afraid. I was only surprised. Lester, you needn't stop her. Were you talking to me, Evelyn?"

"No one," said the dwarf with a slow effort and in a harsh imitation of Evelyn's voice, "cares about me. I don't expect much. I don't ask for much. I only want you, Betty. Lester's so cruel to me. She won't cry. I only want to see you cry." It tried to lift its hands, but they only waggled. The body drooped and the head fell on one side. So askew, it continued to emit sounds mostly indistinguishable. Now and then a sentence stood out. It said at last, clearly and with a slight giggle, "Betty

235

looked so funny when she cried. I want to see Betty cry."

Jonathan said under his breath, "God be merciful to us all!" Betty said, "Evelyn, if you want to talk, come and talk. I can't promise to cry, but I'll listen." Richard said, "Must we waste time?"

The dwarf's head jerked and turned as far as it could from one to the other. It gave back a little. Before those three, as if the consciousness of their eyes oppressed it, it fell together a little more. It said, with a final great effort, "You hurt me when you look at me. I don't want you to look at me. I want to look at you. Betty, you used to be frightened of me. I want you to be frightened of me."

Jonathan said with a sudden decision, "We can't do anything. Let's do what we can do. If we're to do it, let's go now." He went to the table and took up the canvas.

Betty said, "Shall we, Lester?" and the other voice, again filling the room, answered, "We'd better. Evelyn can't manage this and I've only one thing to do with it— to take it back. Let's go."

Richard went quickly past Jonathan to the table. He picked up his glass; he waved to the others and they came to him. He tried to speak and could not. But Betty did. She too took her glass; she held it up; she said, "Good luck, Lester!" and they all drank. Richard flung his glass to the floor. As it smashed, the dwarf with a little squeal turned round and began stumbling towards the door. The three friends went after it.

It was very late when they came into the street, but in the light of a near standard they saw a single taxi moving slowly along. The driver was a big man; he saw

Jonathan's lifted hand, slowed and leaning back opened the door. They stood round the dwarf while, slowly and in utter silence, it scrambled clumsily in. Before either of the young men could speak, Betty had followed it and sat down by it. They sat opposite, Jonathan could not quite remember giving the address, but he supposed he must have done, for the door was closed on them and the carriage moved off in the night. In spite of Betty's face opposite him a macabre horror fell on Jonathan; all he had ever read, in fiction or history, of fatal midnight drives recurred to him: discrowned kings fleeing, madmen carried off to Bedlam, or perhaps sane men by careful plottings certified as mad, gagged men borne to private assassinations, gangsters taken for rides by gangsters, and through all a ghastly element of another kind —arrest of heretics, seizure of martyrs, witches clutched or witches clutching—in all the cities of all the world midnight and dark coaches rolling and things unnamable for good or evil about to be done. Something still deeper—there and then, or had been, one plain simple act which could only be done in such a night. Unless this night were now about to give place to a more frightening day—a dawn on some town where such creatures lived as this opposite him or his own imagined insects and had their own occupation, grisly, unseen in this sun, but visible to sickness in another light so much like this but not this.

Beside him Richard leaned back free from such distress, for he had already known that distress. He had been used to think that nothing could shock him; he had been wrong. The universe is always capable of a worse trick than we suppose, but at least when we have known it we are no longer surprised by anything less. Jonathan's horrid nightmares, oppressive as they were to him, were less distressing than the pain of a mother listening to her child choking with bronchitis in the night. Richard's endurance now, like hers, was of present and direct facts. He had seen something which, in the full sense of the words, ought not to be, and never before had he felt the full sense of the words. This was what everything that ought not to be was—this quiet agreement that it should be. It was a breach in nature and therefore in his own nature. His own self-indulgence was of this kind; his dispassionate consideration might be and might not—that depended on him. And now in this happier world he had thought to enter, a thing as extreme struck him. He could not disbelieve Lester when she spoke of going; he could not even doubt that it ought to be. But except for that "ought to be" the coldness in his heart was indistinguishable from the earlier chill. The new birth refused him. He was as yet ignorant of the fact that this was one method of its becoming actual. He despaired.

But Lester, when she had walked in the dead City, piercingly aware of her own rejection, had known that despair, and its inflexibility had entered her and grown in her. She no longer drove her one-time friend with her old impatience; her strength was now the other side of her willingness to wait "a million years" or to know she was not even to be allowed that. In their swift passage to the dark coach she had felt the rain on the false flesh; she had felt it as the premonition of that lucid flowing water of separation. A double charge was laid on her, to expel this thing from the streets of London, and then herself to go. The falsity must go to its place of origin to be destroyed; to go, so literally, dust to dust. The City must have what belonged to it in the mode in which it belonged. She thought no more of tubes and tunnels filled with horrors. Matter was purified and earth was free, or to become so. But instead of the tunnel flowed the inexorable river. She too must go.

She saw the taxi roll through the streets; she saw the four sitting in it. She knew that, if her new sight strengthened, she would see even more clearly the whole construction, not only of the vehicle, but of false mortality and true mortality. She almost did see Richard so, in his whole miraculous pattern, all the particles of him, of the strange creature who was in every particle both flesh and spirit, was something that was both, was (the only word that meant the thing he was) a man. She loved him the more passionately for the seeing. And then she saw Betty move. She saw her turn to that contorted thing in the corner which, under those vivid and suffering intelligences, was now beginning to lose even the semblance of a woman, and she saw her put her living hand on its dead paw. She heard Betty say, "Evelyn!" and then again, "Evelyn, let's talk!" and through a dim mumble she heard Evelyn say, "I don't want you now." She saw—and could not see farther—a fixed pallid mask of a face molded in and looking out of the false flesh with a scared malice, and she too cried out, "Evelyn, don't leave us!" She even made an effort to dominate it, but that failed at once; the false flesh she could command but not now the thing within the flesh. Evelyn said, "I hate you." The dead paw—now hardly five-fingered—made an effort to shake off Betty's hand and when that tightened on it, jerked and pulled in order to get away. As it succeeded, the taxi came to a stop.

Chapter Ten

THE ACTS OF THE CITY

On the vigil of the hallows, it was gloomily and steadily raining. Few people were out in the streets of London and the curtains at most windows were again drawn together. Even delight in the peace could hardly find satisfaction in keeping them wide on such a night. Unpropitiously, the feast approached.

The Clerk was sitting in his hall. He had remained secluded there since he had dismissed the false woman into the outer world, and with that (as he believed) the spirit that had interrupted his work. He was a little more troubled than he wished to admit to himself, and that for two reasons. He had been more pricked than he had allowed by Betty's silence about him when she repeated to him the tumultuous records of the world's future. There was, to his mind, but one explanation—that some new weakness had taken her, and when he had been defeated in his operation he had even been able to use that as an explanation. This other being—now imprisoned and banished from him—had affected her and silenced her. The future was not therefore as she had said. The alternative possibility—that the future was as she had said and that he would so soon have utterly vanished from the world—was too dreadful for him. He encouraged his mind into illusion. Illusion, to the magician as to the saint, is a great danger. But the master in Goetia has always at the center of his heart a single tiny everlasting illusion; it may be long before that point infects him wholly, but sooner or later it is bound to do so. It was infecting Simon now. It was hurrying him.

He was reluctant to do what he was being driven, by that scurry in his mind, to intend. He knew well that for the greater initiate to fall back on the methods of the lesser initiate was unwise. In sorcery as in sanctity there is no return. The master in any art who abandons the methods of his mastery and falls back on prentice habits runs a fearful risk. No lover, of any kind, not even the lover of himself, can safely turn from maturity to adolescence. His adolescence is in his maturity. The past may be recalled and redeemed in the present, but the present cannot be forsaken for the past. Lester was exposed to the true method; Evelyn was seeking the false. But the magician runs a greater risk even than Evelyn's, for if he begins to return, his works begin to return to him. All this Simon had learned many years before, but till now it had never been a temptation to him; now it was. He had begun to fall back on crude early methods of magic. He had already conceded to his need the making of the false body; now he was about to concede more. To recover Betty by spiritual means would mean much careful planning and working. He sat with his eyes fixed on that window through which he desired to see her spirit come, and he knew he must first suspend and separate her physical life. Her body, especially with this new knowledge, this love relation to another, was her safeguard. He must at once, by easy and quick methods, overthrow her body. The great face that gazed towards the window was more like the face of Jonathan's painting than anyone, even Jonathan, had ever seen it before.

He turned his mind to his paramour. She was then sitting at her solitary dinner, in her house at Highgate, and presently she felt herself beginning to breathe heavily and her left hand began to shake. She knew the signs, and she set herself to making her mind empty. Such communications demand a technique not dissimilar to that of prayer. First she thought of nothing but him; when she had nothing but his image in her mind, she set herself to exclude that too. Her coffee was before her; no one would come till she rang. She sat— that woman only just past fifty, though since that very morning she had aged and looked full ten years older— gazing out over the coffee, a statue of quiet meditation; and the image of him faded from her mind and she sank into an inner stillness. It was in that stillness, the stillness of the threshold of a ghostly temple, that she heard her own voice saying aloud, "Hair. Bring me her hair." She heard it clearly the first time she said it, but she heard herself repeat it several times before she acted, where once she would have moved at once. But she was stiff tonight and tired, and in great wanhope, and it was only slowly that at last she raised herself, pressing on the arms of her chair, and went clumsily upstairs to Betty's room. There, peering among the bristles of the brushes, she found two or three short golden hairs. She picked them carefully out, put them in an envelope, and going downstairs got out her car and drove down to Holborn. It was an hour afterwards that the maid found that, for the first time in her experience, her mistress had left the dining-room without ringing.

When she reached the house she found Plankin

just about to lock the door. As she reached it and he waited for her, she almost thought that the small carved hand showed through the darkness palely lit and in motion, waving her to go on. Plankin said, "Good evening, my lady. It's a nasty night." She nodded to him and he nodded back. He said, "It's good to belong to the Father and to be inside. We'll be in our beds soon, most of us. The Father's got good beds for those he takes care of," and as she went down the hall she heard him behind her still saying, "Good beds; good beds."

Round the corner, through the small door. The hall was dark. She switched on one light—the single light that was just over the door. It did not penetrate far—just enough to let her dimly see the Clerk sitting in the throned chair and something shining upon his knees. He was waiting for her. She went straight across to him, took the hairs out of the envelope and gave them to him. He was sitting quite still and holding on his knees a little lump of what seemed paste. It was that which shone. He took the hairs from her and laid them on the paste; then he began to mold it. It was very small, not more than two inches long, and as he pressed and molded it he made it less; presently it was not much more than an inch. Then, as if he needed more, he put his hand inside his cassock and took it out again full of all kind of soft amorphous stuff, also shining. He added that to what he already held and worked at it. There was in the hall now only the light over the door and the phosphorescent glow of the image.

When it was finished, it was a rough shape of a woman, nothing like so finished as that other larger shape he had made that morning. He stood up and put it on the seat of his chair. He said to the woman by him,

"I will make the enclosure now. You shall hold it when we are ready," and she nodded. He took three paces to the front of the throne and bending his great height he began to walk backward round it in a circle, drawing after him the point of his left thumb upon the floor. It left behind it a softly shining trail as if it were the streak of a snail's path. When he had finished the circle, he took a pace nearer the chair and began another circle, and when that in turn was finished, he went in turn to the four points of the compass and joined the two circles by four straight lines. As he did so the air within the circles grew heavy and stifling, as if they formed a kind of round thick wall which shut out health and easy breath. He stood up and paused for a few moments as if to recover, then he lifted the fixed endoplasmic shape in his hands, turned and took his seat again upon the now secluded throne. He nodded heavily at the woman, and she came and knelt in front of him with her face towards him. She seemed much older now than she had been when she entered the hall; it was the fallen face of a woman of ninety that stared at him, and was still ageing, and the hands she put out were older too, thin and faintly tremulous. He gave the image, built round those golden hairs, into them, and she held it at about the height of her shoulders, a little above his knees. The only sound now was that of the rain upon the roof.

The Clerk said, "Call her; call her often!" She obediently began; she could not make her voice anything but flat and lifeless, but she began automatically. "Betty! . . . Betty! . . . Betty!" and presently the repetition seemed to strengthen her. While she called, the Clerk put his hand again inside his cassock, but this time near his breast, and drew out what seemed a long needle. It too was bright, but with the brightness of actual steel; it was not like the doll and it glinted in the efflorescence of the doll. There was about it almost a natural beauty, but the presence of that slip of loveliness accentuated the strange horror of the rest. The Clerk took it in his left hand. It had at its head a tiny gold knob, and on this he settled his forefinger, holding it about half-way down, between his thumb and his second and third fingers; the fourth came round to the ball of his thumb. He said, "Louder!" In that oppressive air, Sara Wallingford could not easily obey, but she made an effort and her body unexpectedly responded. Her voice came out with a summons that was like a thin shriek: "Betty! . . . Betty!" And all the time she held up the doll to her master. The Clerk leaned forward and raised the needle.

For almost a minute her voice shrieked alone and then it was no longer alone. Other shrieks from the house beyond answered it and joined with it. The sudden multiplication of sound sang in her ears; she jerked and almost dropped the endoplasmic doll. She recovered herself immediately, but in that half-second's loss of control the Clerk had stabbed at the doll. The needle struck the tip of her middle right-hand finger, and as he pulled back his weapon a drop of blood stood out and oozed onto the fixed jelly. The Clerk looked at her; his eyes drew her yet more upright on her knees. Her finger continued to bleed; the shoulder of the doll showed crimson from the drops.

She went very white and had stopped her high old woman's scream. It was he and not the secrets for which she had cared, and she did not know much of them, but something she could not help knowing and what she knew made her afraid. His great face loomed over her and would not let her go. The face was the face of the Exile of Israel, of the old Israel and the new, and all Israel else was free to the Return. She saw, unknowing, as she looked up, the face of all exile, the face of the refusal of the Return, and it seemed to her as imbecile as it had been in the painting, though now indeed she had forgotten the painting. She tried to let go the doll, and failed. Her left hand could loosen it, but it remained fixed to her right, sealed to it by the blood. She held it in her left and tried to pull her right free, but she could not. She felt indeed all the pain of the rending flesh, but the flesh was not rent. As her blood ran into the doll, so her heart's indifference passed into her flesh; her brain knew what ought to be, but her body refused her brain. The organic nature of her blood made her one with the doll and more intimately much than the golden hairs could unite Betty to it. She realized the substitution that was taking place; she was likely to die in Betty's stead.

She knew she was about to die. She knew that the Clerk would not spare her and that even the thought of sparing would not occur to him. She had hated all things for his sake and so did he, but now his hate was against her too. But she was allowed justice; she was allowed to hate even herself for his sake. After that instinctive effort to escape, she accepted that; she even gloried in it. Her heart flung itself up into that great alien sky of his face and was absorbed in it. She had but one thing to ask and that unvocally; that he should strike to kill before the doll had become even more she than Betty. She had a vague and terrible fear that the substitution might be so complete that Betty would not die. Let him stab before that happened! let him strike both of them into whatever waited! let her have but the chance to meet her daughter there, and see which of them could rule!

She was conscious of one other thing, though she did not properly know what it was. There passed through the face above her a series of vibrations, waves passing down it from forehead to chin. They reverberated in her as a kind of perpetual drumming, increasing as the face changed sea-like down from brow to point, and dying as the pause came, and again beginning as from beneath the hair the wave issued and swelled and sank and swelled, change after change of heavy cloud in that now to her almost shapeless sky. These waves, could she have realized it, came from the drumming rain—heavy, rapid, continuous; October closing in a deluge. The vigil of the saints was innumerably active in the City and all London lay awake under it.

As if her prayer had moved the opaque cloud to yield to it, the slender steel flashed and struck again. She saw it; and, whether through his error or her shrinking, she felt the sudden sting in her forefinger—as if she were to be united to the image, member by member, blow by blow. But, for all the sudden pain and fear, it was not her mouth from which even now those screams were issuing; she after her first wound had become dumb. They came from two sources. The first was within the double barrier; it was held between her hands. In the head of the rough endoplasmic shape a hole opened and out of the hole came screams much like her own had been. It was the most startling and the most dangerous. It had been the first sound of this which caused her to quiver and deflected Simon's aim, for it meant that a weakness and a peril were already within the circle. The wall had not yet been broken by any pressure from without—as the operation in Betty's bedroom had been. The magic here was mechanically shrilling under some turn within it; it was beginning to twist upon itself. The thing done was in active and antagonistic return.

But the noise was multiple; that scream was not solitary. Rising through the drumming of the rain—of which all this time the Clerk had never been entirely unaware, as it is said that those in deep prayer can hear and even consider sounds without distraction—came the screams from beyond the threshold, but now from only just beyond. Those who screamed were already at the door. The house had thrown them from its upper rooms, or rather that which had entered the house. All in the bedrooms and in the offices and the rest had been locked and silent and asleep when through the night and the rain that single taxi had rolled to the outer door. It stopped; the driver leaned back, put out his hand and threw it open. Richard had been the first to descend; then Jonathan and Betty; lastly, the reluctant thing that had first got in. Jonathan gave some silver to the driver and the vehicle disappeared into the darkness. They turned to the house; the carved hand glowed; and then, as they passed it, Betty put out a hand with a movement as if she brushed a twig away and the thing went out suddenly. The dwarf, driven first of all the company, flinched as if it had itself been struck. It reached the door and was halted, for though alone of all in London, it might of its nature have passed through that door yet the high and now dominating spirit who controlled it knew that neither her husband nor her friend's lover could. Jonathan began to use the knocker. Richard looked for a bell and could find none, until a thought struck him, and taking a step or two back he peered by the light of a sheltered match at the center of the carved hand. He saw there a discolored spot in the palm, something which might have been a bell, the nerve of the physical machinery of that house, whose brain (now secluding itself into imbecility) lay in the round hall within. They could not hear the sound of the bell, nor was Jonathan's hammering and occasional kicking at the door much more than a relief to his own feelings. The noise seemed deadened and only an echo of itself. Presently, however, a window went up above them and a voice which Richard recognized as the doorkeeper's said, "What's all this? You can't see the Father now. It's too late."

"We've something for him," Jonathan called, "something of his own."

"You can't do anything for him and you can't give him anything," the voice of Plankin said. "It's late; it's too late."

Another voice interrupted him. It came from the dwarf, but they knew it for Evelyn's and as it sounded the dwarf in a paroxysm of strength beat on the door with its hands. It cried, "Let me in! Let me in!"

Plankin, unseen above them, said, "I don't know, I'm sure. It isn't right to open the door after dark. The Father doesn't wish it. There's things in the dark that might frighten us."

Evelyn screamed, "Let me in! It's raining; you can't leave me in the rain." She added, more quietly and sniveling, "I shall catch a dreadful cold." The dwarf struck again at the door and this time there broke out under the false hands a deep booming sound, as if the previous faint echo had now passed into a cavern of great depth. Jonathan had ceased to knock and Richard took his hand from the discolored palm. This, at last, was the proper summons to that gatehouse; that which they had brought must itself demand entrance. At its call—dead woman and inorganic shape—the gatekeeper, if at all, would come down and open. They could not now hear Plankin for the noise, any more than they could see him for the night. They waited.

The door began to open—less than a crack; they could hardly have known it had not the dwarf, tearing and scrabbling, flung itself at the crack. Both its possessing spirits urged it there; there, with a yelp of delight, it pressed. The threshold shook; Betty and her friends felt it move, and the door, as if of its own accord, swung more widely back, revealing Plankin half-dressed and carrying him with it. He stared at the intruder, as he staggered back. The dwarf sprang jerkily into the lit hall. Betty and the others followed and as they did so the eyes of the gatekeeper changed. Dismay came into them; he gasped; he threw his hands to his head; he cried, "Oh! Oh!" Richard, as he saw and heard, remembered a phrase from their interview of that morning—"a tumor in the head." As he recollected it, and saw the dreadful consciousness of returning pain, he heard a clamor break out on the floor above. The dwarf had thrust past Plankin and was scuttling away down the hall. As it pierced into the house the clamor grew—a hubbub of cries and thuds and shouts and hurrying feet and crashing doors. This was the Return and this the operation of inflexible law.

They appeared; they came, stumbling and roaring, down the stairs—all those who carried the Clerk's mark in their bodies. First, an old woman, in a nightgown,

eyes running tears and hand clutching her side where
the cancer had begun again to gnaw, and she had been
waked by it with only one thought, and that all confused—to be healed, to get to her Comforter. A few steps
behind came a young man partly dressed, coughing and
spitting blood onto the stairs, and feeling vainly for the
handkerchief he had in his first waking spasm forgotten.
And after him a still younger man, who as he came was
being twisted slowly back into deformity, his leg wither-
ing and drawing up, so that he was presently clinging to
the banisters and hopping down sideways. Others followed, some with unseen ailments and some with open
wounds, but all hurrying with one instinctive desire—to
get to Simon, to find their Father, to be healed and at
rest. Only one of all that household was not there—one,
the paralytic, who had waked to find her flesh turning
again a prison, she already half-immobile, and now lying
part in and part out of bed anguished and alone in her
room. The rest were down the stairs and in the hall and
hurrying as best they could round the corner into that
corridor in the wall to the hole that gave on the center
of all. In front of them, and quicker than any, went the
dwarf, and as if in a miserable retinue they followed,
Plankin the first. The hunt for the miracle-monger was
up; they rushed to be again sealed his own, but there
was something dangerous in the way they went.

Betty had paused in the open door till the scurry
had gone by. Her hand was in Jonathan's, who still
carried the canvas of the painting under his other arm.
Richard was on Betty's other side. At last, she too began
to move; she went quietly and her face was very serious
and calm. As they went down the hall, they saw that the
walls there and still more those of the narrow corridor

when they entered it were running with drops and thin streams of water. Richard looked up. He saw that, here and there, the rain was beginning to come through the roof; he felt a few drops on his head, on his face, on his eyelids. But for the most part the rain was not yet upon the walls; it was the condensation of something in the air, some freshness of water that lay on them, but left the air dry and sterile for want of it. The walls absorbed it; under it they changed to a kind of slime.

When they came to the hall it was not so. There the roof was still sound and the walls, as far as they could see, still dry. Before them the diseased throng were hurrying across the floor and the three friends could not clearly see the dwarf beyond them or the two encircled figures beyond it. The woman, as all this crowd burst in, did not move, but the Clerk turned his eyes. Plankin was coming so fast that he outwent even the dwarf, who indeed seemed to pause and totter as it took there the first step, so that the others all broke out around it, and came first to the invisible barrier. That perhaps would not have held against any indifferent human beings; it was not primarily meant for such protection—much less against divine scepticism or heavenly joy. Brutality might have trampled it, scattered about the outer circle, tottering and crawling round it, surrounding it, beating with their hands on an invisible wall, wailing and moaning, and one howling dog-like. The Clerk took no slightest notice; he was looking, and his eyes were very wary, at the other thing that now began to advance.

It walked more steadily now, as if it had found some center of determination in itself. When Lester's influence had been on it, there had been in its movements an irrepressible jerkiness. But now that jerkiness had passed;

it moved inflexibly, as if it neither could nor wished to stop. When it had almost reached the barrier, Betty pulled her hand from Jonathan's and ran after it. She caught up with it; in a swift and strong motion she caught its hand; she exclaimed, "Evelyn, do stop!"

The Clerk had been watching it come. Now he stood up. As he did so, he released from the intensity of his concentration the endoplasmic image in the hands of his paramour; it fell; and she, unable to let it go, fell forward also at that sudden unbalancing release. The Clerk had, at the same time, taken a step towards the barrier, so that she fell against the chair, and the doll, to which her hands were still fastened by her own blood, lay on the seat. She lay propped there and she turned her head, so that she saw, at a little distance, not only the dwarf, of which she knew nothing, but handlinked with it her daughter, her rival and enemy. That Betty was wholly free from her. She saw her almost as Jonathan saw her, beautiful and good, very much Betty. That Betty was quite unlike the doll she helplessly held. The doll was all she had of Betty and even the doll was becoming, as her blood soaked into it, less and less like Betty and more and more like herself. She was being, by an operation which her own will had in the beginning encouraged, slowly substituted for Betty. She lay, rigid and fixed, propped by the edge of the chair, and into the insatiable image through those two small pricks her blood continued to drain.

The Clerk made a quick savage motion and the clamor of the diseased creatures ceased. He looked round the circle, collecting their pitiable eyes; then he raised his hand, pointing it at the dwarf, and he said, "Drag it away!"

Most of them ignored him. A few of those least diseased did look round at the dwarf, but they looked back
at once. It was not disobedience but impotence that held
them there. Someone—it was difficult to know who, in
that throng—said feebly, "Make us well, Father!" The
dwarf, dragging at Betty's hand and pulling her after it,
advanced another few steps. Now it was right up against
the barrier and had, with a definite and powerful thrust,
got one foot just over the circle by some half an inch.
There it seemed to halt, as if it could press no farther.
Betty still clung to its hand; it was all she could do. She
called out, "Lester, do help me! I can't hold her."

Indeed nothing—neither the Clerk's frown nor
Betty's clasp—could now affect the mad determination of
the lost spirit. Evelyn was overridden by the fear that
even this refuge in which she somehow was might be
snatched from her. She saw the barrier almost as a material wall; if she could get this body within it, she would
be safe, or as safe as she could be. The attraction which
that point exercised on the mere material image was
strengthened by her own will; a false union held her and
it. Since the house had been entered, there had been no
need for Lester to drive the shape; it had been only too
urgent to hurry on. Only Betty still clung to it. She
flung out her other hand behind her, as if to Jonathan;
and Jonathan sprang forward and caught it. As if aware
of them for the first time, the Clerk lifted his eyes and
saw the three friends.

Jonathan and Betty were too occupied to meet his
eyes, but Richard did. And as he did, the sudden recollection of what this man had offered him rose bitterly
in his heart. This fellow had offered to rule Lester for
him, to give him back his wife or not as he might choose

—he! He had been still lingering by the door, but now suddenly he too moved. If Lester was to go from him, she should go with all honors. He walked forward to join the others and when he had reached them he took the canvas from under Jonathan's arm. He said, "Father Simon, my wife wishes us to return your property. Take it."

He lightly tossed the canvas towards the Clerk; it flew over the circles and struck Simon on the shoulder. The Clerk gave a sudden squeal. Richard went on, holding himself very upright and imperious. "If I had not been a fool in the past, you would not have been able to——"

"Darling, must you be quite so savage?" Lester's voice half-laughing interrupted. "Tell him what you ought to tell him—that will be enough."

Richard had forgotten his commission. Now he remembered. He said, "Yes . . . well . . . but I think it's too late. Lester is free of you, and Betty is free, and the world will soon be free. But just before it is—I was sent to offer you everything—all the kingdoms in it and their glory. You were to be asked to meet those others who are like you; you were, all three of you, to be . . . how do I know what? masters, for all I do know. But I think we've come in time. Let's see if your friends will."

A sudden silence fell. Richard listened—all of them, even the Clerk, all except Evelyn, listened—for that other voice. It did not then come. Lester was still clearly aware of what was happening. But she was also aware of a certain difference in her surroundings. She had seemed to enter the house with the others, even to come as far as the hall, but when the others had gone right in, when Richard had gone and had begun to speak, when she had

broken in on him with that gay but serious protest, she
had become aware that she was no longer related to that
deformed image. It had itself released her, merely by
entering the hall. For as it did so and she for the first
second with it, she had found herself once more in the
rain. It was driving down over and past her onto—the
Thames? some wide river, flowing, flowing on beneath
her; and the pale ghastly light in the hall had changed.
Within the rain a fresher light was opening. It shone on
the rain and on the river; and the room with its com-
panies was still there, but it stood on the river, which
flowed through it, and in the rain, which fell through it.
The light was like dawn, except that it had in it a tinge
redder than dawn, and the same tinge was in the river
and the rain, exquisite and blood-roseal, delicate and en-
riching. Only she felt again the awful sense of separation.
It was like a sharp pain in a great joy. She gave herself
to it; she could no other; she had consented long before
—when she married Richard perhaps—or was consenting
now—when she was leaving him. Her heart sank; without him, what was immortality or glory worth? and yet
only without him could she even be that which she now
was. All, all was ending; this, after so many preludes, was
certainly death. This was the most exquisite and pure
joy of death, in a bearing of bitterness too great to be
borne. Above her the sky every moment grew more high
and empty; the rain fell from a source far beyond all
clouds. Below her the myriad drops, falling in slanting
lines, struck the great river in innumerable little explo-
sions, covering the whole surface. She saw each of them
with an admirable exactitude—each at the same time as
she saw all, and the flowing river and the empty sky, and
herself no longer bodily understood, but a point, a point

reflected from many drops and pierced by many drops, a spark of the light floating in the air. But she was not very conscious of herself as herself; she no longer thought of herself as bearing or enjoying; the bitterness, the joy and the inscape of those great waters were all she knew, and among them the round hall, with those mortal figures within it, and its window open, as she now saw it, on the waters. Even Richard's figure there had lost its immediate urgency; something once necessary and still infinitely precious, which had belonged to it, now lay deep, beyond all fathoming deep, in the current below, and could be found again only within the current or within the flashing rain. Of any future union, if any were to be, she could not begin even to think; had she, the sense of separation would have been incomplete, and the deadly keenness of the rain unenjoyed.

The rain did not seem to her to be driving into the round hall; if it did, it was there invisible to her. The window was open, and she became aware that towards the window, from a great distance, two forms were moving. They came walking upon the waters, great-headed, great-cloaked forms, forms like Simon, two Simons far beyond the hall, coming towards the hall and Simon. She thought at first there were more—a whole procession of Simons, but it was not so; there were but the two. They were going directly towards the window, one behind the other, and as she saw them she had a sudden sense that never, never would she have asked either of them to bring her a drink of water in the night. She would have been terrified of what they brought; there would have been something in the glass—as if the Richard of past days had put secret poison in the drink; and much worse than that, for human malice was but human malice, and comprehensible and pardonable enough to any human; but this would have been a cool and immaterial—and the worse for being immaterial—antipathy to—to? to all, a drink the taste of which would have been a separation without joy. They came on, as it were below her—not that she had at all a place to see them from— and as they passed or seemed to pass, she had a moment's terror that it was not they but she. The great-headed, great-cloaked, steadily walking forms were wholly unlike her, but yet they were she—double, immense, concealed, walking through the unfelt rain on the unyielding water, antipathetic, relegated to antipathy; as if in the shadowy City of her early death she had gone another way and through the deep tunnels and tribes had come out on this water, and (grown in them to this size and covered in them with this wrapping to hide herself) were walking on to some quiet and awful consummation. This had been the other way, the way she had just not gone. Behind them, as they went, the faint roseal glow in the waters and the rain gathered thicker and followed and deepened as it followed. The color of it—rose or blood or fire—struck up the descending lines of rain and was lost somewhere in that empty upper sky above her; but below it was by now almost a wall which moved after those forms; and absorbed and changed the antipathy they diffused; and all behind them the freshness of the waters and the light was free and lovely.

On earth—that is, among those earthly—the turn of the night had come. The morning of the feast imperceptibly began, though none of them knew it—none? the Clerk knew. As a man feels the peculiar chill that comes, especially in early spring or late autumn, with the rising sun, so he, long before any sun had risen, felt a new coldness in the hall. The air within the charmed circle was heavy, but as the Acts of the City took charge and the nearness of all the hallows grew everywhere within the outer air, it became dank and even more oppressive with a graveyard chill. More than humanity was holy and more than humanity was strange. The round hall itself and its spare furnishings and the air in it were of earth, and nothing could alter that nature. The blessedness of earth was in them and now began to spread out of them. There too were the hallows, and their life began to awake, though the City itself seemed not yet awake. Invisible motions stirred and crept or stepped or flew, as if a whole creation existed there unseen. The Acts of the City were at hand. Simon's eyes were still on the dwarf, which by now had pressed still farther into the barrier, as if it was working its way through some thick molded stuff which could not quite halt it. It was delayed also by its paw, being still caught in Betty's; for all its spasmodic tugging it could not quite free itself from that young passionate clasp. But it had dragged Betty herself very near the barrier. Her other hand was in Jonathan's and his arm was round her. As her foot touched the outer circle, she looked round at him and said, "Don't hold me now, Jon. I must go with her."

Jonathan said, "You'll do nothing of the sort. What's the good? Let her go where she wants. It's I who need you, more than ever she can."

Betty answered breathlessly, "No, really, Jon. I *must* go; after all, we did know each other. And you're different; you can manage. Besides, I shouldn't be the least good to you if—— Let me go, darling. I can't leave her to die again. I was glad she was dead the first time, so I must be with her now."

Jonathan tried to resist, but all his energy and all the energy of his art was in vain. He set his feet; they slipped. He dragged at Betty's slim form; it advanced. He said, "Don't; it's hell. What shall I do?"

Betty, faintly, panted, "Hell? it won't hurt me; of course it won't. I *must* go; darling, let me."

Their voices, quiet enough, were dreadfully loud in the hall where there was no other sound except always of the rain. Jonathan called, "Richard, come and help me!"

Richard said—and if there was an impurity in his answer, it was hardly avoidable; a deadly touch was in his heart and more than Jonathan he knew that certain departures must be; if he spoke with the least possible impatience, it was but mortal—Richard said, "I shouldn't worry. You won't have her if you keep her; when she wants to go she ought to go."

His eyes were still on the Clerk and the Clerk's on Betty. At this moment, suppose as he might that he still had his whole ancient purpose in mind, it was a dream and an illusion. The sight of his daughter and slave, whole, well and free, distracted him. He forgot the theory of magic, the principle of the physical and spiritual categories of identity, the philosophy and metaphysic of Goetia. Spells had failed and images had failed. He was more a common man than ever before and he forgot all but the immediate act. That remained: killing remained. He saw the body of Betty, and the hand that held the needle crept slowly up his side. Inch by inch she drew nearer; inch by inch he raised the weapon. He fixed his eyes on her throat.

They were all now in a world of simple act. The time for thought, dispute, preparation was done. They were in the City. They were potent to act or impotent to act, but that was the only difference between any of them. The eyes of the woman who lay, incapable of act, against the abandoned chair, were also on Betty and greedy with the same murderous desire. The diseased creatures, also incapable, who lay around the circle, trembled and moaned a little with their helpless longing for the act of healing. She and they alike yearned towards act and could not reach it. The dwarf-form was still in motion and its motions as it forced its way on were both its own and Evelyn's—it magically drawn to its origin, she spiritually driving to her refuge. Betty felt that invisible soft mass press against her everywhere —against head and breasts, hands and thighs and legs. She gasped out to Jonathan, "Let go—you must. I may; not you. Only one of us, and I knew her." She wrenched her own hand free from his and struck it backward against him, as Lester had struck at Richard, one gesture whether accursed or blest. In the fierceness of her knowledgeable love, she struck so hard—all heaven in the blow—that he loosed his arm from her and fell back a pace. Richard caught and steadied him. At that moment, as Betty entered the circle, the rain broke in.

It came with a furious rush, as if it had beaten the roof down under it. But in fact the roof had not fallen. The rain drove through it and down over all of them, torrential, but torrential most over the center of the circle as if the center of a storm was settled there. Under the deluge the doll on the chair at once melted; it ran over the woman's hand and wholly disappeared, except for a thin film of liquid putrescence which covered them, pullulating as if with unspermed life. She saw it and under it her hands still bloody; she shook them wildly and tried to tear at them, but the thin pulsing jelly was everywhere over them and her fingers could not get through it. For the first time in her life she began to sob, with a hideous harsh sound; and as her obstinacy melted like the doll under the rain she scrambled to her feet and made for Simon, the tears on her aged cheeks, clutching at him with those useless and helpless hands. He did not notice her; it was his misfortune.

As if the barrier itself had also disappeared under the rain, the dwarf-figure began suddenly to move loosely. It slipped and almost fell over; then it righted itself and tottered on. But at the same time it began to lose even the rough shape it had. The rain poured down on it; its head ran thickly into its shoulders; then it had no head nor shoulders, but still it staggered forward. The paw that Betty held became damp mud in her grasp and oozed through her fingers; its legs, such as they were, bent and came together, and then it had no legs and was only a lump which was madly bumping on, and then at the edge of the second circle it lost power altogether and toppled down, dropping just within that circle and falling in great splashes of mud over Simon's feet. He had, so far, the adoration he desired.

Betty had stood still where she had lost hold. Simon looked once at the splashes; then, as quick as the holy rain itself, he flung himself forward and struck with his steel at his daughter's throat. The weapon touched her, swerved, scratched and was gone. The two young men had moved, but something had been before them. The bloody and filthy hands of the old woman, blind with her tears, had caught Simon's upper arm as he launched himself, and the thrust was deflected. The hand that held the steel was pulled away and, opening as it fell, dropped the weapon. Betty put out her hand and lightly caught it. She glanced at it curiously and as she stepped back to Jonathan gave it to him with a smile. The Clerk furiously and with a strange cry flung himself round after his mistress, and as they swung in a clutching frenzy and she falling backward before him, he saw across and beyond her the window of the hall, and there he saw and knew his end.

There stood in the window two shapes which he at once recognized. They were exactly alike; their huge all-but-skeleton heads were thrust a little forward; their cloaks of darkness were wrapped round them; their blank eyes were turned to him. They had, in the beginning, been exactly like him, but his human flesh, even his, carried a little the sense of its own experiences, and theirs only indirectly and at one remove. They had therefore the effect now of slightly sinister caricatures of him—as the doll, though more horribly, of Betty and the dwarf of any woman. It was the nature of that world to produce not so much evil art as bad art, and even Jonathan's painting was more truthful to its reality than any reproduction of its own. But each reproduction had its own proper quality. The heavenly rain drove on these shapes without visible effect; they were, however perversely, of human flesh, and indeed, in so far as they were anything, were Simon himself. The grace drove against them from behind, as if it were driving them back to him; or perhaps it had been their coming which stirred and shook the unseen clouds and left a void the living waters rushed in to fill. The roseal glow behind them in the waters was now very deep and filled the window with what was becoming not so much a glow as a fume of color. An opaque cloud gathered. It had been so when that other Jew ascended; such a cloud had risen from the opening of the new dimensions into which he physically passed, and the eyes of the disciples had not pierced it. But that Jew had gone up into the law and according to the law. Now the law was filling the breach in the law. The blood of all victims and the fire of all avengers was in it—from Abel to those of London and Berlin—yet it was merely itself. It was an act, and as an act it followed of its own volition, wave-like, high-arching. The shapes began to advance and it also. The Clerk stood rigid, at his feet the body of his mistress; across the floor those other Clerks came on.

He made, within himself, one last effort. But these were too much he; all the years, in the most secret corner of his heart, he had sustained them so. His thoughts had shaped their brains, his words their voices. He had spoken in himself and in them. What he now said to them, he must say to himself. He began to bid them stop, but as he did so he found himself stiffen into an even more fixed rigidity. He tried to look them down, but he could no more catch any meaning in their eyes than he could see his own. He moved his hand to trace against them in the air a significant and compelling figure of magic, and he felt the earth shake under him and the burden of the air weigh on him to crush him as he did so. To unmake them he must unmake himself. There was only one other possibility; he might attempt, here, with no preparation, to unite them again with himself and make them again he. He must act and the act might be successful. He consented.

He crossed the barrier; he went forward. They too, each head slightly turning towards him, continued to advance, in the steady measure of his own steps as his of theirs. He began to murmur spells, of which the beating rhythm mingles with those which sustain flesh, but he felt again a creeping in his own flesh and desisted. In the seclusion of the circles, protected by them, he might have found and practiced a distinction. Here, in the confusion of the rain, he could not. It beat on him and he could not think; it drove against him and he could not see. He went on against it, but the growing roseal light confused him still more. It bewildered him and he lost sight of the shapes until suddenly they loomed out of it very close to him. He unexpectedly thought, "This is death," and knew himself weaken at the thought.

He managed to pronounce a word of command. They stopped, but then also he too stopped. He obeyed himself. He knew he needed time—time and shelter from the rain and the rose-light and the rose-smell; which was not only a rose-smell but a smell of blood and of burning, of all those great crimson things. He smelled crimson between him and them, and saw it too, for that rich color had ceased to over-arch them, and was sweeping down and round them, gathering and thickening, as if from light it were becoming liquidity, and yet he could not feel it. It grew and shut them in, all three, two not able to speak and one not daring to speak. Only through it there went out from all three a blast of antipathy. He hated them, and since they held his hate they hated him. The hate seemed to swell in a nightmare bubble within the rose which was forming round them, cloud in cloud, overlying like petals. Simon made a quick half spring as if to overleap it, and so did they; but he failed and fell back, and so did they. The smell of the rose was changing to the smell of his last act, to the smell of blood. He looked down; he saw below him the depth of the rose. A sudden fresh blast of rain fell on him and drove him deeper, and so those others. It flashed past him in an infinity of drops, as of points falling—at first crystal, then of all colors, from those almost too dark to be seen through to those almost too bright to be seen. They fell continuously between him and those other faces, in which he could now see those waves passing which his devotee had seen in his own face. The bright showers of the hallows flashed, and beyond him he could see only his multiplied self; and all he could do against them was only done to himself.

The rose began to withdraw. He felt himself carried with it and slipping more deeply into it. The smell of blood was in his nostrils; the touch of burning on his flesh; this was what the crimson must be to him. He stared, as he sank and as that in which he was held moved in its own fashion, at the rain of swift-darting points between him and himself. The City, so, was visible to him. "If I go down into hell, thou art there"; but if I go down into thee——? If even yet he could attend to those points, he would escape hell; he would never have been in hell. If he could not, he had his changing and unchanging faces to study. He stared at them, imbecile; imbecile, they stared back—farther and farther, deeper and deeper, through the rose and the burning and the blood.

At the moment when the Clerk met the other Clerks, when the rose-light began to thicken and swim and gather round them, the three friends also felt that final blast of rain, falling on and even through them. Jonathan and Richard shrank under it, as under a burst of ordinary rain. Betty, still fresh from the lake of power, the wise waters of creation, lifted her face to it and felt it nourishing her. It was she who saw, as the driving torrent dwindled and passed, a fume of crimson rising, as if the rain had so fallen on the shaping rose that it sent up a cloud as of the smell of rose-gardens after rain. The smell lingered, but the cloud sank. As if she looked down a great distance she saw a small pool crimson in the light, and that too vanishing, till it was no more than the level of dark wine in a wine cup, and within it, before it vanished, she saw the whole City through which she had so often passed, vivid and real in that glowing richness. But she lost that sight as she realized that the City opened all ways about her and the hall in which she stood, in which also the daylight now visibly expanded. She heard the early noises of London outside the hall. She sighed with delight, and turned to the morning joy; smiling, she turned to her lover. He looked back at her, he still young and already a master in a certain knowledge of that City. Yet it was not he—it was Richard over whom the Acts of the City more closely hovered, and he whose face, like Lester's once in Betty's own room, was touched with the somber majesty of penitence and grief and a young death.

But there were others in the hall. The diseased, except for an occasional sob, were silent now, the clear light showing them more pitiable. The body of Sara Wallingford lay where she had fallen; she had not moved. It was neither she nor the sick whom Betty and her friends first saw. Before them, in what had once been the circle, were the two dead and living girls. They seemed to be in their earthly shapes, their earthly clothes. Betty took a step or two towards them and there, in an overpowering ordinariness, they stood, as any three young women might, deciding occupation, exchanging chat. It was Evelyn who spoke. Her eyes darting from Betty to Lester and back, she said, "Don't you interfere with me. I won't let you. I won't. Don't try."

Lester said, "Look, Evelyn, we've often gone out together; let's do it again. Come with me today and we'll think what there is to do."

Betty made a motion to speak, but Lester smiled at her and she ceased. The voices and the words might have been of any moment in the past. Lester went on, "Come, you might as well. I'm sorry if I've been . . . stupid. It was wrong. If I ever made use of you, come and make use of me. I only want you to. I do. I do. Let's go and see what we can find!"

Evelyn said, "I suppose you think that's kind. You think it's clever to be kind, don't you? I always hated being with you, and I daresay sooner or later I can find someone else there, thank you."

"Yes," said Lester, "I'm afraid you may."

The words, to all but Evelyn, brought a sinister thought of that other strange world. But Evelyn was past noting even that. When her shelters had melted round her, she had not known in her despair what she would do; and now she only knew that she would not let herself be caught. Lester and Betty were trying to catch her, to keep her, to pain her; they had always hated her. But she would beat them. She made a rush; she ran between them; she dodged the hands that were not flung out; she cried, "Let me go" to those who had not held her. She ran to the window; the yard outside was very lonely and spectral. She almost hesitated. But she looked back over her shoulder and saw Lester move. She cried out, "You thought you'd got me, didn't you?" They saw the immortal fixity of her constricted face, gleeful in her supposed triumph, lunatic in her escape, as it had had once a subdued lunatic glee in its cruel indulgences; and then she broke through the window again and was gone into that other City, there to wait and wander and mutter till she found what companions she could.

Betty looked at Lester, and they were silent. Then Lester said, "We might have found the waters together, she and I. Well, I must go. Goodbye, my dear. Thank you for being sweet."

Betty exclaimed, "But what about——?" Out of sheer courtesy to those who might hear her, she checked herself, but her eyes were on the unhappy throng, and she made a small gesture with her hand. She did not know who they were nor how they came to be in that house, but she saw what they were suffering. Lester shook her head. She said, "They are for you, my dear. You can do it; you've done harder things. It'll take something out of you, of course, but you can. Goodbye." She looked across at Richard. She said, "Dearest, I did love you. Forgive me. And thank you— Oh Richard, *thank you!* Goodbye, my blessing!" She stood, quiet and very real, before them; almost she shone on them; then the brightness quivered in the air, a gleam of brighter light than day, and in a flash traversed all the hall; the approach of all the hallows possessed her, and she too, into the separations and unions which are indeed its approach, and into the end to which it is itself an approach, was wholly gone. The tremor of brightness received her.

Betty was the first to move. She looked at those who remained in the hall, besides her own friends. She was, since Lester had spoken, clear what was to be done. But she felt a little as she had done on Highgate Hill, though now even more at peace. A troublesomeness was approaching, the result of the act to which she was, by her friend's word, committed. The act was to be hardly hers yet without her it could not be. But now that other companion for whom on the hill she had sighed and called was with her; the extra grace involved an extra labor; without the labor, of what value the grace? She said impulsively, "Jon, I will try not to be tiresome."

He did not answer directly, but he put his arm about her shoulders, and said, "What about your mother?"

They went to her. They knelt and looked and touched and spoke. She showed no sign, lying there living but inert. It would be long before she came to herself and then she would not come to herself. When presently she woke and tried to move, she would wake without knowledge, without memory, lost to all capacity and to all care. She would not know who she was or where she was or who those were that were about her or what they did—not even what they did for her, for the things that were done—the dressing, the feeding, the taking into the air—would be things to which she could attach no words. She had given herself away and her self would be no longer there, or rather (as if it were a newborn child) would have to be cared for and trained afresh. But since in that gift she had desired the good of another and not her own, since she had indeed willed to give her self, the City secluded her passion and took her gift to its own divine self. She had, almost in a literal physical sense, to be born again; at least she had to grow again, and over the growth her daughter was to preside. That tenderness was to meet her needs and (if she could ever speak) to answer her stumbling words. She was now

almost in that state to which her master had willed to reduce their child; the substitution was one of the Acts of
the City. Her spiritual knowledge lay unconscious, as it
were in the depth of the separating and uniting waters;
her body under the common sun. Resurrection must be
from the very beginning and meanwhile Betty was to do
for her mother, while she lived, all that love could do.

But it would be certainly, for a long while, a thinner
and wanner Betty who would do so. For now, when it
was clear that she could do nothing there for her mother,
she and Jon then rose from their knees. She said, "Well
. . ." and she kissed him. Then she saw Richard. They
looked at each other; she smiled and put out her hand,
and he came slowly across. She went to meet him and
gave him also her mild lips. He said, "Thank you for the
picture." She pressed his hand and then she had turned
again and gone across to the nearest of those sick and
sorry creatures who were lying or crouching there. Her
immortality was strong in her as she came to him; it happened to be Plankin. She took his hands in hers; the joy
of the City in her, she kissed him on the mouth; she
looked into his eye. She said, after a minute, "You'll be
well." He looked at first bewildered; then slowly relieved; then suddenly joyous. He half-scrambled to his
feet from where, his head on his knees, he had been sitting, and uttered some sort of incoherent cry. Betty said
clearly, "That'll be all right," released herself, and went
on. She passed, so, round the whole circle, holding,
touching, healing—simply and naturally, and with all
the gaiety that she could. But though her voice did not
falter nor her hands lose their strength, yet as she went
on she herself changed. She grew paler; she had to pause
to recover as time after time she rose and left renewed

271

wholeness behind. Jonathan had followed her all the while and presently, as she came near the end, she was leaning on his arm for the necessary step or two between one and another. As the high heavenly power in her was poured into those tormented beings, so the power, and still more quickly the joy of the power, passed from her. She who had risen from the waters was still that she and could not be lost unless she betrayed herself, but these energies were for a purpose and were to be spent on that purpose. Have and not-have; not-have and have—sometimes on the first and sometimes the other; but by both she and Lester and all came to the City, though the union of both and the life of the union, the life of that final terrible and triumphant *Have!* was yet far beyond them and even to envisage it would be to refuse the way to it. Her miraculous life passed into those others and she herself, without any apparent gain to herself from her voice and smile and gesture and free love, was left wholly to her old. At the end she wavered and nearly fell. Jonathan held her and they turned and came, but she hardly, back towards Richard, who took her other arm, and so she paused, white and worn, supported by her lover and her friend. She murmured, with a last flashing smile, "That's done!"

All those whom she had healed were on their feet —moving, chattering, tidying themselves. They did not seem to know what exactly had happened; at least they showed no awareness of Betty and did not even look at her. Someone said, "I knew the Father would help us," and someone else, "It might have been a dream," and someone else. "Goodness! what a fright!" And then a whole noise of voices broke out and a little laughter, and Betty looked pleadingly at Jonathan, and the three began to move slowly towards the door. The morning of the feast was bright in the hall. As they came near the door, and Betty's white frailty was only just holding up and holding level, Plankin suddenly ran up to them. He said, "Excuse *me*, miss and gentlemen, but there's one more upstairs—Elsie Bookin who does the typing. She used to have the paralysis, and if she thinks she's got it again I daresay she couldn't get down with the rest of us. But she may feel bad, and if so be as you were going upstairs, I'm sure she'd be thankful."

Jonathan began to say something. Betty pressed his arm. She looked at Plankin and the faintest of wry smiles turned her lips. With a final effort she pulled herself up. She said, "Oh well. . . . Yes. Jon, do you mind . . .?"